REPRISAL

Colin T. N~

REPRISAL

Colin T. Nelson

North Star Press of St. Cloud, Inc.
St. Cloud, Minnesota

For

Pamela Nelson

This is a work of fiction. All characters and situations depicted are fictional and any resemblance to actual people or real events is purely coincidental.

Copyright © 2010 Colin Nelson

ISBN: 0-87839-358-4
ISBN-13: 978-0-87839-358-5

First Edition, June 2010

Printed in the United States of America

Published by
North Star Press of St. Cloud, Inc.
P.O. Box 451
St. Cloud, Minnesota 56302

www.northstarpress.com

Fairy tales do not tell children that dragons exist. Children already know that dragons exist. Fairy tales tell children that dragons can be killed.

---G.K. Chesterton

PROLOGUE

A
fter making a cut from just above the left ear across the forehead to just above the right ear, she rolled the skin up over the top of his head to expose the skull. She smiled at the beautiful glistening glow of young bone.

This was her favorite part.

The skull was such a distinct color and a Divine feat of perfect engineering. The pieces came together in thin jagged lines as tightly as the ancient Greek architects did with the marble in the Parthenon. If her assistant wasn't standing next to her, she'd love to take off her glove and stroke the smooth, cool surface.

Although a small woman, Dr. Helen Wong was proud of her strength, particularly in her fingers. She reached for the Stryker saw and spoke into the microphone hanging above her head, "I am preparing to cut the skull laterally to expose the brain." On a boy this young, the skull should come apart easily; she could always resort to brute force if necessary.

She sighed. It was a pity to destroy the beauty before her. The saw whined and Dr. Wong started her cut.

In spite of all the modern tools, Dr. Wong knew that fingers were often just as effective. And what difference did it make to this lifeless body? Because murder was alleged, Dr. Wong performed the autopsy.

She worked as the chief medical examiner for Hennepin County in Minneapolis. Her job was to determine the medical cause of death. She felt the pressure from local law enforcement, the FBI, and the prosecutor to expedite her findings.

She'd already read the police report summary and knew about the case from the media. More than a dozen young Somali men had disappeared without explanation from Minneapolis and St. Paul. A few had shown up in Somalia as "freedom fighters" and had been killed. The rest were still missing. The victim in this case had returned for some unknown reason, only to end up dead in Minneapolis. The suspect in custody was charged with first-degree murder.

As to the body slanting down on the aluminum table before her, there wasn't any doubt really, as to the cause of death. The young man's throat gaped open like a quartered watermelon from a cut that started below one ear and slashed across to a spot just below the other ear. The laceration extended down through all the tissue and muscle in the throat to reach the spine. Except for the bone in the spine stopping the weapon, the killer might have severed the head.

Unusually deep, she pondered. *Strange. Why? What kind of person would do that?* She momentarily felt sorry for the public defender who had to represent the killer.

"Turn in the tox results yet?" she barked at her assistant and instantly regretted her tone. She'd ordered the minimum tests to be run. He nodded in response. She hurried to finish, mindful of her appointment with the dean of the University of Minnesota Medical School later that afternoon.

Dr. Wong felt she had been cheated. Her male predecessor had filled the medical examiner's position for the county government and, at the same time, was a professor at the medical school. It meant a double salary and much more professional visibility. She was determined to get the same arrangement for herself during her appointment.

She knew the local prosecutors called her "Chopsticks" behind her back because of the crude surgical techniques commonly used in autopsies. The racism angered her, but she performed expertly and when necessary, she testified in court convincingly. Excellence was her defense.

Prior to opening the skull, Dr. Wong completed the external exam quickly and noted that she found no identifying marks on the body. No other trauma except for the lacerated neck presented itself. Since the cause of death was clear to her, she scanned the body quickly. She studied the young black boy's skin that had turned a shade of gray, like ashes.

She probed along the body with her long fingers. Underneath the latex gloves, her hands looked delicate but hid an immense strength that showed only when she squeezed muscled parts like the biceps.

The feet were heavily calloused, unlike most other people who lived in Minnesota who wore shoes twelve months of the year. They seemed to be tinged the color of a rotten plum. Hard to tell what that meant since the blood had been drained from his body earlier. She preferred performing autopsies on lighter skinned bodies since trauma to the underlying tissues was easier to spot.

One thing bothered her: the same red discolorations covered both his palms. *Unusual. What caused it?*

Dr. Wong was in a hurry, and she assumed they were simply abrasions, which she noted, speaking into the mike hanging above her. She thought they could've been the results of a struggle. It didn't matter since it had nothing to do with the cause of death.

After the exterior exam, she hurried to perform the usual Y incision in the chest. To assist the team, the autopsy table had a body block, a plastic brick, which rested under the body, lifting the chest area in a high, curved arc while the arms and neck fell away. The incision traveled down the length of the body. Dr. Wong preferred to use a good pair of garden pruning sheers instead of the expensive autopsy equipment. The sheers were stronger and cheaper. A small sheen of perspiration popped out from her forehead.

She measured the subcutaneous fat of the abdomen. Looked at the peritoneal surface. She found both lungs adherent to their respective pleural cavities. After her visual check, Dr. Wong used her fingers to feel around inside the opened cavity. She began to remove the organs. They would be observed, weighed, sometimes sliced like a loaf of bread for further analysis. In this case, she saw no need beyond weighing.

The contents of the stomach revealed the remains of onions, tomatoes, meat, and what looked like pie crust. Dr. Wong and her assistant had become pretty good at guessing what the person had just eaten. It was like a game for them.

"Gyros sandwich?" the assistant said.

Dr. Wong chuckled. "I don't know." She sifted through the contents with a scalpel. "There's no pita bread. Looks like some kind of fried meat, not grilled. This is a new one, I guess."

She spoke into the microphone while examining the heart, "The atria and auricular appendages appear normal. The valves appear normal in circumference and are thin and delicate." She droned on until the exam of each of the organs was completed, including the kidneys, prostrate, coronary artery, spleen, liver, pancreas, and thyroid.

Dr. Wong could do this in her sleep. While speaking, she thought ahead to the meeting with Dr. Johnson at the university. When she set her sights on a goal, she seldom missed. Still, her success wasn't guaranteed yet.

As she lifted the brain out of the skull, she spoke aloud, "The vessels at the base of the brain appear to be intact. There appears to be a very subtle contusion of the right temporal tip in an area measuring approximately one-and-a-half by one-and-a-half centimetres."

Dr. Wong wondered which outfit she should wear for the meeting with Dr. Johnson. What color would be best? Something serious but also not too formal. She glanced at the sweep hand of the digital clock on the wall.

"Come on Henry. We've got to finish up," she told her assistant.

"If you have to run, I'll sew it up and clean things," he offered.

"Thanks. I've got the meeting this afternoon." She turned back to the mike. Dr. Wong spoke again to indicate the time they finished then stepped back. She'd wash thoroughly but quickly and still have plenty of time.

Outside the exam room, she stripped off the gown, face mask, protective glasses, and gloves, throwing them in the cleaning receptacle. Into the bathroom for washing and a quick check on her hair and makeup, then she'd go home and change.

Dr. Wong climbed the stairs from the basement lab to the modern office complex that housed her office, three assistants, and the support staff. A skylight in the middle of the space provided a welcome square of sunshine, especially during the long Minnesota winters.

Outside, the warm sun on her face reminded her that she needed to start using sun block in her make-up again. Uncovered from a layer of winter snow, the ground around the office revealed new mysteries popping up in the greediness of growth.

Dr. Wong climbed into her Lincoln Navigator and sped out of the lot.

Like the dirty clothing she'd left in the cleaning bin, she left any thoughts of the routine autopsy behind.

Later, of course, she recognized her mistake.

But then, how could she be blamed? The year she started medical school, it didn't even exist.

The small pox virus, variola, proved to be one of the most successful killers in human history. Thanks to a farsighted world-wide program, by 1979 the virus had been eradicated from the planet. Vaccine production stopped. Human immunity against the disease waned year to year to the point that today, everyone in the world is defenseless and susceptible to infection.

ONE

Although never convicted of a crime, Zehra Hassan had to go to jail.
One of dozens of public defenders in Minneapolis, she forced herself out of the office and down Fourth Avenue toward the concrete building known as the Public Service Facility. In spite of the bureaucratic name, it was still a jail. She never liked going there and, especially today, dreaded the first interview with her new client.

She'd been appointed to defend the terrorist accused of killing a missing Somali boy who'd returned to Minneapolis. Zehra remembered her first appearance with him. One of the arresting cops who was a friend of hers, approached her after the hearing.

"Watch this guy, Z. He's bad news."

When even the cops were worried about a defendant, that concerned Zehra.

Hot sun pressed like a weight across her back. For May, this was unusually warm. Bright light glanced from the tall glass buildings surrounding her. Heat rising off the sidewalk clutched at her legs.

Zehra opened one of the doors to the PSF and thought of the air-conditioned reward on the other side. Once in, she still felt clammy and hot.

"Hey, Joe," she called to the deputy sheriff at the metal detector. "What's up with the air?"

Joe grinned when he saw Zehra. "The computer's aren't programmed right. They tell us they're workin' on it"

Zehra took a deep breath, patted her damp forehead, and headed for the elevator that would take her down two floors into the suffering and struggles of the inmates below. Pulling the back of her suit over her hips, she slowed down and waited.

When she'd first moved to Minnesota years ago, she thought of it as the tundra. "Siberia with family restaurants," one of the filmmaking Coen brothers had said after they left themselves.

Certainly, the first winter matched her expectations. Then she experienced her first spring. Formally hidden under snow banks, caches of unexpected objects appeared. People uncovered life in a variety of colors with a diversity of animals and plants all greedy for new growth. The spring thaw also uncovered other odd things: sinners; unexplained mysteries; and even a dead body on occasion.

The elevator came, and Zehra rode alone as it descended. After graduating from law school and working in the prosecutor's office for a few years, she'd switched to the defense side. One of the necessary difficulties of the job involved meeting clients who were dangerous enough to be held in custody.

When the elevator opened, Zehra rushed out into a small room with a beige tile floor. The bright fluorescent light above caused her to see a metallic reflection of herself in one of the thick windows in the wall. She liked her face, her large hazel eyes—unusual for someone with her dark complexion. Thick black hair curled around the edges of her chin. Then, there was her nose—too long. A remnant of her distant relatives from Iran.

The heat made her chest feel clammy and damp.

When Zehra moved forward to press the button on the intercom, a deputy looked up at her and waved in recognition. She heard the loud metal clank as the lock shot open in the door. She pulled on the cold handle, walked through, turned left.

Zehra's parents were part of the flood of educated people who fled to the United States after the fall of the Shah for more opportunity, a chance to become naturalized citizens, have children, and work hard.

She'd grown up in Dallas but moved to Utah for college, mostly because she loved to snowboard. After graduating, she moved to Minnesota for law school, followed by her parents after they wilted in the hot weather of Texas summers.

Zehra walked through the thick dead air of the jail toward an interview room. She missed the colors of her garden down here. She found an open room and stepped into it.

Against one wall, two metal chairs flanked a plastic table. She set her briefcase on the table next to a red button, the size of her palm, that protruded from the wall. If she hit the button, several deputies would charge into the room.

Zehra pulled out the thin file she had on the new client. It read: *State of Minnesota vs. Ibrahim El-Amin.* With the amount of publicity generated by the disappearance of many young Somali men from the Twin Cities, the police and FBI had worked overtime to discover what happened. The murder seemed to be the first crack in these cases, since this victim had also disappeared earlier like the others. No one knew why he'd come back or how.

Zehra stood—she never liked to meet new clients sitting down. She had to control the meeting. Not that she believed much of what defendants told her. So many lied, made excuses, denied, and minimized their behavior. The savvy ones threw in a few truths like glue, to try and hold together their preposterous stories.

Around the control desk, she saw two deputies escorting El-Amin toward the second door in the room.

He had closely cut curly black hair and a short, flat nose. Dark skin that shone under the lights and a ragged beard. A short man, he walked slowly, erect and proud. He wore the jail's private-label clothing line—an orange jump suit. The deputy pushed on his arm. El-Amin jerked it away and came through the door.

He paused. His eyes rose slowly and looked at Zehra. They glistened black and focused, surrounded by deep cavities of smudged gray making him look old.

Even though his shoulders were narrow, Zehra saw wiry strength in them.

Behind El-Amin, the door closed, and the lock scraped through, metal against metal. Zehra nodded. "Hello, Mr. El-Amin. I'm Zehra Hassan, your lawyer." She held her hand at her side.

He didn't respond. Continued to stare at her. His eyes probed her face, shoulders, chest, then circled her hips and legs. She'd seen this before—the Stare, although it usually came from the street gangsters.

But this defendant was different. He wasn't a gangster and at twenty-six, was older. She held his gaze for a moment, then broke it off.

They both sat, and El-Amin used his left hand to push himself away from her. He had strong hands with thick calluses edging each finger.

Zehra took a deep breath. Considering that she had ambitions to be the first Muslim judge in Minnesota, defending a Muslim terrorist wouldn't help her career at all.

"I've been appointed to represent you in your murder case," Zehra began. "You speak English?"

He bobbed his head.

"First, we should talk about bail. Is there anyone who could afford to come up with some money . . . ?"

"I want a male lawyer," he demanded.

She'd heard this before, too. "Sorry, you get me."

"Are you Muslim?"

"That's irrelevant."

"In my country, women are not allowed to work like this. It is contrary to the Qur'an."

"Well, this isn't your country, and women do work like this here," Zehra said. "Do you want to talk about your case or religion? 'Cause if it's religion, I'm leaving."

He leaned back and refused to speak. His nostrils flared as if he smelled something.

Zehra took a deep breath. Most defendants were desperate to get out of custody. Not this one. And the bullshit about Muslims really set her on edge.

As an American-born Muslim, she knew the difficulties faced by people like her—trying to be good Americans and good Muslims at the same time. It was the discrimination and the crap suffered by Muslim women that upset her and had led to law school. Most Americans knew more about micro-breweries than Islam and how close its theology related to Judeo-Christianity. Along with other females in the United States, Zehra was passionate to modernize the role of Muslim women.

And here she faced the very problem they all faced—a radical, extremist who probably hated all women and had probably killed an innocent young man.

She thought to herself, *Is there a way I can dump this case? Can I beg a male, Christian colleague to take this bronco?*

"Okay. Let's look at the Complaint," Zehra sighed. She pulled out a document written by the prosecutor that alleged facts to make the defendant guilty of the charge of first-degree murder.

"It says that on March 19th a witness was standing on an open porch at the back end of the Horn of Africa deli on Cedar Avenue. The witness saw a young black man come out of the patio next to the deli through a wooden gate in the fence below the witness.

"Just as the guy got through the gate, another dark man, wearing a mask of some sort and identified as you, came up behind the younger one, grabbed his forehead with the left hand. With the right hand, he cut the younger one's throat with a knife. Then the killer fled."

Zehra glanced at El-Amin. His expression remained frozen.

"A week later," she continued reading, "a confidential, reliable informant, a CRI, reported to police you were at a coffee shop near the crime scene and bragged about a knife you had. You bragged that you 'brought a little lamb to Allah.' When police executed a search warrant at your apartment, they found a knife and a shirt. Both had been cleaned, but forensics later determined the victim's blood showed on both items."

Under brows hooded low, his eyes moved from the paper to Zehra's eyes again. He crossed his muscled arms over his chest.

A creepy feeling crabbed its way up her back. At this point, after reading all the accusatory facts, most defendants raved about how they were "all lies" and insisted they were innocent.

Still, Zehra's training as a defense lawyer asserted itself, and she started to see holes in the state's case. "When the cops did that line-up with the witness and he picked you, it's highly suggestive. The light was bad during the crime and after, as well. I don't know if it it'll stand up to cross—"

"It is not important. There are bigger things."

"What things? You think a murder one case isn't important?"

"You are not qualified."

"Damn right. If I could pull the plug on you, I would so fast"

"I have a right to a lawyer, don't I?" His lips lifted above white teeth.

"You got one."

"You . . . are a woman and an infidel."

"Aw . . . shit." Zehra moved her chair back. It felt hard to breathe around El-Amin, as if there were a vacuum sucking the air out of the room. She wanted to get out of this case. Besides, he made her feel uneasy.

Mostly, he stood for all she hated and fought against.

El-Amin raised his arm with a finger pointed up in the air. "Men have authority over women because Allah has made the one superior to the other," he quoted from the Qur'an.

Zehra felt a drop of sweat course down her neck. The stuffy room became claustrophobic. She breathed faster. "Don't quote me that crap. I know the Qur'an."

He interrupted her. "I have the right to a trial, and I can command you to have one."

"You have a right to a trial."

"I want a jury trial with a new lawyer."

"You'll get your trial," she shouted at him.

"I did it."

Zehra's words caught in her throat. "You killed the Somali?"

"It was necessary."

She stammered, "Well . . . I could talk to the prosecutor about a deal . . ."

"Do not talk to them."

Zehra'd never had a defendant admit guilt but still demand a trial. *What's wrong with this idiot?* She shoved her chair back and stood. "I've had it. I'm out of here."

"I know that I have a right to represent myself."

Zehra felt the anger rising in her until a thought struck her—she might be able to get out of the case. If he insisted on defending himself, she could be relieved of representing him.

She started to stuff the papers into her briefcase, not worrying about the order. The room felt small, stuffy. She wished she were drinking a cup of tea and working with her garden plants.

El-Amin stood and leaned toward her. He smelled of onions. Through gritted teeth, his said, "I will not have anything to do with you. I will be disgraced." His eyes shone with fury. "You do not wear *hijab*, you have bare legs. It is not of the law of Allah."

Zehra snapped. She jammed her finger into his face. "Listen you jerk, I'd be happy to never talk to you again. And don't tell me about the law of Allah. I know it better than you do." She stopped for a moment. "Have you ever read the Qur'an yourself or do you let others interpret it for you?" Her shouts bounced off the close walls.

"A woman cannot understand the words from the Prophet like a man."

Zehra felt her face flush hot with anger. Sweat stood out on her forehead. She knew better than to argue with him, but she hated all that he said. She stood but didn't trust her legs to support her. "Get out of my way," she yelled at him.

"No woman talks to me like that." He reached for the chair, gripped the edges, and started to lift it.

The silence in the room crackled with tension. Zehra heard the lights above humming. Thick air dulled any outside sounds. The chair scraped across the floor.

Zehra watched his eyes. Knew it was time and slammed the red panic button with her fist.

El-Amin had the chair off the ground. He twisted his shoulders to get better leverage. She could hear him grunt as he strained to swing it toward her.

Zehra backed into the corner. The block walls felt surprisingly cool. She had her arms up. Clanking sounds echoed around the room. El-Amin swore something in Arabic.

Two deputies burst through the door and clamped their arms over El-Amin's shoulders. The chair clattered to the floor. One deputy seemed to enjoy the opportunity and twisted El-Amin's arm behind him until Zehra heard something crunch. El-Amin screamed and dropped to the floor. He stomped on El-Amin's back.

Another deputy arrived and helped the first two drag her client outside the interview room. "You okay, Zehra?" he asked her. "Sorry . . . we didn't see anything until you hit the button. I . . . I'm so sorry."

She waved her hand at him. "Don't worry, Jack. I gotta get out of here." She stumbled back to the elevator and rode up to civilization above. Her blouse was drenched, and Zehra longed to get out of the sticky clothing.

She burst through the doors outside and felt the comforting smell of fresh air. Closing her eyes, she let the sun's warmth penetrate her wet face. Tangled thoughts flew through her brain. Nothing like this had ever happened to her before.

Even though El-Amin said he was guilty, her reading of the file told her there was a good chance he was innocent. Why would he want a trial? Zehra shook out her damp hair as if to shake off the creepy feeling he left with her.

That's not to mention the way guys like El-Amin had hijacked Islam in a perverted way to serve their violent ends. That infuriated her.

She took a deep breath and watched as a sparrow lifted off a nearby tree. It paddled upwards along the stones on the side of the old City Hall where Peregrine falcons sometimes swooped down from the ramparts to snatch prey like the sparrow.

Zehra started toward the cool of her office, plotting how she was going to dump the case.

TWO

The fact that Americans weren't immune to the disease, had been the key to everything.

Mustafa Ammar closed his leather bound copy of the Qur'an. He rose from his knees, completed his prayers, and removed the old, tan cotton robe. Underneath, he wore a blue Hugo Boss suit with a white shirt open at the collar.

Several years earlier, as part of his planning, he had successfully embedded himself in the Minnesota company called Health Technologies. He worked there as Michael Ammar, a genetic scientist--a perfect cover for his real work. After his prayers, he prepared to leave for the office and the labs.

Today, his immediate problem was a lack of information. With the launch date set for less than two weeks from now, Mustafa worried about the last minute details. Years of planning and struggle and setting up a network of believers, would finally pay-off. Could he control things until the release?

As he had intended, El-Amin had been accused of killing the Somali boy. Mustafa was certain he wouldn't reveal anything, but Mustafa still worried. He needed information about law enforcement. What were they doing on El-Amin's case? Would they uncover anything?

The scream of boiling water in the teapot startled him. He moved to the kitchen and poured hot water over loose tea leaves. Smelled the comforting aroma. Sitting in the hard chair beside the window, Mustafa thought back over years of work leading up to this point.

The key triggering everything was the fact that the deadly disease of smallpox had been eradicated from the world in the late 1970s. Drug companies stopped making vaccines. The Western infidels continued blissfully shopping, eating, and getting fat, confident that smallpox was a mass killer of the past. And even though people no longer had an immunity to it, that was okay since the disease didn't exist.

Except for two places.

He'd learned there remained two repositories of the virus. One, located in the Maximum Containment Laboratory at the Center for Disease Control in Atlanta, Georgia, was under the heaviest security. The other was located in Vector, an old city

14

in Russia. During what the infidels called the "Cold War," both the United States and Russia agreed to maintain the virus in safe deep freeze, so that in the case of an unexpected break-out, vaccines could be developed from the saved virus.

Mustafa sipped the tea and enjoyed the floral fragrance. He and his brotherhood saw this as an opportunity to strike at the West in a fashion more devastating than anything ever done before. Let others set off bombs in subways. What did that do? Kill a few people. And a week later, everyone forgot about it.

The Al-Qaeda attack on the World Trade Center first gave Mustafa a hint of what could be done. Not the destruction itself, but the ensuing panic. What if he could do something even worse, more widespread, and unstoppable that would lead to panic and death on a nation-wide scale?

He'd be blessed by Allah and revered the world over for his courage and vision.

The security at Vector was a joke and was bought-off cheaply. He'd already taken one shipment from them for testing on the Somali boys. The second one would be coming. He'd meet it himself. Once here, the delivery systems to spread the plague were also simple. The virus attached itself to the moist membranes of human mouths, noses, and throats. Like a greedy parasite, it exploded in uncontrolled growth. Unlike a parasite, the virus spread easily and killed quickly.

Finishing his tea, he cleaned up the few dishes in the kitchen and left for work. He pampered himself here in America. He justified it as part of his cover. Leaving the house, he climbed into the new BMW and started for Health Tech.

The company had also given him the place for the launch: the school where he volunteered as a science teacher to high school children. In two weeks the school-wide science fair would occur. He had volunteered to help prepare the projects—giving him access to all areas of the school. The fair would bring the students with hundreds of their parents. Like sacrificial lambs for Allah, they'd be cut down mercilessly.

Mustafa weaved his way skillfully through heavy traffic to the company. All around him, drivers strained to go faster. Most of them talking on cell phones. Probably about banal subjects like shopping or the insatiable need for Americans to watch sports. Not that many of them participated. Most sat on couches and drank beer. Mustafa worked hard to maintain his body and the fighting skills he'd learned from the brotherhood.

How far he'd come in his life, he marveled.

Born in Egypt, his parents fled from the British oppressors to the Netherlands where Mustafa had earned his undergraduate degree. Then they moved to Dearborn, Michigan which was the "Ellis Island," for most Middle Eastern people entering the

U.S. There, he'd earned his doctorate in molecular biology and had been confronted by the new groups at the mosque he attended.

It was ironic he thought. Before his commitment, he'd been lackadaisical about his faith like most Americans. The group at the mosque had befriended the lonely young man he was and convinced him to commit his life to ending the West's oppression and attacks on Islam.

The memory of his grandparents' deaths made that easy.

In Egypt, under the harsh rule of the British, they'd joined in an uprising. As carelessly as brushing off the sand from their shoes, the British soldiers massacred hundreds, including Mustafa's grandparents. His parents fled with him. Although their hearts remained in Egypt, they were too afraid to return. Now, they'd fallen for many of the temptations of Western society and become soft, unfaithful Muslims.

Mustafa pulled into the employee's parking lot at Health Technologies. He walked through the warming air to his office, nodded at the stupid secretary that he shared with three other people, and walked into his office.

As usual, his desk was immaculately clean. The walls were bare of any personal mementos or photos.

Mustafa set his briefcase on the credenza under the window. He looked outside. In the middle of a sinfully huge expanse of grassy lawn, a fountain shot water high into the air. In the morning sun, it looked like thousands of sparkling diamonds falling into the pool below. It reminded him of the pictures he'd seen of his dead grandparents. Thousands of pieces of glass shone on the ground next to their bodies where plate glass windows had shattered under the hail of bullets. Their blood, his blood, stained the gray dust beneath them.

He could never forgive.

Mustafa turned abruptly when he heard a loud knock on the door frame. He spun around.

Another scientist, John Posten, officed next to him. He grinned at Mustafa. "Hey, Michael, you stud. How many women'd you score this weekend?" Posten waited and when Mustafa didn't respond, he went on, "You're so buff and good looking. That your secret?"

"Lots of exercise. Good food. You know."

Posten looked down at the tub around his waist. "Yeah . . . gotta work on that myself. Get your prayers in this morning?"

Mustafa felt a red hot surge of blood shoot into his face. The rage always started with the shaking in his legs. Why didn't Allah strike these kafirs dead? These stupid fools. He hoped the one standing before him would be the first to die. Mustafa fought to appear calm. "Of course. Five times a day. You should try it yourself."

Posten's mouth curled down. "Yeah . . . s'pose it wouldn't hurt." He started to turn. "Hey, got time for a muffin in the cafeteria?"

"No thanks. Too much work. I'm leaving for Egypt in a few days."

"Again? How come you get the cool assignments? What're you doing this time?"

"Well, since I speak Arabic and the company wants to expand our contacts in the Middle East, I guess they pick me. I'm presenting another paper. It's called, 'Use of the IL-4 Gene to Produce Interleukin-4.'"

"Cool stuff. You know it better than anyone. Yo, bro." Posten started to walk away. He stopped. "Hey, you're going to the company party aren't you?"

"Of course." Mustafa watched him waddle out the door.

Sitting at his desk, he checked his corporate email. Amongst the usual worthless dung, he saw one from another employee, Joseph Hassan. Mustafa vaguely remembered him. Older man, Muslim. Hassan wanted to meet for lunch. Mustafa paused. Hassan . . . wasn't that the name of El-Amin's lawyer?

He twisted around to his briefcase and grabbed the morning edition of the *Star Tribune*, the local paper. There it was: El-Amin's new lawyer was a woman named Zehra Hassan. Could she be related to Joseph? In America, the name Hassan was unusual. It just might be possible, he thought.

This could be the key to getting the information he wanted about the El-Amin case. He knew his good looks attracted women. She'd be easy to fool. And if necessary in order to control her, there were other measures he could take in the meantime.

He banged his desk with a closed fist in triumph. Allah always provided. Mustafa tapped a quick response on his computer to Joseph and agreed to meet.

THREE

I t constituted one of the biggest pleasures of his life, but Paul Schmidt was afraid to tell anyone about it.

In his two-bedroom home in St. Louis Park, a first-ring suburb of Minneapolis, he kept everything locked in the basement. In this densely urban setting, people didn't do his kind of hobby. People owned guns but few treasured or collected weapons the way he did.

He'd grown up on the outskirts of St. Cloud, a town on the edge of the pine forests of northern Minnesota.

He missed the woods but realized there wasn't much work for people with his skills in St. Cloud. The town had been named after an Indian chief and that lineage carried down to him from his grandmother, a one-half Ojibwa Indian.

Paul was proud of the heritage and knew it showed in him. The dark skin, dark straight hair, tall lanky body, and a quiet personality. From his father, he'd inherited the German sense of order, competence, and duty to country.

Tonight, he walked through the living room where he'd hung the heads of the big game he'd successfully hunted. They'd become like friends visiting and occasionally, he even talked to them. Paul stepped down the narrow wooden stairs to his basement in anticipation. A closed, faintly musty smell met him.

He'd built a crude but serviceable workbench seven feet long across the wall in the largest room. Paul flicked on the overhead lights.

He organized his tools in specific order. Some were hung on pegboard mounted behind the low bench and others stored in the drawers of low file cabinets. Paul found the cabinets at thrift shops and was proud to have never paid more than four dollars for one. The presses for reloading shells occupied the far corner.

Although he liked guns better, his knife collection was extensive, and he particularly loved the antique ones he'd found. All were carefully sharpened since a knife without an edge was as good as trying to cut with a pencil.

Tonight, he'd simply clean some of the rifles, not that they really needed it since he kept them spotless. The sweet familiar smell of cleaning fluid and the special gun oil comforted Paul.

His passion was restoring older weapons. He found them from many sources, brought them back to his workshop, and set them on the white butcher block paper covering the table.

Usually, they came to him covered in rust, oil, or even mud—hiding the beautiful craftsmanship underneath. He loved the process of carefully cleaning and uncovering the original features. Many weapons had old stories or mysteries about them that Paul could discover when he scraped away the outer layers of age and abuse.

His friends would think his fixation was weird.

And maybe it was, but he loved the technical sophistication of arms and the historical romance. If he lived in northern Minnesota, he'd fit right in. In fact, next to small engine repair, gun repair was a major industry.

After high school, when the Army recruiter in St. Cloud had talked to his best friend, the midfielder on the high school soccer team, Paul became interested too. Paul qualified for the Rangers and took to the training with gusto. He loved the order, the mission, the clear rules, and the self-reliance he learned.

After his successful discharge from the Army, Paul knew he wanted to continue serving the country in some way. He returned to Minnesota, finished college, and then law school.

With the help of his parent's friend, a congresswoman, she persuaded the FBI to hire him in 2000. Things went well until the disaster in Milwaukee almost cost him his job.

The recent Somali murder case offered him the way to rehabilitate his career and help his country.

His biggest challenge would be the political ones in the Bureau itself. Even after all these years, the memory of his screw-up caused his shoulders to tighten. He felt immense guilt and at the same time, furious anger at the Bureau. It had been his fault of course, but they'd hung everything on him as the sacrificial lamb, with no more concern than someone might have in shaking out a wet rag to toss into the dryer.

Then, after his demotion, he was the one who'd taken the call three years ago from a teacher at Hiawatha High School in the southern suburb that started the FBI investigation.

He remembered her breathy, anxious voice.

"This is Gennifer Simmons, that's Gennifer with a 'G,' and I'm worried about something."

Demoted to answering the phone on the public tip line, Paul droned, "What's the problem?"

"Our school has a big Somali population and there's a boy, well I should say he's a man 'cause he seems much older than the other kids and . . ."

"What about him?"

She paused. "I . . . I don't know if I should do this because a teacher's first duty is to her students but, well, I'm really worried." She gulped a deep breath. "We call him the 'Pied Piper' since he's always getting the younger boys to follow him. And he lectures them, talks about infidels."

"Yeah?" Paul tried to be patient.

"His lecturing and getting the boys to follow him wasn't so bad, I guess, but when he came to me a couple times with maps of Minnesota and asked me to show him where to get across the border into Canada . . . well, I got really worried. But I'm not sure I should be telling you"

Paul's feet clumped to the floor as his brain raced. He grabbed a pen and notepad. "We're definitely interested. Who is this young man and where can I talk to him?" Was he being too alarmist? No . . . after 9/11 he knew to react to anything.

"Well . . . that's just it. I don't think you can."

"This could be a matter of national security, don't you see that?" he shouted.

"But . . . he's gone."

"He's gone? Where'd he go?"

"I don't know. He and three other young men just disappeared."

THE FBI RESPONSE WAS INSTANTANEOUS. In a few months, many other Somali young men disappeared from their homes and schools. No one—friends, family, religious leaders—knew where they went or why. Then, a few showed up, fighting in Somalia, and the FBI cracked open the case.

But now, Paul didn't think the Bureau was going far enough in their investigation, and it scared the hell out of him.

In his basement, Paul walked to the stand up steel locker in the corner. He felt the damp coolness. He withdrew several of the weapons from the locker, both handguns and rifles. Paul laid some of his handguns on the table.

There was the cute little Glock 29, the subcompact with the powerful 10mm upgrade from the Glock 26. He held the grip in two fingers, as it was designed, and set it down. So light, it almost felt like a toy. Next to it, he put his larger Glock 21 that boasted a heavy .45-caliber shell. He marveled at the fact the Austrian Glock was made of high-strength nylon-polymer, much more resilient than carbon steel.

His cell phone rang.

Usually, his friends texted him, so it was unusual for a call. Paul wiped his hands on a paper towel and walked over to pick it up.

Didn't recognize the number, clicked on receive, and said hello.

"Paul, sorry to disturb you, but I've got some questions," Zehra Hassan said.

His breath caught in his throat involuntarily at the sound of her voice. He'd met her in law school, dated her for a short time, then they drifted apart. He still remembered how attractive she was, flawless skin and big, almond shaped eyes. "That's okay. I'm not doing anything important. What's up?"

He had initiated contact with her a few days ago. She'd been surprised, but Paul insisted he called as a friend to see if he could help her. She probably saw through that but agreed. He told her of the difficulty the police and FBI had in figuring out what happened to the missing young men.

It was a lucky break for the FBI when the witness came forward about the victim, Mohamoud Ahmed, and identified the suspect. The distrust of authorities in the Somali community made investigation difficult. Their loyalty to their clans trumped all other duties.

And Zehra didn't trust the reason for his call. He'd told his boss about the possibility of using Zehra to gain information about the murder case in the hopes of getting an advantage for the FBI.

After Zehra agreed to talk, Paul suspected she'd use him for the same reason.

"I just met my client, Ibrahim El-Amin, this afternoon. Since you've worked on the case, I wondered if I could talk to you. I mean, you said to call."

He sat down in the straight-backed chair at his bench. "Sure. What's he like?"

"I hate the son of a bitch. And he hates me . . . well, all women."

"Did he do something to you?"

"Other than to try to hit me, no," she said. "He stands for everything I've worked against all my life. These traditional Muslim guys from over there are jerks. They treat women like they're camels. Quoting me the Qur'an. Can you imagine?"

"Can't help you there," he chuckled, remembering how tough she was. "You know how badly we want to take this guy out." She didn't respond, and he knew why. Making contact with her hadn't been an accident, and Paul knew she had her suspicions, but he couldn't tell her everything right now. Primarily, the case was the most important aspect to him, not her. It involved connections much larger than she imagined. He'd have to be careful. "What else?" he asked her, fishing.

"Since I only watch the gardening shows, I don't catch all the news. What's the background?"

"The young Somali men disappeared from many families and locations, and it remained a local police case until a few developments this year." Paul paused, careful how much he could reveal to her. "One of the boys, Shirwa Ahmed, blew himself up in Somalia last October to become the first American suicide bomber. Then, recently, Burhan Hassan was found shot dead in Mogadishu."

"Odd."

"Yeah. One of 'em was studying engineering and suddenly left."

"What ages?"

"Anywhere from seventeen to their late twenties."

Zehra sighed. "Why in the hell would they want to go back to Somalia? I thought most people couldn't wait to get out."

"Somalia hasn't had a functioning government since 1991. It's ruled by tribes, and that remains true today. It's a pretty primitive place in many respects."

"So why did these guys go back?"

"The Somali community here has many answers to that."

"I know, Paul, but what do you think?"

"The FBI's theory is they were recruited to fight in a group called the Shabaab militia. They're 'freedom fighters' for the Somalia homeland."

"So, what's the problem with that?"

"Shabaab is a militant Islamic group aligned with Al Qaeda." Paul paused. "You can imagine that rang a few bells in the FBI and in Washington."

"Yeah, I guess. So, how does the victim in my case fit in?"

"He disappeared from a high school a year ago. His parents reported sporadic contact with him by cell, but they always felt the calls were monitored by someone else because Ahmed didn't speak freely."

"I saw that in the evidence material. He said he was on a jihad for Allah, and it was the purest he'd ever felt. A true believer."

"Right. Without his parent's knowledge, he showed up here and was murdered."

"Had he been recruited by the Shabaab?" Zehra pried.

"That's what the Bureau and the police think."

"But . . . you hesitated. Is that what you think?"

He had to be careful what he said to Zehra. "It's what I think, too," he lied.

"I still don't understand why he came back. Or why he was murdered."

Paul chuckled. "You sound like a defense lawyer—what's the motive? The simple answer is, he didn't cooperate. Many of these guys come back to recruit their friends. Ahmed wouldn't do it, so he was killed—by your client."

Zehra didn't respond.

"Come on, Zehra. You're too savvy to believe this killer is innocent. You're no bleeding-heart liberal."

"I didn't say he was innocent. I just don't know." She paused. "The ID isn't great, especially since the killer wore a mask and glasses."

Paul remembered the lush resonance in her voice when it dipped into lower registers. Their affair had been pretty hot. They'd come close to having sex, but at the last moment, she backed-off, saying the Muslim guilt would be too much for her. "You know I can't say anything." He cleared his throat. "What do you think happened?"

"The Shabaab theory sounds plausible. I wonder if the organization is strong enough here in the Twin Cities to have enforcers."

"They sure as hell do and frankly, it's asshole guys like your client who scare me. What if they start directing their kids to attack us here? On some jihad?"

"Scary thought."

"Zehra, I know you have an ethical duty to keep your talks with him confidential and to zealously represent him in court but remember, if you learn of any possible criminal activity that's going to happen . . ."

"Paul, how stupid do you think I am? Just 'cause I'm representing him doesn't mean I like this jerk or believe him," Zehra snapped. "I'm just as worried about terrorists as everyone else!"

Neither spoke for a while.

"Sorry. I just don't want you to get into any trouble."

"Trouble? What the hell are you talking about?"

"Just be careful; that's all I can say."

Zehra said, "El-Amin's demanding a speedy trial. So, we'll set a trial date as soon as possible."

"Can you be ready by then?"

Zehra said, "I don't think he cares."

"Okay." His voice softened. "What are you going to do now?"

"Relax. I've got lots of watering to do in my garden. When I bought this place, I looked for the biggest balcony I could find. I've got about a dozen pots out there with lettuce, flowers, strawberries, and a few unidentified things. It's so crowded I can hardly get around to water, but I'd die without my garden. It keeps me sane."

Paul sensed they were done and said, "Zehra . . . I want you to be careful with this case."

"What do you mean? The guy's in custody, and the deputies all love me."

After Paul clicked off the phone, he went back to work. He lifted his most expensive prize onto the table. The Browning BAR rifle with the telescopic sights. He'd splurged to buy the most luxurious one, the Safari model, which had the engraved steel receiver and upgraded walnut stock. He ran his fingers down the slightly oily barrel to feel the smooth precision of the engineering.

He thought of Zehra. When she was first assigned to represent the killer, Paul told his superiors he knew Zehra, providing him an excuse to contact her. It seemed like a good idea then. Now he realized how difficult it would be.

FOUR

Carolyn Bechter could feel tension rumble up from her groin, through her stomach, and into her chest. She took deep breaths to calm herself. As one of the "seasoned" reporters for TV Channel 6, she thought this was the story that would catapult her out of obscurity. She'd missed breaking the story of the disappearance of the young Somali men. Of course, she covered the arrest of the terrorist El-Amin and was assigned to cover the murder trial when it began. But she competed against all the other local to national journalists. After years of declining responsibilities, this story *had* to work for her.

She paused in the lobby of Hiawatha High School, in a southern suburb of the Twin Cities. Just outside, protesters were gathering. Carolyn knew other media people would be here soon, but she was the first.

She could feel the immensity of this story.

Carolyn stopped at the front desk and showed her ID.

While Carolyn waited, she thanked the cheap-ass station owners for at least setting up the "Tip-Six" website. Corny as it sounded, it actually worked. When it was introduced two years ago, her producer assured everyone that the tips coming in would be distributed equally. Not true.

As an older reporter, Carolyn fought a losing battle against the newer, blonder, and lower-paid reporters who caught the eye of the producer—pig that he was. The perky, new reporters always got more choice assignment with more face time on the screen. The more they jiggled, the more stories they got. For years, Carolyn struggled to make a name for herself. But now, even her producer told her she was "branding out." His term to describe the fatigue that viewers felt when they saw her yet again, after fifteen years with Channel Six.

She'd show the self-centered prick.

When the tip came in about the protest, Carolyn happened to be there, had grabbed it, and run with it.

"Hey," the receptionist said. "It's like, gonna happen over there." She pointed and looked at her watch. "We've been cut-back to part time, so I've gotta boogie." She looked at Carolyn with stupid eyes. "Sorry, but you're on your own."

Carolyn sighed. Years ago, her presence at a school like this would have brought out several people, all interested in seeing the face they watched nightly or trying to get on camera themselves. Not anymore. The twit of a receptionist didn't even recognize Carolyn. Of course, the poor girl wasn't Carolyn's demographic. She had the over-forty-five crowd. This girl's group got their news from the Internet.

She thought of her former husband, Matt, who had soared while she'd stalled in the secondary market of the Twin Cities. He'd moved to Los Angeles. The passion between them always teetered between love and competition. So far, he'd won. Carolyn tried to dismiss him. It didn't matter anymore. Let it go.

And passion? Well, she hadn't been laid in months.

She felt the rumble in her lower body. This story could do it for her.

A middle-aged woman entered the lobby. She had short, curly brown hair, a frumpy brown outfit, sans makeup. Her smile was crooked and weak and as she came closer she said, "Are you . . . Carolyn Bechter?"

Of course I am you idiot, Carolyn thought to herself. *Don't you recognize me?* She forced a smile back. "I am. Who are you?"

"I'm a teacher here. Gennifer. I just came out to see what was going on with these protests."

"Oh? Tell me."

"You don't have a camera man?"

"Uh . . . no. For these background stories, we usually don't send one along," Carolyn lied.

"Oh, I can't say anything."

Carolyn waited. Silence was her greatest interviewing trick.

"Well . . ." Simmons shifted her weight onto the other hefty thigh. "I guess the Muslims are protesting that they want more time set aside for their prayers. They pray five times a day, you know. And since they just wash before, they use all the lavatories."

Carolyn nodded.

"But I guess the Christian Evangelical group is also going to protest. They want prayer in the school too. And to be able to use the bathrooms when they want."

"What do you think?"

"Oh . . . I can't say. I'm just here to see what happens. I don't want my students getting in trouble. We have a large Somali population in our school, you know."

Carolyn sighed; convinced this source wasn't a source at all. She'd learned over the years to keep trolling until she hit something big. "Nice to talk with you." Carolyn moved outside.

Across the grassy field next to the administration building, several people, obviously Somali or Middle Eastern, gathered in a group. Most of the girls wore long dresses in spite of the warming weather. Most wore head coverings. The boys stood separate from them and carried a few placards that asked for more prayer time.

Carolyn thought they'd picked up that American practice pretty quickly. She wondered how many were illegals but still had learned to demand "their rights."

On the other side of the field, another group of students walked forward slowly. This group looked all-American. Short hair, long pants, tan t-shirts, and jeans. Boys and girls mingled. They were chanting about more prayer themselves.

For a moment, it struck Carolyn—why the protest? Weren't they asking for the same thing? Who instigated the protest?

As an investigative journalist, she questioned everything, looking for an angle that she could exploit before other media arrived.

When the second group got closer to the first, there were some shouts back and forth but no violence. Nothing looked too coordinated, and Carolyn wondered if the tip and her trip out here had been another waste of time.

Then she saw a lone man, an adult, behind the Somali group. He moved among them quickly and spoke to various students. He was a tall man, dark skinned with a long white shirt, buttoned to the neck. *Don't these people ever get hot?* Carolyn wondered.

Something about the man caught her attention.

She couldn't hear what he said, but the way he darted from one student to the next looked unusual. Carolyn knew her instincts were almost always right on. When the man left the group and headed for the building, Carolyn followed him.

Catching him just before he entered a side door, Carolyn called out, "Excuse me, sir? Carolyn Bechter, Channel 6 TV news . . . can I talk . . ."

His head swiveled around, and black eyes jerked back and forth. He focused on her. "What do you want?" he said in good English.

"Uh . . . I just want to know what's going on here." She felt her high heels sinking into the grass as she hurried over to the man.

"Our students have rights that should be protected."

"What do they want?"

"To be treated equally. To be allowed to practice their religion in peace."

"What's your name?"

His eyes darted to both sides again. "I must leave now." He ducked through the door.

Carolyn grabbed the handle, but it had already closed and locked. When she turned around, two men in short-sleeved colored t-shirts passed her. "Excuse me, I'm Carolyn Bechter, Channel 6 TV news . . . do you work here?" They stopped and recognized her. Good. The power of celebrity always got her information.

"Yeah. Nice to meet you in person. I watch you a lot." The older man hesitated, and then stuck out his hand to shake hers. "Jim Miller. I'm in charge of the entire physical plant here. How can we help?"

"Did you happen to notice the man I was just talking to?"

"Ben? Yeah, he's worked here for a short time."

"Who is he? What's his name?"

"Ben Mohammad. 'Course, every other one of 'em's named Mohammad. He was just hired as our outreach coordinator. We've got a large Somali student population, so they hired Ben. Lots of these parents can't speak English and are working too hard to participate much in the school, so I guess, Ben's supposed to 'reach out and touch 'em.'"

"Do you know anything else about him?"

"Naw . . . he lives in South Minneapolis, near Somali-land, over by Augsburg College. I think he works part time in a deli there . . . I don't know." Jim's brows furrowed. "Why are you interested?"

Easy . . . easy, Carolyn thought to herself. All her experience taught her to not raise suspicions, or the information source would stop. "We're just covering the protest. I'm looking for a human interest angle. You know, make the story real by showing real people."

Carolyn couldn't help but think this might be her last chance—thanks to high-def TV. In a few years, the lines in her face, even with make-up, couldn't be hid. She'd be out on the street. Then where would she go? She hadn't saved a penny, and the little she had in her 401K dipped every day to new lows. Maybe print journalism? What a joke! They were even more strapped for funding that TV. Maybe an obscure position on, God forbid, a public TV station. She shook her head.

Jim started to back away. "Hey, where's your camera guy? Don't you always have one for TV?"

"He's on his way. What are Ben's duties?"

"Uh . . . I don't know. You should talk to the principal." Jim started to turn.

The younger man said, "I think he takes some of the boys on projects. Ya know, like field trips and stuff like that."

In spite of the Pepto Bismol she'd popped, Carolyn felt the rumbling start inside her again. "Field trips? He takes the Somali boys on field trips? Where do they go?"

Jim pulled on the other man's arm. "Come on, Kenny. We got work to do." They spun around and walked away.

The rumbling in Carolyn's stomach told her one thing: she had stumbled onto something important. She didn't know what. From all her year's experience, she could feel it. She'd stick with it until the story cracked open. Carolyn would be a hero again.

FIVE

Monday morning in Courtroom Two, Zehra stood before the Honorable MaryAnn Gorden Smith, the "Hot Tub" judge, and arraigned her client. "My client doesn't want a female lawyer," Zehra said. "He wants to represent himself."

Prior to coming to court, Zehra had researched all the rules governing this issue. She desperately wanted out of the case.

The judge stopped flipping papers and frowned at her.

"I know, Judge. But my client has a right to represent himself, and he demands it."

Judge Smith peered at El-Amin, standing behind the low wooden wall at the side of the courtroom. He crossed his hands in front of himself at his waist. "Are you sure this is what you want to do?" she asked.

He closed his eyes and spoke, "I will not have a woman represent me nor have a woman judge me."

The prosecutor, Steve Harmon, stood behind the table reserved for counsel. "I want the record to note the defendant wants to go pro se. He can't change his mind later."

"I want my trial as soon as possible," El-Amin shouted.

To make clear her disagreement, the judge twitched her head back and forth. "Well, it's your right but . . ." she said to El-Amin and looked back at Zehra and Jackie Nyguen, the lawyer who would second-chair Zehra. "I don't have time for this today. We'll settle the issue of representation later. For now, you've still got the case." She bent her head to the papers and flipped them to dismiss the lawyers.

"Wait." El-Amin said in a deep voice.

The judge's face jerked up. Annoyed. "What?"

"I will not have this woman represent me. I understand that I am able to represent myself?"

Her lips tightened. "It's not advisable in a case this serious."

"I demand to represent myself."

Zehra jumped in, "That's his right, your Honor. You could relieve me of my duty to represent him." Zehra knew the judge was too quick to fall for that but hoped she would give her a break.

"I'm not going to deal with this today or you, sir," the judge sneered. "For now, everything remains the same. You're representing him, Ms. Hassan." She gathered the file together and tossed it aside as if tired of a bad paperback novel.

"But your Honor . . ."

"What is it you don't understand?"

"I know you've appointed the public defender, but the defendant wants to go pro se, and he has a right . . ." As her voice rose, Zehra knew it was too shrill.

"That's enough out of everyone," Judge Smith shouted. "Counsel, you sit down." The judge turned to the defendant. "Deputies, get him out of here."

As they moved away from the bench, Jackie whispered, "Way to go, girl. What a bitch. Why do you call her the 'Hot Tub' judge?"

Zehra sighed, "Several years ago, the governor worked with Smith in the state legislature. She was a successful lawyer and prominent in legal circles. Well, the governor's wife and Smith became friends, as Smith was always politically savvy. After legislative sessions, they'd go back to the governor's mansion to relax in the hot tub. When the next judicial opening occurred in this county, guess who got it?"

Jackie nodded. "You're shitting me! Is she smart?"

"Very. But MaryAnn uses every advantage she has. I'm sure the governor didn't miss those boobs on his new choice as she splashed in the hot tub."

AFTER THE COURT HEARING, Zehra and Jackie walked down Fourth Avenue, two blocks to the Public Defender's office, past a parking ramp edged in flowers. Spring flowers gloried in the morning light—purple, blue, and dark-green leaves. A fresh breeze lifted them as if they were dancing. Purple crocuses partnered with the miniature irises to move in rhythm with the wind.

Reaching the tall office building, they walked around the coffee shop on the main floor and rode the elevator to the seventh floor, all of it occupied by dozens of lawyers, law clerks, support staff, investigators, and the law library.

In the lobby, Jerry Zimmerman stalked around the room, telling everyone about his newest case. "In this crazy job, you think you've heard everything. No . . . they always throw you a curve." He jerked his head from one person to another but really just wanted their attention.

Jerry's squat body moved faster as he talked more. Black hair scrambled to cover the top of his head but failed. "So, I'm interviewing this new guy, who's charged with burglary of a jewelry shop at the Mall of America. First of all," he stopped and pointed at Jackie. "You'd pick a store in the busiest mall in America to rob, right? Smart idea?"

Zehra laughed to herself. There were so many of these clients. She'd often been in the same place Jerry found himself.

"Get this. He decides to commit the 'perfect crime,' but he lacks a basic tool—the getaway car. That doesn't stop our little criminal. He must've watched too many motivational DVDs, telling him he can be all that he wants to be—a successful criminal. So, he takes the bus out to the Mall."

Jerry moved again, poking the air with his upraised finger. "Into the Mall, no disguise of course, he heads to the jewelry shop. When he gets there, the clerks are almost closing up for the night. He smashes a case open, shovels the stuff into a garbage bag, and boogies. To his credit, he actually got out of the Mall before security could stop him."

"What happened?" one of the secretaries asked.

Jerry stopped dead, hung his head. "Ah . . . you know how they caught him?" Jerry waited to deliver the punch line. "The putz was standing outside waiting for his get-away car—the bus!" Everyone laughed. "He's got the jewelry still in the garbage bag in his hot little hands when he's nabbed. And he wants a fuckin' trial!"

Jerry wiped his eye and said, "I should write sit coms. You can't make this stuff up."

"You can do it, Jerry," Zehra called to him as she walked into her office. Jackie followed, and Zehra dropped her leather briefcase on the chair next to her desk. The office occupied a corner, shaped like a badly designed triangle. Large windows opened onto the condo high rise next door. At least Zehra faced east to catch the morning sun—something vital for her during the long winters.

She turned to her computer and opened her email. Scrolling through the messages of upcoming birthdays, how stupid the judges were, a used car for sale until she saw one with an unknown sender. That wasn't unusual since her address was a government office that anyone could access.

She opened it, started to read, and gasped.

It read: "Death to the infidel!"

"What?" Jackie's head jerked up.

"I don't know. I don't . . . probably some nut." Zehra showed her the message.

"You get stuff like that?"

"Never. I don't feel good about this. Another reason for me to bail on El-Amin."

She saved it and sent an email to the IT guy in the office to see if he could find the source. It bothered her and she felt a low grumbling in her stomach.

She looked at Jackie as she settled in the chair. Glad to have her help, Jackie started working as a public defender two years earlier. She'd come from a corporate law firm but found the work boring, even though it paid almost twice what she made as a government lawyer. She wanted the action of courtroom trial work.

Shiny dark hair curved around Jackie's round face. Large brown eyes almost distracted Zehra from the beautiful, flawless pale skin—that made her jealous since Jackie didn't have a wrinkle anywhere. Unlike most Vietnamese women, she had an ample figure that she kept trim with yoga classes, four times a week. Some day, Zehra agreed, she'd come along for a class, although between snow boarding in the winter and biking in the summer, she kept herself busy.

"Like those killer glasses, Jackie," Zehra said about the square "Buddy Holly" glasses she wore.

Jackie worked hard, was sharp, and anxious to help.

Zehra remembered her own training as a law student in the prosecutor's office, the county attorney, a few years ago. She thought of her mentor, Charlie Pollard, how much he'd taught her, and how excited she'd been to learn. She'd told that to Jackie.

"Did you like working as a prosecutor?" Jackie asked.

"Sure. There are pressures on both sides. They're different, but I learned a lot over there. I met a lot of cops and began to see the world from their perspective. I went with them on ride-alongs and even spent some time at the gun range."

"You?" Jackie's eyes opened wide.

"Yeah, can you imagine? Me, essentially a pacifist, shooting pistols?" But I wanted to learn. Who knows? I may join the NRA."

Jackie laughed and asked what they needed to do today.

"Bobby Joe Washington's coming in this morning," Zehra said.

"How'd you get him? I hear he's like one of the best."

"Right. He's one of the only investigators to be trained in the FACS, the Facial Action Coding System."

"Is that like the TV show where the expert can tell if a person's lying just by looking at their face?"

"Yeah, I think so. Plus, our chief assigned him, specifically. BJ's not happy about it, but, as usual, he'll do a good job. He went to work as soon as we got the discovery evidence. I hope to hell, he'll have something solid for us today. Otherwise, we're in deep shit."

"Why's he unhappy about working on this?" said Jackie.

"Well, I can't blame him. The chief figures since BJ's black, he'll have a better chance of getting access to the black, Somali community than the white investigators."

"I don't know . . ."

"Of course not. It's stupid. The same reason I was assigned the case—the Chief thinks just because I'm Muslim that should somehow make a difference. I argued with him, but he wouldn't listen. We're all stuck with this piece of crap. The Somalis don't like American blacks, generally. It's not gonna work, but the chief's real worried about how this will play in the press."

Jackie said. "I bet you're like, so pissed."

Zehra raised her eyebrows at Jackie. "I'm working to get out of it, if I can. This guy's a real bronco." She threw up her arms. "How the hell does he expect us to 'defend' him when he says he's guilty?"

SIX

"Come on, Barry. You owe me one," pleaded Zehra. "Think of all the crap I did for you on that robbery . . . the one where the defendant called you four times a day to complain. Who took all those calls for you?"

"I know, I know. But not this case. I don't want the press."

"I'm not asking you to take it for free. I'll take the two sex cases you got."

"Awe . . ."

"Think of what it'll be like in front of the jury, Barry." Zehra coaxed him. "Facing those nice people as your perp, who diddled little girls, sits right next to you. Do you want that? I bet he can drool and smell at the same time."

"He's innocent," Barry joked.

"Get off it. This is your last chance to dump those whining perverts."

"No way, Zehra. I'm sorry you got stuck with this one, but I don't want to have to deal with all the shit . . . including 'Chairman Mao.'" Barry referred to the chief public defender, who, although he wasn't Asian, resembled the round, cruel face of Mao Tse-tung.

"Go to hell, Barry."

Zehra sighed and leaned back in her broken chair. Her office contained a beige, laminated desk, a tan bookshelf, two other chairs, and a low credenza.

To avoid the beige jail cell effect, Zehra brought in a Persian wool rug. She could also use that for her prayers, as a faithful Muslim, at least a couple times a day. Two large frames with colorful cloth stretched over them hung on the wall before her desk in her favorite color, red. Photos of her extended family lined up across the credenza in a variety of frames. Inside the door, Zehra had a round mirror to check her hair before she left the office.

Zehra pulled open the bottom drawer and spied the secret she'd smuggled in: a Hostess cream-filled chocolate cupcake. Utterly horrible and disgusting, but she loved to nibble one occasionally. If Jackie wasn't there, Zehra would have taken a bite. Thank God, Jackie sat across from her. Zehra wondered if there was a twelve-step program for people like her who ate too much junk, especially things that had more chemicals than food.

Jackie shook her head. "What do you want me to do first?"

Zehra closed the drawer, turned to face her. She sighed. "I hope our investigator, BJ, comes in here in the next ten minutes and tells us he's cracked the case open and it's gonna be a slam-dunk. I need a miracle." Zehra looked at Jackie. Zehra forced the thought out of her mind for now. "Until the judge relieves us of representing this 'camel jockey,' we've got to prepare. We need to challenge the search of his apartment. Check out the warrant and give me some research on the legality of it. After all, there were two other guys living there. How do we know which guy owned the knife and shirt?"

"Prints?"

"None. Then, there's the line-up. Try to knock that out. I'm worried we're not gonna get this all put together in time." She looked over at Jackie. "With a trial date in a month, that means the Omnibus hearing to challenge this stuff will come up in about two weeks. If I'm forced to try it, I don't want any accusations of malpractice 'cause we're not ready."

"You'll want to see the crime scene. There's the investigation of witnesses . . ."

"I've already got BJ working his butt off. I hope to hell he scores. The only problem with him is he's an adult ADD."

"Huh?"

"He starts off with great ideas and energy but then loses interest. The trick to working with him is to keep him focused. Like the DNA. I've been after him to get the test results." She opened her Blackberry and tapped into her schedule. "Oh, damn! I forgot the appearance this afternoon with the hockey jock." She glanced at her watch.

"Tough case?"

"Depends on how you look at it. I've got a U of M hockey player who was filmed having sex with a woman in the stairwell of a parking ramp. Indecent exposure is the charge. It's only a misdemeanor, and I told him to plead. We'll get it off his record later. Know what he tells me?"

"What?"

"He has a constitutional right to freedom of expression. Can you believe it? I'm gonna have to give him a crash course in constitutional law this afternoon when I kick his expressive butt."

"How about the autopsy of our victim. Still want to go over it?"

"Yeah," Zehra said. "You never know when something small will pop up for us."

Jackie tapped on her laptop. She finished and looked at Zehra. "I'm like, amazed at you—you're so thorough. I really appreciate the chance to work with you. A lot of the younger women look up to you."

"Thanks, but I don't see myself that way."

"It must be tough being the first Muslim in the office. Me—I'm Christian, Catholic. A result of the French co-opting the Vietnamese aristocracy into converting in order to receive special treatment during the occupation."

"It's hard to be a Muslim in America period, although we're the third largest religion in this country. Particularly after 9/11, you can't believe the looks I get everywhere I go. Even though I'm female, I still get the looks." She took a deep breath. "You should try getting on a plane."

"What?"

"When I'm seated, I don't dare go to the toilet and never, never go to the one in the front, near the cockpit. Many times, I've been afraid some of the passengers would take me down out of their own fear. Of course, I'm so claustrophobic, I have a hard time flying anyway."

Jackie remained silent for a moment. Then said, "But you're so pretty, so small. I can't imagine . . ."

"Well . . ." she sighed. Some days the effort was just too much, too discouraging. Before Zehra could wallow much deeper, her cell phone rang. She answered to hear her mother's voice.

"Zehra, you've got to come over for dinner tomorrow night. I'm fixing the lamb dish you like so much."

"Thanks Mom, but I'm too busy, and you know I'm not eating much meat anymore."

If she didn't love her mother so much, these conversations could become a pain in the neck. She nagged Zehra constantly about getting a good job at a big company and marrying. After all, she was thirty-two. Couldn't she find a nice Muslim man, preferably a doctor or engineer?

Of course Zehra would like to be married some day. Most men she dated were Christians because the Muslim population, besides Somali, was small in Minnesota. Although they shared a religion, that was about it. Even the way Somalis practiced Islam was a product of culture and history—foreign to Zehra's experience. In the meantime, her mother's words echoed the loneliness she often felt. Zehra imagined that she lived in a large bell of quiet isolation that seldom rang.

Her mother said, "Well, you could stand to put a little weight on. Now, could you be here at six-thirty? We'll have a cup of tea before . . ."

"Ah, Mom. I'm so busy . . . oh, all right" Zehra hardly waited for the response in order to get her mother off the phone. Zehra feared the true reason for the invitation.

"Okay, dear." A pause. "Oh, one last thing I forgot. I've invited a nice, young friend to come too. I'm sure you'll like him. Good-bye."

Snapping the phone off, Zehra shook her head. Probably another loser!

"Something wrong?" Jackie looked at Zehra closely.

"My mother. Still trying to set me up. In her generation, arranged marriages some-times happened amongst Muslim women. I guess it had some merit to it—my parents were arranged, and they're still happily married. But, I don't like the idea at all. I try to be nice to my mother, but I just get mad at myself for not saying, 'no.'"

A penetrating voice carried into the office from the hallway.

"That's BJ," Zehra told Jackie.

The resonant sound of singing was followed by a large black man. He turned sharply into the office and pulled up straight until he finished a phrase. "Jazz," he told them. "Beautiful, beautiful music. Too bad the kids don't learn this stuff in school. A lot better than gangsta rap for them." He nodded to each of them. "These black kids are losing their roots if they don't understand jazz."

Zehra looked up at him. He stood over six feet, had a shaved head, a gray goatee, and liquid brown eyes that never stopped moving. When speaking, Zehra noticed he over-enunciated his words, like Denzel Washington. Probably because BJ also had large, beautiful teeth like the actor, which seemed to get in the way when he talked. Some-times, to kid him, she called him Denzel.

Jackie asked, "Do you play jazz?"

"Got my own group. 'Gabriel's Horns,' we call it. I play the trumpet. We just put out a new CD."

"BJ, I was just telling Jackie about the FACS training you had."

"Yeah, cool stuff."

Jackie offered him her chair. "How's it work?" she asked.

"Well, it's a system for breaking down human facial expressions into a series of muscle movements, called action units."

"You mean like every time I wrinkle my face or smile, you're checking me out?" Jackie said. "Wicked."

"Exactly," BJ said. "We memorize about seventy muscle and head movements, and the combination of those can tell us what a person is really thinking. It's not per-fect, but it helps me when interviewing people to have a sense if they're lying or not."

"Is it something new?"

"Researchers developed it in the seventies, and law enforcement is starting to use it. There was a famous case of a woman in South Carolina who went on TV to plead for the return of her kidnapped kids. I saw the video in training. The woman's cheeks lifted in a smile while the corners of her mouth tried to suppress it. The dis-connect between a smile and her pleading led investigators to question her further. Turns out, she killed her two kids and made up the kidnapping."

"Awesome."

He took the chair and scowled.

"Don't tell me, BJ . . ." Zehra held her breath.

His eyes darted from one to the other. "I warned them sons of bitches," he said. "This wasn't gonna work. 'Oh, no,' they said. 'You're black. They'll open doors for you.'" BJ waved his hands in the air. "May as well've sent Linda, the white chick that works next to me, for all the good black did me."

"We all warned Mao," Zehra said. "None of us want this case."

BJ kept talking, "Besides, I was a cop for twenty years. Some of these cases are just too close to home. This is ugly—a young kid slashed to death. You know I'll do my job, but how about a nice auto thief instead?"

"BJ," Zehra said, "Did you interview the main witness, the one from the porch, to see what he says?"

He stopped abruptly and sat still. "Z, we didn't score."

"What happened?" The tension tightened the muscles low in her body. In her mind she saw a digital clock clicking over, crossing off the days until she had to start the trial.

"I ain't got shit for you. He wouldn't talk, and none of them other dudes would either. I can't wait to tell Mao they wouldn't even open the door for a black man." His eyes drooped in defeat. "Sorry, I can't help."

Zehra took a deep breath. "We'll keep working . . ."

BJ raised his eyes slowly to meet Zehra's. She loved those warm looks. "I got more bad news," he paused. "The DNA? I just heard the results from the testing of the saliva and blood on the mask. It matches our boy exactly."

SEVEN

At the seven o'clock Monday morning meeting in the FBI office high in the Federal Building, Paul refused the pastries everyone else ate. The open boxes circled the conference table twice while people sheepishly took seconds. Paul watched them stretch their mouths open to cram in dripping purple Bismarcks. People ate in silence.

"Hey, Jimmy," one of the agents called across the table. "Don't forget that Wellness meeting this afternoon for weight control. If you go through it, you get a reduction in your co-pays in the health plan."

Paul was anxious for his boss to speak.

After allowing for a round of tea-colored tepid government coffee, Paul's boss, Bill Conway, cleared his throat. He had been the senior agent in charge of the Twin Cities for six years. "Folks, listen-up," he started. "We've got a lot to cover. Sorry about the coffee. With the budget cuts, we had to stop the Starbucks." He brushed crumbs off his yellow necktie and tried to smooth it over the protruding belly below.

Several of them pushed back from the table and crossed their legs to listen.

"I got off the phone with the director in Washington this morning." Conway paused for the effect. "He called at five o'clock, his time. That's damn early here. Now, I don't like to get these calls 'cause they usually mean the director's unhappy." His gaze bounced from one face to another. In spite of the sugar surge, most of them looked half awake.

"The director's been getting calls from lots of big-shot politicos, including our own esteemed senators. They're worried. And you all know how things work in government when the shit rolls downhill—in the end, we gotta shovel."

Mavis Drews, the oldest female agent in Minneapolis, sat up. "I thought we got pleas out of three of these recruiters, Bill. What more do they want?"

Conway moved back to his edge of the table. He looked at his administrative assistant who scrambled through a pile of files. She pushed one toward him.

"Here . . . here we go. Yeah, we got convictions on these three." He raised the files in the air to demonstrate. "What they're saying, confirms our theory. These guys were recruiting for the freedom fighters in Somalia—the Shabaab, which we know has links to Al-Qaeda." Conway had thick hair combed over his head, gray-green eyes, and a jowly face. It lent a level of seriousness to his statement.

"But they didn't plead to that, did they, Bill?" Joe Fancher asked.

"We got one for lying to us during the investigation. But the other two pled to providing material support for terrorists. They admitted going to Yemen, then back to Somalia to handle the new recruits from the Twin Cities and then, turned them into terrorists there. They call 'em 'born agains.' Got eight years on this last defendant. Trouble is they're not talking about anything else." When he threw the files on the table, doughnut crumbs scattered. "That's a problem. I admit we got a few loose ends."

Drews said, "So, what does the Director want? We broke the case, arrested the suspects, and got convictions." She looked around the long table and pumped her fist into the air tentatively. "What the hell else do those idiot politicians want?"

"No, no . . . he's happy about that. Congratulated us. No, the calls are coming from Congress people and agencies about what happens now."

Drews pressed on, "What happens?" she snorted. "What happens is we busted 'em!"

"I know, Mavis. But let's go down the road a little ways. If these slugs were recruiting for terrorist fighters in Somalia, how much does it take for them to turn these kids loose in the U.S?" Conway had a hoarse, smoker's voice that gave him a very Karl Malden tone. "And what about the Al-Qaeda ties. Is this a way for them to attack us?"

No one spoke for a long moment. Finally, Mavis said, "Yeah . . . guess you're right. It's the eight-hundred-pound gorilla in the room."

Conway was used to spending more time behind a desk and reading histories of the Second World War, than running the streets and chasing bad guys. He looked forward to his opportunity to retire at full pension in two years.

"One of these kids who disappeared blew himself up with a bomb in Somalia," Conway let his words hang in the air above the table. "But I got more headaches than that," he moaned. "None of you have to deal with all the agency calls I get."

Paul had mixed feelings toward the agent in charge. Although Conway had reluctantly taken Paul into the Minneapolis office after the mess Paul made in Milwaukee, Conway had come to like him. The phone call from the teacher a few years ago worked as well as Paul hoped it would. It had opened the case of the Somali recruiters and given Paul a chance to be assigned to the investigation, which he helped solve.

But Paul knew Conway, near the end of his career, lacked the energy to fight anymore. He seemed out of touch, telling stories of his past that weren't exactly true. He spoke "fight," but he really meant "don't rock the boat." Paul suspected they had only uncovered the tip of an iceberg. From the outside, the FBI looked in control of everything. From the inside, Paul knew they scrambled, dependent on the Somali informants to help them and telephone intercepts.

He warned Conway of his concerns, but the old guy didn't have the energy to probe deeper.

"So, I'm getting calls from everyone even remotely tied to Homeland Security. You wouldn't believe it. I've never heard of half these agencies! No wonder the government's running in the red. Who's paying for all these people?" He leaned back with a deep laugh.

"What's going on?" Paul asked.

Conway looked down at his assistant again. She paged through more papers, giving him one with a long hand-written list on it. He shifted his bulk from one leg to the other. "Okay, here goes." He glanced up over the tops of his glasses. "You ain't gonna believe this." Looked down again and read. "Immigration and Customs Enforcement, the Coast Guard, Federal Protection Services, the Army Medical Research Institute, TRIPwire, Customs and Border Protection, Cyber Protection . . . and the frickin' list goes on. I got a congresswoman in Mississippi asking me if we got a fence on the northern border with Canada!"

Laughter lapped around the table like waves on a lake shore.

"She probably doesn't even know where Canada is," Fancher said.

"And you all know how the agents at Immigration Customs and Enforcement have screwed us in the past," Conway shouted. "Early on in the case, we both had informants covering the same suspect. I argued with them to butt out, that their interference could blow the suspect. They made a premature takedown that almost blew this whole case." He looked up at the ceiling.

"Turf wars," said Fancher. "They want the brass ring as much as we do."

"ICE thinks they've got the resources, but they don't," Conway said. He glared at the group. "I'm sure as hell not gonna be the one to tell the Director he's lost the case to some dumb-ass border agents. You know what he'll do to me? So, no leaks to them, period." He thumped the table with a thick fist.

Mavis said, "What do you want to do, Bill?"

He screwed-up his face. Sighed. "Dammit, I wish I could smoke in here. Well, for now, the plan is to hold steady. We're making progress, and the calls from Washington are finally slowing down."

"Yeah, yeah, I think that's right," said Fancher. He reached a hand out for another pastry, lifted it, and at the last moment, tore it in half.

"We've got the ringleaders in jail. The billions of dollars spent on computers at Homeland Security are monitoring cell calls and emails, looking for keywords. Any alerts come to me directly."

"Keep the telephone intercepts in place," Mavis said. "Keep our informants fresh. Good idea." Mavis puffed her breath out. "It's getting better. Especially, the suburban Somalis. They're a little more integrated into the community . . . but that's not saying much.

The clans don't agree on many things, they look down on each other, won't cooperate much, fight amongst themselves and distrust almost everyone except their own people."

"Local police helpful?"

"Yeah, but they get the same response we do."

Conway's eyes surveyed the agents around the table. "There's a Somali elder; can't remember his name or even pronounce it for that matter. He says that a combination of our investigation, national attention, and more vigilant parents has caused the recruiting to drop. 'It's over,' he says." Conway paused to wait for comments or support. "Well, I guess we agree to keep on truckin'."

Paul spoke, "I'm not sure that's a good idea, Bill."

"What else do you think we can do?"

"As you know, I've got myself 'embedded' in the murder case going on now. The defense lawyer's a friend of mine. Although she can never reveal confidential things, of course I'll get information from their investigation. It'll be like working with an informant."

"To what end, Paul?" Mavis asked.

"I'm not sure. But remember, I got the first call five years ago. Something was going on way back then."

"The Shabaab militia?" Mavis said.

"Didn't really pick up traction until 2006. So, what were they doing here in the high schools long before that?"

"Laying the ground work, obviously."

"I think there's more . . . Didn't you hear the news this morning? On Minnesota Public Radio? There's a new wave of protests breaking out in the Somali community. Nothing like we've seen before. What's it mean?"

"Paul, you're a great agent, but you've just come off probation," Bill interrupted. "In my experience the simple explanation is usually the right one. We've got the explanation now. I used to tell that to Reagan all the time when I was in the Attorney General's office. He liked it simple." Conway looked back at the group. "The activity's down, so I think we've succeeded."

"But why did the Ahmed boy come back? None of the other missing men has returned. Why this one? And why was he killed here?"

"Let the local prosecutor figure that one out. It's not our jurisdiction anyway." He turned away.

"But Bill . . ."

"Back off." Conway spun to face Paul. "Let me tell you something. You didn't get all the goddamn pressure from the press, the public, congressmen, the Director, or the agencies before we finally broke this case. It was hell. Right now, we've got the case solved, the organizers are in jail, and things are quiet. If you poke some hornet's nest, all the shit starts over again. And for what? You 'think there's more,'" Conway imitated Paul's voice. "But until you know you've got something solid, I don't want you stirring things up again. Am I perfectly clear?" He poked Paul in the chest with a pointed finger.

Bill was so close to Paul's face, he could smell stale cigarette smoke on Conway. Paul knew him well enough to understand the order and dismissal. He looked from one agent to another as he scanned the room. Good people, good agents, but like most groups, once a decision was made, it was difficult to alter the course. People became attached to their agendas and ideas.

He took a deep breath trying to accept what his unconscious mind told him— he'd continue the investigation on his own. If he screwed up again, his career was over. But the chance to redeem himself pushed him forward.

EIGHT

Zehra dreaded going home to her beloved parents.

She drove her ancient Audi. This old one was all she could afford on her government salary. Her mind swirled with plots to get out of the meeting she knew her parents had set up--with some nice, boring Muslim guy. What could she do?

Her parents lived in the western suburb of Minnetonka. Everything in this state carried the names of Indians from long ago. At least, they were remembered in some fashion. Zehra'd come to learn that Minnesota was misunderstood by most of the country.

Thought to be populated by either stoic Scandinavians or Mary Tyler Moore wannabes, Zehra discovered the people surprisingly diverse. Along with a significant Native American population, the state also held the country's second largest group of Hmong people from Laos and the largest Somali population. The Minneapolis and St. Paul schools reported over one hundred languages spoken in their classrooms.

After growing up in the heat and humidity of Texas, Zehra liked the change of seasons and the brittle winters. She wished for a large, middle-class Muslim community, born in America like her. Americanized, but still faithful to the teachings of Islam, she spent much of her time educating others about the similarities between Christianity and Islam. Zerha didn't mind the effort because it was part of her larger desire to help the progress of American Muslim women.

Zerha curved into her parent's drive. They owned a rambler on the edge of a small pond. She shut off the engine and looked over her shoulder at the gold Dodge parked in the street. Must be the dreaded guest.

Mother . . . she complained to herself . . . *if I didn't love you so much.* Like many Muslims, family meant everything to the Hassans, Zehra included. She climbed out slowly with the bag of organic pita bread. Normally, she didn't drink much, but tonight she brought a large bottle of Chardonnay. She'd probably need it.

Before entering, Zehra stopped to savor the best part of coming home—her mother's gardens.

Zehra inherited this garden obsession, but since she lived in a condo, her garden consisted of potted plants. Considering the short growing season in Minnesota, she indulged in every opportunity to enjoy the colors, textures, and scents of her gardens.

Water splashed across the roses from a sprinkler, and Zehra could smell fragrant, damp black earth and freshly mowed grass.

Zehra loved the orderliness of her mother's plans, even though it appeared as natural as Nature. It was as complicated as law school had been. When her pots weren't challenging enough, Zehra came home to help her mother.

Unlike her work as a defense lawyer, where it was often difficult to find the truth or to reach a final, successful result, gardening offered both.

And the truth surfaced in that beauty of Nature's work . . . along with Zehra's help.

She walked up the stone path that led to the front. Wafting out through the screen door, spices met Zehra's nose. She stopped at the door and looked sideways at the garden.

In the back stood the alliums—tall stalks with flower bursts that looked like fuzzy, purple tennis balls. In front of those were the bleeding hearts. Nodding white flowers hung from arching stems that resembled a row of nuns with white habits, leaning forward to give thanks for the rain.

Zehra smiled at the peaceful feeling, and then forced herself to open the door to walk into the house. The narcotic perfume smell of a hyacinth drew her inside in spite of the fate that awaited her.

Her mother, Martha Hassan, came out to meet her, wiping her hands on a paper towel. She wrapped Zehra in her small arms and hugged. "So nice to see you," Martha said.

"Killer gardens, Mom."

"Just trying to keep things alive. If I could get your father to help more . . ."

Her mother avoided the living room to pull Zehra into the kitchen. She set the pita bread on the counter, dipped a bread chip into the lemon hummus her mother had been mixing, tasted nothing but garlic, and put the wine next to the bread. Like a lot of older Iranian women, her mother gladly took on all the trappings of an American, including her name. So did her father, Joseph.

"How's work? I don't know how you can defend those guilty criminals," Martha asked. "Isn't it dangerous?" She avoided the living room.

"No . . . just a pain in the butt."

"How can you represent this terrorist?"

"I don't want to, believe me." An uncomfortable twinge raced through her lower body when she remembered the email. Zehra pushed the thought away

"These crazy ones give all us Muslims a bad name. Remember after the Oklahoma City bombing, we were afraid to let you and your brother outside for days? I was scared to death our usually wonderful neighbors would do something to you. Why do you insist on defending these terrorists? I'm so disappointed."

"I said I don't want the case, Mom. I'm trying to get rid of it," she sighed.

"Well . . . why don't you go back to medical school?"

Zehra stopped her. "Okay, Mom. Let's go meet him."

"Huh? Oh, yes. He's such a nice man. And so handsome." Martha's face glistened like the edge of the sweating wine bottle.

Pulling Zehra by the hand, she led her back into the living room. As they entered, a tall man stood with his legs together and his arms flat against his sides. He nodded and waited for the introduction.

Oh, brother! Zehra thought, *here we go.*

"Zehra, this is Robert Ali. He's got a good job at 3M."

He stuck out his hand to grasp Zehra's. He nodded again and said, "Hello, Zehra. I'm an accountant at 3M, but I'm also interested in the theatre."

"How interesting." She looked up into a narrow face with a sharp nose and large nostrils. She marveled at the contrast in colors—pale face surrounded by thick black hair, black eyes, black nostrils, and a black, pressed dress shirt.

"After your mother told me all about you, I was anxious to meet you."

Zehra shot her mother a glance. "Oh, I'm sure she told you everything." She felt like an abandoned dog in a pound that Robert inspected for possible purchase.

"I've got a role in a play at the White Bear community theatre."

"How interesting."

"How do you like your job?"

Zehra said, "Well, right now, with the case I just got, I'd be happier teaching snowboarding."

"My role is Marc Antony in *Julius Caesar*. That's by Shakespeare, you know." He emphasized the playwright that any sixth grader would recognize.

"I know. How interesting."

"Do you like Indian food?"

"Huh? Yeah, the spicier, the better."

"The early reviews in the paper, the *White Bear Lake Community News*, said my performance in rehearsals has been outstanding. I think it comes from my naturally out-going personality and my love of fun."

Zehra felt dizzy. "Mom, where's Dad?"

"He's still stuck in Arden Hills at his job. It might be described as part time, but he works like it's full time." She whispered to Zehra, "He told me he's working with a nice young Muslim man. A bio-engineer." Her eyebrows bounced upward. Louder, she said, "The lamb's almost ready. Lamb is Robert's favorite dish." She smiled at him. "Isn't it?"

"Oh, yes. I tried to get the director to substitute lamb in the food scene but not too many Americans are used to it."

As they filed into the kitchen to check on dinner, Zehra looked at her mother. Pretty, in an old-world way. Long nose, deep, expressive eyes, dark skin, and long hair cut below her shoulders, which she hid during the day when she usually wore *hijab*, the head covering worn by millions of Muslim women. The irony struck Zehra again. All the Americanized habits still couldn't eliminate a few of the old-world ones. When she looked at her mother, she saw intelligence and love.

In their own way, her parents had fought battles, too.

It started with the struggle her parents faced when they decided to leave Iran, years ago. Ruled by the Shah and supported by the United States, they were part of the educated elite. But her parents sensed trouble. Available at the time, dual citizenship enabled them to come to America.

They came as Muslims who looked like they had a perpetual tan. A few Iranians had opened doors previously, but after "students" captured the U.S. embassy and the Ayatollah took power in 1979, they faced suspicion and hostility. They were forced to hide their own identity and religion for a long time. Anyone who looked dark and Middle Eastern was suspect by many Americans.

The struggle continued over the years.

Thank goodness, things progressed so that Zehra lived a much different life, although hers presented its own, new struggles. She knew she'd inherited her mother's drive and was grateful for it. The support of her parents comforted her all the time and provided a rock through tough periods—except for arranging men to meet her.

Zehra marveled that in spite of the difficulties her parents experienced, they were the most patriotic Americans she knew.

Her mother lifted a pot of water onto the stove to boil for rice. The lamb stew contained some of her early-season herbs from the garden. She spoke without looking at Zehra, which always meant her mother was uneasy about something. "I still can't get over your defending that crazy man. I saw you were interviewed by the *Star Tribune*. Sounds like you're having trouble? I'm worried."

Zehra sighed. "It's tough. The Somali people are wonderful, what I know about them, but they won't cooperate with the police or FBI. So getting any trust or communication with them is hard. El-Amin refuses to cooperate with me. He represents all the things I hate about extremist Islam, but I'm forced to defend him. I don't want to have anything to do with guys like him."

Her mother's face jerked around. "The men are the worst."

"Well some, I guess. This guy's bad. Always quotes me the Qur'an . . ."

"Do you read it often?" asked Robert, who'd followed them into the kitchen. He stood straight with his hands cupped together in front of his waist.

"Yeah, I do. I mean, not every day, but it gives me peace. I also like the old poet Rumi. I know it's old fashioned, but I still like him."

"I absolutely love Shakespeare. I'm not sure the Qur'an is very relevant for us today in the U.S."

He leaned closer to her, and she smelled stale breath.

She said, "I disagree. I think it's more important than ever to study the Qur'an. There's so much misunderstanding in America about Islam. We need to be able to quote the Qur'an accurately. If some of us who are moderate and progressive don't stand up and teach others, we'll always be associated with the fringe extremists. And women will always be subjugated. Things are changing, and we should be a part of that." Hopefully, the speech would scare off the proud thespian for good. No such luck.

He looked into her eyes with a basset hound's expression in his own. "You're so interesting, Zehra." He paused for one second and then said, "It reminds me of my passion for the theatre. I hope to have, well . . . I should have a leading role this fall in our new production. Maybe you'd like to see it?"

"Uh, I'll check my schedule."

Her mother interrupted them. "You go on and on about that new stuff, Zehra. All those things you want to change. Don't you understand that as things change more, you must cling to the principles that have sustained us through so much? The Qur'an says . . ."

"Drop it about the Qur'an. I'm sick of people telling me what it says. I can read it for myself, and I don't need anyone to interpret it for me." Her mother's eyes softened, and she looked away. Zehra regretted her sharp tone. The new case, the jerk for a client, and the set-backs in the investigation—they all upset her. "Look, Mom. I'm sorry. It's not you."

Martha avoided any more argument by going to the simmering pot. She stirred and added more spices.

Zehra's Casio watch beeped.

Robert picked up her wrist in his limp grasp. "What's this?"

"Oh . . . Casio makes this watch for Muslims that goes off five times a day to remind me to pray. Stupid, but I like it."

Martha turned the heat lower on the rice and wiped her hands. She looked up at Robert. "You're faithful? Join us. You can wash in the bathroom on the left, down the hall."

He nodded. "I'll wash now. How 'bout you, Zehra?"

"I'm lucky to get in two prayers a day. I'm so busy."

"You should really be more faithful," he said and walked away, his khaki pants bunched in puddles around his shoes.

Zehra shook her head behind his back and followed her mother into the other, larger bathroom and performed the ritual ablution or cleansing to ensure they were in a state of physical and spiritual purity.

They washed their hands and faces and arms up to their elbows. While they washed, Zehra also meditated to cleanse her mind and heart from worldly thoughts and concerns, even her recent argument with the odd man down the hall. Martha handed her a scarf to cover her head and hair.

Together, they moved into the living room. Robert followed and stood next to Martha. They all raised their hands parallel to their ears with the palms facing out. Then they knelt on their knees, said more of the prayers, and bowed fully to the floor so that seven parts of their bodies touched the ground. They faced northeast, the shortest path to Mecca from North America. Robert stepped in front and prostrated himself until his forehead touched the carpet.

Zehra felt stiffness in her back, so she relaxed as she knelt.

"Allahu Akbar," they recited. God is great.

They stood upright, folded their hands over their chests, and repeated the opening discourse of the Qur'an.

"All praise belongs to God, Lord of all worlds, the Compassionate, the Merciful, Ruler of Judgment Day. You alone do we worship and to you alone do we appeal for help. Show the straight way, the way of those upon whom You have bestowed Your grace, not of those who have earned Your wrath or who go astray."

Zehra and her mother completed the obligatory prayers and remained silent as they each privately petitioned Allah with their own requests. Robert moved off to the side by himself.

Standing, Martha hugged Zehra and went back into the kitchen. Zehra knew she could escape this loser easily. She frowned at the thought of her mother's machinations. But it was impossible to stay mad at someone who had just prayed with you.

NINE

Running late for a full morning of court appearances, Zehra grabbed her purse and briefcase from her desk. As she hurried toward the door, her phone rang.

Caller ID showed it was her boss, the Chief Public Defender.

"Get up here right now," he demanded.

Zehra could tell from his tone of voice not to protest about her own late schedule. In five minutes, she sat before Bill Cleary. He'd been in the job forever and had gone from a crusading young lawyer to an overweight bureaucrat, protecting his position. He popped open what was probably his tenth can of Coke for the day and leaned forward.

Everyone called him 'Chairman Mao' behind his back because of the way his face had exploded into a round moon, along with his body. Too many cheap hotdogs and fries eaten in the Government Center plaza, Zehra thought. She studied his face, trying to anticipate the problem.

The moon face clouded over. "I just got off the phone with Judge Gordon Smith." He scowled. "And I don't like these kinds of calls. Know what I'm talking about?"

"I can guess."

"Zehra, you're good, one of our best, but I'll get to the fucking point. I don't give a shit if you want off this case or not. You're on it, you're trying it, and you'll do a good job. Got that?"

"Bill, don't you have any consideration for me? Just because I'm Muslim, doesn't mean I'm the best for this case."

"Yes it does. With this kind of publicity and the press chewing on my ass every day, you're exactly what I need for this case. If deflects all the racist and religious crap they always try to throw at us." His heavy cheeks quivered with anger. "It's window dressing, I know. But you're gonna do it."

"So, you're going to let an idiot like Gordon Smith tell you how to run your office?"

"Of course not. I don't give a rat's ass about her." He looked like he was lying.

Zehra tried to remain calm. Her voice rose, "What the hell does that have to do with our mission to give the best possible defense to everyone? You don't give a damn about that anymore," she shouted.

"Careful . . ."

"Maybe you don't remember that this bronco attacked me. I shouldn't have to do this." She thought about the email. "Then, I got this strange email." She explained.

"I don't know. What can I do? Have IT track it down. In the meantime, be careful."

"So, I'm off the case?"

"No."

"She stared at him. "I won't forget this."

"You don't finish this case, I'll send you back to traffic court for the rest of your career."

"That's bullshit."

Mao's eyes glazed over and Zehra knew he was done with her.

Ten minutes later, carrying a stack of files against her chest and lugging her heavy purse over her shoulder, Zehra struggled through the door into the courtroom. Jackie followed behind her.

"Thanks for letting me come with you," she told Zehra. She pushed her thick-framed glasses higher on her little nose.

"Oh, you'll have fun." Zehra raised her eyebrows to send the real message.

"How many cases have you got?"

"Let's see . . ." Zehra reached one of the low counsel tables in the middle of the courtroom and dropped her load. "Eleven for this morning. Not too bad."

Zehra felt the energy surge in the courtroom—people moving in all directions at once, the constant buzz of conversation, the public drifting in and out, and the clerk shouting out the names of cases to be heard by the judge.

The only quiet bubble of space was directly before the judge where lawyers and their clients made their formal appearances.

Most of the lawyers in the courtroom worked for the government, either assistant county attorneys or public defenders. A few private lawyers represented clients, but, in reality, most criminals were poor and had appointed counsel. Since public defenders worked the courtrooms every day of the week, they were some of the best lawyers in the county.

When Jackie asked her about a career as a public defender, Zehra had told her not to expect big money. "Instead, you'll get lots of freedom, responsibility, and an opportunity to have tough cases dumped on you at an early stage in your career. Dealing with the clients we represent is a tough part. And a lot of us stay because we believe it's an important part of what we call justice."

"That's what I want—the experience in the courtroom. It sounds like the most fun." Jackie dropped her shoulders. "I've put everything on hold in my life for our case. My boyfriend, Josh, is so great. He just adores me and says whatever I need to do is cool with him."

"Hey, Zehra, I heard you got the El-Amin murder case," a voice from behind them called.

Zehra turned to see Charlie Pollard, the county attorney she'd worked with many years ago. He was a friend and had been a mentor to her over the years. She smiled and gave him a quick hug. "Yeah," she said, nodding. "I guess I specialize in 'broncos.' This guys' a treat."

"What's the defendant like?"

She rolled her eyes. "Maybe I shouldn't have switched sides."

"That bad, huh?" Charlie looked older than she remembered, his hair thinner, his eyes sagging. "I've hear rumors through the grape vine . . . be careful of this guy, Zehra. Even the cops are spooked by him." "You know you're always welcome to return from the 'dark side' to work with us."

Zehra laughed. "Too much bureaucracy for me."

He said goodbye with a little flip of his hand and left to meet with the defense lawyer on his case.

"Nice guy," Jackie said.

"Most of the prosecutors are. We've got our problems; they've got theirs."

"It's busy today." She squinted at the horde.

"Let's look for our client, 'World Premiere.'"

"Huh?"

"That's his name."

"Seriously?"

Zehra shrugged.

They walked to the public area of the courtroom and searched the crowd. Outside, in the hall, they called out his name. Zehra looked at her watch. "He always runs twenty minutes late so he should be here."

"Ms. Hassan." The slim black man strode toward them. He tipped from side to side with an exaggerated shoulder roll that matched the rhythm of his walk. The baseball cap, red and white, was too large for his head and turned at a precise angle to his face. He smiled at them, exposing a golden front tooth.

"World Premiere," Zehra reached out her hand to shake. With some of the male public defenders, the black clients gave a 'soul' shake, with a turn of the wrist and a bump of the fist. None of her clients ever shook with her that way.

"W'as happ'n here, Man."

"Well, you've got the Disorderly Conduct case. Nothing too serious."

"Man . . . they should drop that! Jus' a bad communication."

"Could be, but the prosecutor won't. Probably 'cause it happened with an employee who works in the building. Prosecutors feel very protective of them."

"Ahh . . . what I gotta do?" His red shorts and basketball shoes, matched the color of his tank top.

Zehra flipped open the thin file containing a Complaint and a single page police report. "It says you wanted your free bus card. When the clerk wouldn't give it to you, you went off on her, yelling, screaming, and threatening to 'kick her ass.'"

"Nah, nah . . . that ain't it, Man. She went off on *me*. Tha's the truth. Here, catch this: how could I go off on her if I jus' finished my last class on Anger Management. Twelve weeks in them classes. I graduated, Man." He leaned back in stiff pride and jerked his head once to emphasize his success. He crossed thin arms over his chest. The tank top he wore revealed the tattoos on his arms. Most were gang signs.

"And . . . that proves it?"

Yeah, it proves it!" He jerked his head again.

"Look, World, or should I call you World Premiere?"

"My mama named me World Premiere. Tha's my name."

"Okay. Look, how 'bout I can get you ten days in the workhouse, stayed for six months?"

"I don't gotta go?" His eyes focused on Zehra.

"Not unless you violate your probation."

"Do it, Man. I ain't got time for this bullshit. I got my bidness to take care of, and I gots to get back to the crib. My baby's mama's there."

After he pled guilty and was sentenced, they both walked out into the hall.

"Hey, thanks," World Premiere told Zehra. "You're a good lawyer. I'll ask for you next time."

When he flashed the golden smile, Zehra saw a young boy trying to act tough but, in the end, a petty criminal. She liked him and hoped he could make something worthwhile out of himself before it was too late. "Yeah, do that. Good luck."

"I kind of liked him," Jackie said. "Awesome outfit. Who's next?"

"Franklin Pierce Anderson."

"Like the president?"

"Hey, I don't think these names up. You can't invent them." They both laughed.

When Zehra went back into the courtroom, she spied him sitting by himself in the public section. "Mr. Anderson?"

A pale, white man stood and stared at them for a moment. When he recognized Zehra, he followed her out into the hall.

The toughest problem with this one would be his body odor. Could she handle his case without passing out?

She turned to face him. He said, "Isn't there a place we can talk in private? I don't feel comfortable with these . . ." he twisted his head as he looked around them. "Criminals."

"Unfortunately, no. We don't have an office here. We can move over to the side of the wall there," Zehra pointed down the long hall. "To our 'private' office."

"Well, all right." He waddled along beside them. He wore a shirt that hadn't been pressed in a long time. His shoes were untied.

Zehra smelled a faint, stale odor near him. She backed off to the usual two arms-lengths.

"This is very embarrassing," Mr. Anderson said when they stopped. "Do we have to go into the court with all those other people?"

"We have to. There's no other way."

"I've seen on TV where the lawyer can take the case into the judge's chambers for privacy." He jiggled has face from side to side so that the old wire-rimmed glasses he wore, already a little loose on his nose, shook with his face. He implied in his tone that Zehra, as a public defender, wasn't a good lawyer because she couldn't "work" the judge.

"Doesn't work that way here," she told him.

He sucked in a deep breath. "Well . . . what should I do?"

Balancing his file on her left arm, she opened it and skimmed over the allegations. "You're charged with Cruelty to Animals. The allegations are that you got mad at your kids, and to punish them, you took their gerbils and placed each one into an air gun. What's an 'air gun'?" She glanced at him.

"It's harmless. It . . . it has a large barrel. It propels things with compressed air. Harmless."

"Well, it says you shot the gerbils across the backyard into the neighbor's yard. When the neighbor got upset, you retrieved the stunned gerbils, brought them back and drowned them in a pail of water in front of your kids." She looked up into his small green eyes, waiting to see what he'd say in response.

"Yeah . . . I guess that's about what happened. But I never laid a hand on the damn kids. Does it say that in the reports?"

"Uh . . ." Zehra pretended to read the police report. "Yeah, it doesn't say that you hit the kids."

"Isn't that a defense?"

"No, it's not a defense. Wanna tell me what happened?"

"Well . . ." he shrugged beefy shoulders. "That's about it. They wouldn't obey me. Thanks to the bitch, their mother, they're totally undisciplined. I had to get their attention. If you don't have kids, you wouldn't understand." He paused. "What should I do now?"

"If you plead guilty, I'm sure we can keep you out of the workhouse. However, in a case like this, the judge'll probably want a probation pre-sentence investigation before he orders the conditions of your probation."

"Probation? For what? Some goddamn, filthy little rats? What the hell's this country coming to? Naw, naw, I'm not gonna do it. We'll go all the way with this one. I'll appeal . . ."

"Mr. Anderson, calm down."

"Don't tell me to calm down, lady. This is my life we're talking about. No one cares about me. About what I'm going through. It's all about the damn rats!"

"Okay, okay. I'll set the case for trial. Of course, you'll have to come back again and sit through two to three days of a trial in front of a jury and listen to all these allegations, I thought you wanted privacy?" She let the words hang around Anderson's neck.

"Two days, huh? I gotta come back?" His eyes shifted up and down the hall where other lawyers met with their clients. Zehra saw him shudder. "I'd rather if we could wrap this up today." He raised a finger in the air. "I want a guarantee, though, that I can tell the judge what really happened."

"Oh, I can guarantee that. I got a feeling the judge may be interested in hearing from you . . ."

By noon, Jackie and Zehra relaxed in her office over cups of herbal tea.

"Damn. That's draining," Jackie laughed. "Can you imagine what my former colleagues would say if they knew what I was doing here?" She pumped both fists up and down. "But this is what I've wanted."

"I don't know where they find some of those people. Imagine, they're living all around us." She dropped her feet from the chair next to her. "Hey, BJ just left me a message. He's coming in." Zehra hoped that he finally found something.

"You couldn't make a reality show about these cases," Jackie said. "No one would believe 'em—they're too real. I can't wait to tell Josh about these. He thinks I've got the coolest job in the world."

BJ walked into the office. "Hey, babes." He sat in the chair next to Jackie. He tried to keep his lips closed, but a wide grin erupted to expose nice teeth, white against his dark face. "I got something for you. I told you I wasn't gettin' anywhere with these Somalis. So, I tried another idea. I'm tight with the security at Richardson High School which has a high Somali population. I checked it out. One of the kids there has a parent who knows El-Amin. And, it gets better."

"Oh?"

"The friend was willing to talk to me. Got a part-time job in a hospital kitchen. He's also an imam at the local mosque, over on West Bank, near the murder scene. He's known our boy for a few months. Not close but sees him. He tells me on the night of the murder, he and El-Amin were chewing *khat* and drinkin' tea at a mosque."

Zehra slammed the drawer on her chocolate cupcakes. "What? You think this guy's legit?"

"Seems to be. The details check out so far."

"This's gotta be tight. You know that."

"Check."

"Why didn't he go to the cops?"

"Scared. Plus, they didn't have the connection I got. They didn't know about him."

Zehra leaned back in her chair and ran both hands through her thick hair. For the first time, she felt a familiar tightening in her lower body. Maybe . . . just maybe, the camel jockey was innocent. In spite of her contempt for him, her competitive instincts as a lawyer rose. And Zehra's sense of justice, sharpened in her own struggles as a Muslim woman, caused her to look at the case in a different light.

"Damn, we got ourselves an alibi." Zehra had to act.

TEN

Frustrated to the point he couldn't sit still, Paul left the office for a long walk. He frequented a Caribou coffee shop on Washington Avenue, across the street from the MacPhail Center for Music. He liked the type of people who hung out there. He knew that Conway's threat was real. What could he do now?

Although the temperatures had spiked unusually high throughout the month, this morning opened crisp and cool. Paul walked the few blocks, drawing in the pungent aroma of damp air. It refreshed him.

He took a small dark roast coffee and sat in the corner where he could look out at the traffic on Washington Avenue, both cars and humans.

Conway was a good man but burned out. At the beginning of the crisis, when the young men started disappearing, Conway worked his best—providing leadership and organization. He'd mastered the complexities in the political jungle of over-lapping law enforcement people. Navigating the multiplicity of egos and ambitions caused more trouble than actually solving the crimes.

The cases forced federal agents and terrorism experts to rethink their assumptions about the vulnerability of Muslim immigrants in the United States to terrorist recruiting. Even the director of the FBI, Robert Mueller, had told the press this may be the most significant domestic terrorism investigation since 9/11. That unleashed all the pressure on Paul's office to produce an answer.

Paul respected Conway for his management. But once the case was "solved" with the discovery of the terrorists in Somali who'd left the Twin Cities, everyone agreed the disappearances were simply recruiters, working to fill the ranks of the militia, Shabaab.

The case had taken months. The pressure to solve it, intense. The human pain and sorrow, incalculable. When an "answer" was provided, naturally everyone breathed a sigh of relief, happy to take a break from the case. That relief rippled up the line to the Director in Washington and fanned out to other concerned people in Congress and the agencies.

It wasn't that Paul disagreed.

He worried the answer was too simple. Why did the Ahmed boy return to Minneapolis? If he had volunteered to be a freedom fighter in Somalia, why would he be killed for that? The teacher who'd called the FBI tip line a few years ago predated the reason for the recruiting—the invasion of Somalia by the Ethiopians that gave rise to the Shabaab militia. What were they doing in the high schools that long ago? Was it even connected to the murder? Were they still in the high schools?

The murder case had given Conway another reason to bow out. Now it was a local police matter, not FBI, although the turf wars still went on. The killer had been charged and awaited trial. Let them take care of the case from now on was Conway's attitude. Luckily, Zehra Hassan had been appointed to represent El-Amin. Paul could use his friendship with her to follow the case and help open the door to more information.

Was the murder connected to anything that threatened national security? He wondered.

He thought back to all the federal agencies in touch with Conway. Homeland Security covered so many different threats. Customs and Border Protection, Coast Guard, Army Medical Research, Immigration, and Customs Enforcement . . . He made a note to check on the medical research agency. What the hell did they do?

He had a friend in ICE, in the investigation arm of Immigration and Customs Enforcement, named Joan Cortez. They met while attending cross-training on security in Washington. He remembered Conway's order prohibiting cooperation with ICE, but if Joan could help him trace the background of El-Amin, it might be worth the risk. ICE may have far reaching information, unavailable to the other law enforcement. Paul waited for Joan to return his call.

He pictured her in his mind. Fun, attractive, tough and extremely ambitious. It'd be hard to get much help from her.

The soft *whir* of the coffee grinders and rich aromas lulled him to relax. Outside, people walked by with renewed vigor. Spring in Minnesota always brought out crazy behavior. After so many months of frigid gloom and gray, the arrival of warm weather released the manic side of everyone.

Paul had worn a sport coat earlier. As the morning heated up, he took it off. Outside the window, he saw a young man in a hooded gold sweatshirt with maroon lettering that said University of Minnesota on the front. He wore a baggy pair of shorts and running shoes.

At the thought of his boss, Paul jerked back to his problems. If Conway discovered Paul's continuing investigation, he would be fired.

All the years he'd worked to get into the Bureau, all the sacrifices he'd made, and the effort to make up for the case that almost ruined his career years ago, would be lost. That case still haunted him. Paul had to admit the bitter memory drove him now as much as his fear for the safety of his family and friends. The government always talked about "national security" but to Paul, that concept was too amorphous. He had to think of the people close to him to make sense of all the hard work he did.

Reluctantly, Paul stood, dropped his cup in the waste receptacle, and left the peace of the coffee shop.

He took his time strolling back to the office. A spring breeze blew up the street between high-rise office buildings. Women, free of heavy winter coats, walked by in short skirts and tight blouses. In response to the hot weather, trees had budded earlier than usual, sporting light green dots.

Paul rode the elevator up to his office. Apparently, no one had told the computer running the heating system it was spring. Hot, stale air punched him in the chest as he turned into the office suite.

Looking out the window, he sat at his desk. Paul was scared and confused. Maybe he should just drop his crazy ideas. The rest of his colleagues might be right. What if he got himself into another mess like before, and was fired? What would his family think? What would he do?

His cell phone rang.

Paul didn't recognize the number but decided to answer anyway. "Paul Schmidt, special agent, FBI."

"Sounds impressive," Joan Cortez chuckled. "Special . . . huh?"

"Aw . . . doesn't mean much. The government gives titles instead of more money."

"And you fell for it?"

"Yup."

"Listen, I got some . . . well, I guess you could say it's good news."

Paul sat up straight in his chair. "Yeah?"

"Good for you, not so good for the local guys."

"About El-Amin?"

"Right. We can't find any criminal background on him in the U.S. Not even a parking ticket. But if we go international, well, you get a little more."

"What?"

"He's dirty." Joan cleared her throat. "He's well funded and linked into an international criminal net."

"What're you talking about?"

"You must know of these criminal organizations, networks, which operate in all kinds of shit that's illegal? One day it's drugs, the next day financial thefts, a little terrorism and weapon smuggling thrown in."

"Yeah?"

"Well, in addition to these disappearing young men, we—ICE—think there's a lot more going on. We don't know what, but a guy like El-Amin is intriguing."

"Where can I find out more?"

"Can you meet me tomorrow, in private?"

"Sure, but what's the problem?"

Joan waited to respond. "I've got to be careful. This is much bigger than my pay grade allows me to tell you. And the shit'll hit the fan if anyone knows I'm cooperating with you." She paused. "You've gotta keep this between us."

"Joan, I'm in the same predicament. I suspected there was more to these disappearances than simply recruiting for Shabaab."

"Meet me at Mears Park in St. Paul tomorrow. One o'clock?"

ELEVEN

V ladimir Zagorsk hurried along the corridor inside the building known as Corpus 6. On one side of him, glass windows looked into a giant steel room. The Model UKZD-25 dynamic test chamber, where small bomblets were detonated, was the largest and most sophisticated in the world.

In spite of the cool temperature, he sweated. Would he be able to do this one more time? If he were caught he could be executed. And although he had a plan to screw the hated Arab who'd buy this, Vladimir's government wouldn't show him any mercy.

He carried a small briefcase with a laptop computer inside, of which most of the interior had been removed to make enough room for the material. To cover his theft from the floor above and allow him to escape unimpeded, he'd stenciled the words, "International Science and Technology Center, Moscow" on the side of the case.

How ironic, Vladimir thought. The center was partially funded by the U.S. Department of Defense—just where this bundle could end up and cause a great deal of trouble.

He forced the thought out of his mind. He needed the money.

One of the 150 scientists who still worked at Vector, Vladimir had easy access to almost all of the forty buildings in the complex. Like many of those others, he was underpaid and the health risks jeopardized the survival of his family. They lived sixteen miles away in Novosibirsk. They'd been offered government housing in Koltsovo, like the other scientists' families, next to Vector. His wife refused, scared to live anywhere near the complex—he didn't blame her and never argued about it.

The Arab, who'd contacted him seven months ago, offered more cash for one shipment than Vladimir earned in five years. Normally, he'd never even considered stealing anything from the complex, but his family's struggle was more than he could bear.

Luckily for him, something had gone wrong for the Arab after the first package, which required another shipment.

Vladimir worried about the contents of the briefcase, glad he'd sealed the protective container around the laptop. A feeling of guilt hummed through his mind at the thought of how destructive it could be, until an image of his son replaced it. Nicky had a chance to get a United States' visa and get out of this hell. That took lots of extra money for the paperwork and even more for the requisite bribes. If he and his wife were stuck here, at least their son could get out.

He left the corridor and slowed down for the stairs. They had been constructed by gangs of prison laborers who intentionally made each step a different size. The rumors said they built them in the hopes some of the scientists from the state would fall and die.

He reached the bottom, took a glance backward at the squat, ugly brick building with windows rimmed in concrete. Ahead, he had two outer security barriers to get through. The first would be easy—he'd paid Fedor enough to look the other way. The second one worried him.

Although Vladimir worked as a scientist in the complex, leaving with a computer case would certainly raise some eyebrows.

He looked off into the distance to the birch and silver pine forests at the edge of the complex. Too pretty, he thought, to surround something as sinister as what went on inside Vector. The tiny green leaves of the Aspens popped out in profusion with the spring warmth. He smelled fresh air. It may hit thirty Celsius today, he'd heard. Of course, that also brought the mud and melting show in Novosibirsk.

As Vladimir approached the final security barrier, he hoped the guard would be weak. He stopped at a small office, didn't recognize the man behind the desk. Vladimir could feel his insides constrict. He forced himself to breathe evenly. *Calm down.*

"Papers." The man ordered.

Vladimir set down the briefcase carefully and pulled out his identification and the fake authorization he prepared earlier.

The security guard ran his eyes over the papers quickly. Then he stopped on the second page. "Hmm." Without moving, he looked up at Vladimir and then his eyes fell to the briefcase. "ISTC out of Moscow, huh?"

Vladimir could tell the truth for this, which made it easier. "It's the special packing materials. You can imagine how careful we must be."

"Of course, of course. But I wasn't notified of this."

Vladimir thought his bowels would let go right there. Now was the point of no return. If it worked, he'd save his family. If not, he could be shot. He reached into his jacket and removed the envelope with rubles and handed it quickly to the guard. Vladimir held his breath.

The man set down his pencil and took his time peering inside the envelope. He nodded once. Slowly, his eyes rose to look into Vladimir's face. Without saying a word, he waved his hand toward the exit.

Vladimir jumped through the door.

Outside, he gulped clean air and hurried past the razor wire surrounding the complex. Above him, sandhill cranes on their migration to North America swam in the warm spring air, happy to be free of the long winter. They stopped momentarily in the field, just long enough to rest and peck for corn.

When he arrived in Lenin Square, the main center of Novosibirsk, he took a cab to the train station. He walked across the large plaza. Ahead of him rose the imposing station. Square, painted turquoise green, the columns and arches shone bright white. He entered under the largest arch.

He boarded the Turkistan-Siberian train to take him south, ultimately to the Caspian Sea where he'd hand-off the case. Unlike the airport with its strict security, the train station offered an easy way to get out of town. No one stopped him as he found an empty seat and put the briefcase directly beside him. It would never leave his sight. Sitting, he grunted from the added weight around his waist. All the bad, cheap food they'd been eating, he thought. With the new money, they'd eat better.

The train pulled out on time and crossed the new bridge over the Ob River. Vladimir looked out the window at the expanse of the west Siberian plain. He rested his hand on the smooth, polished frame that surrounded the window. With the spring sun pouring into the window, the wood felt warm under his fingers. The plain stretched over forests, fields, and factories. The city still ranked as the largest industrial center in Siberia.

He arrived in Turkmenbashi, on the eastern shore of the Caspian Sea, late in the afternoon. As he left the train, he cradled the suitcase with both arms. He reviewed the instructions once again. He was to meet the Arab at the New Independence Monument right at sunset. Vladimir pulled his sleeve back to look at his watch. An hour to go.

He'd have just enough time to make the transfer and get back on the train to return home—good, as he felt uneasy. Not only was he anxious to get rid of the case as soon as possible, but the entire city made him feel he was watched all the time.

The first president after independence from the Soviet Union, Saparmurad Niyasov, had relied upon a personality cult to rule with absolute authority. Huge photos of his face covered billboards, buildings, and posters everywhere. Many streets carried his name. And the crazy monuments he'd built! There was the low, square, dun-colored block building topped by a giant bull. Balanced on the bull's horns, floated an immense globe. It boasted the name, "Turkmenbashi on Top of the World."

Vladimir wandered toward the port. The sun had already dropped over the sea to the west, leaving the water colored in blues and grays. A milky light shone around him, illuminating buildings in an eerie glow. He smelled the moist, salty air from the quiet water. A lonely bell clanged.

When he arrived at the Independence Monument, shadows reached out like fingers toward him from low buildings. The monument consisted of an egg-shaped mound on the ground, covered in gold ornamentation, and topped by an immense spire. He would meet the Arab in front of the tall statue in front.

Vladimir reached the point and looked up at the statue. Carved from dark stone, it looked like a fierce Tartar. Full hat, full beard down his chest, he dressed in a long coat that dropped to the statue's feet. Around the coat, a black cape billowed out as if the wind were blowing it. In his hands, he held a curved, gold scimitar.

Vladimir watched as three crows landed on the scimitar. They cawed their annoyance at his presence.

When he turned around, the Arab stood before him.

Without smiling, the man greeted Vladimir and reached for the briefcase. For a moment, he hung on. "The money?" he asked.

"Of course. I will do it now." The Arab reached into his coat for a cell phone. A few taps on the keyboard, and he looked back at Vladimir. "Done. Transferred to your account, as before."

Vladimir waited a few minutes, then keyed in his own cell phone to check the bank account. He didn't trust these Arabs and despised everything about them. If it weren't for the money, he wished they'd rot in hell with their terrorists. Satisfied the money had moved, Vladimir handed the case to the Arab.

He accepted it. "Thank you, Mr. Zagorsk. You have done a great thing for Allah. This will help destroy His enemies."

The feeling of guilt returned to Vladimir.

He peered into Vladimir's eyes. "You don't seem well? Don't worry. It is part of Allah's plan for all of us."

He hoped the Arab would never be able to find him, later. But it was a risk he was willing to take for the sake of Nicky. "What will you do with this?" From behind Vladimir, the crows suddenly rose from the scimitar in a cawing clatter and circled twice before heading toward the sea to the west.

"That is beyond what you need to know."

TWELVE

Zehra and BJ stopped before the security checkpoint at the Hennepin County Government Center in Minneapolis. The courtrooms and the prosecutor's office occupied most of the space above them.

"Why are you working so hard on this one?" BJ asked. "The guy's a scumbag."

"I know and I hate everything he stands for, so I've got two good reasons to coast. Except for a couple points: if he's convicted and appeals, he'll allege inadequacy of counsel—they always do. I've got to protect my butt. Also . . ." Zehra stopped walking while the flow of people continued around them toward the elevators. "I guess, well, I guess it's my sense of justice. What if he's really innocent? I'm not saying he deserves it, but if I slack on this I've lost my chance to work for a just system." She looked at the African-American standing next to her and knew he understood.

They arrived at the County Attorney's floor and asked to see Steve Harmon, the assistant county attorney prosecuting the Ibrahim El-Amin case.

He burst through the door in the lobby, shook both their hands. "Zehra, BJ, two of my favorite defenders." He invited them through the open door. "Can't talk you two into coming back to work with the 'good guys'?"

"Well . . . there are days . . ." Zehra said and looked back at BJ, who laughed with her.

After filing into his small office, they sat. "Coffee? Water?" Harmon offered. His blue eyes sparkled.

Zehra shook her head. "You should drink tea, Steve. Better for you. How are things going with the 'crime fighters' here?"

Harmon, jacketless, leaned back in his chair and lifted his hands behind his head, where he locked his fingers. Harmon was in his mid-forties—the hardest kind of prosecutor to work against because he was very experienced and clever but young enough to still have energy and drive. Dark hair thinned over his head, which was balanced by a close-clipped beard. The silver flecks throughout shone against his tan skin.

Zehra never forgot how generous he had been to her, when she worked as a prosecutor a few years ago and needed his advice. However, his nickname was "Hardball Harmon" and he wouldn't offer help now. She looked behind his shoulder and saw the family photo with his teenage kids—a boy and a girl. His boy wore a sweatshirt that named St. Thomas, a local college. Her eyes lingered for a moment because he looked about the same age as the victim in her murder case.

Harmon interrupted her thoughts. "You remember how things are around here. Between my boss, the cops, victims, and the press, I don't have much time to prosecute!"

"Both sides have their problems," BJ said.

"And my problem is," Zehra started, "El-Amin hates women and particularly, me—a Muslim infidel. In the end, I'll have to try the case anyway."

"Yeah . . . the hardest for me are always the 'not-so-innocent' victims," Harmon said.

BJ laughed in recognition of the problem. "Yeah, I remember. Before I worked here, when I was a cop, we'd arrive at the scene of a shooting. Two coked-up dudes fighting over a woman. The first one to pull the gun became the defendant. They're both strapped so it could've just as easily been the other way around."

Steve dropped his arms and leaned forward over his desk. Energy popped off him. "And you should hear 'em demand their rights! The truly innocent victims—the kids, the rape victims, the old people who get mugged—that's what bothers me. That's why I keep working on this treadmill."

Zehra shifted in her seat. This talk could go on all afternoon. Better to save it for a happy hour somewhere else. "Steve, we're here to give you notice of an alibi witness BJ found. We'll file the formal notice and give you the whole statement when our secretary finishes the transcript, but we wanted to talk about it first."

Suddenly, Harmon's eyes narrowed, and he leaned over the desk. The light stuff was over. This was business, and he changed completely. "What alibi?"

BJ started, "I've been checking and found a guy who says that during the murder, he was with El-Amin at a mosque. He's an imam and knows El-Amin well."

Harmon gulped a big breath of air. "Yeah . . . yeah. Have you checked this guy out? He's probably a cousin to El-Amin, putting-up for him."

"Oh, I know, but in the end, Steve, he's gonna alibi the defendant."

"Details, man."

BJ stretched his long body out in the chair. "I'll give you the whole Q and A, but the long and short is the imam knows our guy, met him often at the mosque, and on the night of the murder, met him and even had tea—Oolong China tea, he remembers specifically."

"Sounds like a drug deal to me—Oolong China?" Harmon chuckled at his joke.

"He remembers 'cause they saw the TV news about the murder."

"Well . . . I've seen this a hundred times. How do we know your guy didn't put the imam up to this?"

"The witness says no."

"Bullshit."

Zehra leaned forward. "I don't think you can say that in front of a jury. What if they happen to believe this dude?"

"Bullshit."

"Look, Steve," Zehra continued. "I'm not sure what my guy wants, but it's part of my job to at least check it out. What kind of an offer can you make to avoid trial?"

"Yeah, I got a great offer for this animal: plead guilty. We won't ask for hanging, which is what he'd get in his own country. Guys, he butchered a young, innocent boy. Wait 'til the jury sees the photos . . ." He had a nervous forced laugh. "Heh, heh."

Zehra remembered it and knew it offered a peek into Harmon's occasional lack of confidence that he tried hard to cover up.

"Maybe so, but doesn't the alibi witness make a difference? Can't you let him plead to something less serious?" Zehra asked. She knew the answer and didn't blame Harmon at all. Still, as the defense lawyer, she had to ask.

Harmon shook his head. "Don't bust my balls on this."

"Remember, dude, the killer was wearing a mask," BJ said. "Your eyewitness can't give a great ID."

"So what? I've also got the DNA. You see that?"

"Yeah."

"It's a match. That's a conviction in my book. You can call all the alibi witnesses you want. I got the DNA. And jurors all watch TV—DNA's air-tight proof."

He was right. Neither Zehra nor BJ said anything for a while. Zehra knew a prosecutor would only drop charges for two reasons: either the evidence was so weak they knew they couldn't prove the case or because of sympathy for the defendant. Neither applied in this case.

The meeting was over. Zehra stood. "Okay, Steve." She reached across the desk and shook firmly. BJ bumped fists with him. "Later," he said.

Back on the public level of the Government Center, Zehra turned to BJ. "Remember we've got an appointment at the BCA lab in forty minutes? We've gotta hurry, 'cause I have to prepare a closing argument for that rape case."

BJ's thick eyebrows pinched down over his eyes. "What trial is that?"

"Oh, I got a guy who raped his teenage cousin—allegedly. He pled not guilty and waived a jury so the judge ordered us back tomorrow at eight-thirty to make the final arguments. The judge already heard all the evidence."

"How can you keep these cases straight?"

She sighed. "I don't know. I wish I had enough time to give them adequate attention. I always feel like I'm just hanging on by my fingernails." She looked up into the air above them. The Government Center had two parallel towers with an open atrium in the middle that rose to the top, twenty-four floors. "This guy's even creepier than El-Amin." Zehra shrugged her shoulders and asked BJ. "How can you keep so calm all the time?"

He smiled. "Faith, baby. Most old cops are angry or screwed-up. That almost caught me too, 'til I found my faith in Jesus again. That and my music. Maybe I should talk to you about it someday," he half-kidded her.

Forty minutes later, they squealed into the parking lot before the sprawling Bureau of Criminal Apprehension forensic lab on Maryland Avenue in St. Paul and rocked to a stop. Built in 2003, it boasted mostly glass for walls, surrounded by red brick, and stood three stories tall.

By going directly to the scientist who did the testing on the mask found at the crime scene, Zehra hoped to find a sliver of something she could use in her defense. It was like trying to find a door just barely cracked open. One she could push open to discover what was behind it.

As they gathered briefcases and notes, they walked to the entrance. Beside the double glass doors stood stone sculptures that resembled ancient Mayan art. A warm breeze blew Zehra's hair over her face and lifted her spirits. She always got a jolt of BJ's peace when she was with him. Grateful for his presence.

BJ checked his watch. "Chill, Z. We'll make it."

They were directed to wait in a large, glass-enclosed atrium that stretched up two stories and was capped by a glass roof. Sun flooded around them and lit up the space. When Zehra sat, the room darkened. She looked up to see puffy, thick clouds moving across the sky. They passed, and the room blazed again.

Of course, everyone in the room stared at the sculpture on the second floor level at the end. It was titled, "Exquisite Corpse."

Zehra had seen it before but was always amused at the sense of humor the artists used. A line of about twenty large aluminum frames, looking like magnifying glasses, balanced on their handles. Inside the row of empty glasses stretched a model of a human body sliced into thin sections from foot to head as if it were awaiting scientific analysis. The slices were colorful, full of blue, green, brown, and blood red sections. Holding the "slices of the body" inside the round frames was a spider web of metal filaments. The most creative part, she thought, was that each slice showed the different types of testing the lab performed: molecular models of heroin, bullet holes, blunt object hits, gas chromatography, and two DNA double-helix models.

The artwork made her feel almost reverent.

She turned to BJ. "Hey, got any new gigs coming up that I can hear?"

"The Dakota. Next Tuesday night." He paused to smile. "'Course we got the slow night and the nine o'clock time slot but hey . . . I'll blow anytime."

In ten minutes, Dr. Betty McWhorter approached them from across the room. Zehra and BJ rose to shake her hand. She said, "BJ, haven't seen you since you left the force. You want to see the respirator for the Ahmed victim?"

"Yes. Thanks for taking your time," Zehra said.

They trailed behind her to a desk in the corner where they received temporary security badges. Through two locked doors, and down a long hallway, Dr. McWhorter led them to a small room. Inside it was empty except for the white table, three chairs, and a sealed box on the table.

"Have a seat," the doctor offered.

Shiny metal trim surrounded the door and the edges of the table. The air conditioning seemed to be on high. Zehra shivered at the chill. She asked, "What can you tell us about the testing you did on the facemask?"

Dr. McWhorter shrugged. A tall woman with bleached-blonde hair cut short under her chin, she moved her bright blue eyes from one to the other. "Well, as you may know, we here in the Biology section conduct several types of serological examinations on evidentiary materials. That includes blood, seminal fluid, saliva, urine along with immunological tests and microscopic exams. For instance, hair, tissue, skin cells, blood, semen, and other bodily samples." She lifted her chin and sniffed.

"Uh . . . what about the DNA testing?"

Dr. McWhorter turned her large body in the chair to face Zehra. "Once we obtain the samples, we perform nuclear autosomal and Y-chromosome STR DNA tests. We compare the DNA types obtained from the questioned materials with DNA types obtained from known sources. In this case, we took samples of the saliva from inside the respirator. There was also a little blood; probably the perp bit his lip." She marked the date and time on the outside of the box with a pen, initialed it, and opened the cover. "Then, we took a swab sample from inside the cheek of the defendant, Mr. El-Amin. Our testing uses capillary electrophoresis to check the match. After you've done a few hundred of these, it's really pretty simple. The technology does most of the work." She sat up straighter in the chair.

"Bottom line, does the saliva inside the mask match the DNA of Mr. El-Amin?" Zehra asked.

"Respirator," she corrected Zehra. "But you're right. Here. You can take it out." She pushed the container closer to them.

Zehra lifted up the small object. "This isn't a mask?"

"A layman would call it that. But this is better, more effective than a mask."

Zehra turned it over. The white cup had 3M 8000 stamped across the top and to the side. She read it—N95. It had a pliable metal strap inside the cotton for a nose clip and four yellow elastic straps around the edges. Looked like a typical face mask, to her. She handed it to BJ.

"What would you use this for?" Zehra asked.

"Oh . . . if you were doing a home project, like sanding and wanted the best filtering protection, this is it. They're routinely used in hospitals. It's designed to fit tightly around the face and has an electrostatic charge in the micro fibers to enhance the filtration."

"Wow. This is top drawer, huh?" BJ whistled quietly.

"It's the best you can get without using a full head mask," Dr. McWhorter said.

"Plus, it fits tightly around the face, so it won't fall off when you're killing someone violently," BJ said. "And, it covers up almost everything. Look . . ." He held it in front of his face without touching his skin.

Zehra agreed it hid most of his face—perfect for a disguise. "But BJ, you'll have to shave your goatee before you become a serial killer." She laughed, and then turned back to the doctor. "I know this is a dumb question, but are you certain about your testing?"

The doctor smiled and dropped her eyes for a moment. "DNA identification is the gold standard, my dear."

"Yeah, I know, but do you think the criminal justice system is relying on this testing too much?"

Dr. McWhorter stood and placed the mask into the box. She taped it shut and cradled it in her arm. With her other arm, she opened the door for them. "We should rely on it—it's foolproof."

THIRTEEN

The day rains had ended in November.

The plains to the west of Mogadishu remained green and offered a few more weeks of grazing land before the driest of seasons descended in December. As the land dried out and the vegetation shriveled, the two shepherds were forced to work their goats further and further from the camps.

The trick was to feed them as much as possible, get through the drought, and make it to the *gu* rains, the next season, starting in April. The desert would blossom once again into a green and fertile land and the people would celebrate as they had for thousands of years.

They both wrapped themselves in long cloths to protect themselves. It wasn't particularly hot, but the wind could do damage quickly.

Most of the days were boring and monotonous. The shepherds didn't mind because tending the goats was their work as it had been for their fathers and the fathers before them. At least they could provide for the clan.

The ground rolled in long, flat scrubland. Flowers that only a few weeks earlier had decorated the hills with color drooped in anticipation of no more water. The goats spread out further than the men could see. That was all right with them, since there wasn't anywhere for the goats to get lost.

Ismir, the younger herder, volunteered this afternoon to round-up the stragglers before they made their camp for the evening. In the desert, night fell quickly and with cold winds. They wanted to have the fire and dinner ready before then.

Ismir scuffed over the worn paths that led to the west. The last of the rain clouds scudded out toward the ocean behind him. He searched into the setting sun to the horizon for the small clumps in the distance that would be the remains of the herd. Far to his left, he noticed something flash.

Unusual. He didn't think there was anything out there. Ismir trudged over the hill to get a better look.

He saw the stragglers from the herd. But to his astonishment, just beyond them, he spied a series of low mud huts. Surrounded by a wire fence, the compound had a more permanent wooden building at one end. This was very unusual. Wood was so scarce out here, no one could afford to use it for something as mundane as shelter.

The flash came from a silver bus. Dust curled around the back end of it, so the bus must have just arrived. From where?

Ismir continued toward the goats and the bus. Scrub brush hid his presence from anyone in the compound, and he moved closer. He knelt down. Who would be way out here? He wondered.

On his stomach, he wiggled almost to within hearing range. The door of the bus opened, and two men got out. They wore white masks.

As they stood aside, several young men, boys really, followed them out of the bus. The boys staggered as if very tired. About ten of them. Ismir didn't recognize any of the people which was odd. He knew everyone in the clan that occupied this area of Somalia. These were strangers.

He inched closer in the long shadows of evening, trying to hear something.

He saw that some were speaking, but the cool wind blew away the words. It appeared they were ordering the boys into the huts.

Suddenly, Ismir felt sad. The boys were black skinned like himself and Somalis, but he could tell they weren't local. They looked foreign. Maybe from Europe. They looked frightened. And for some reason, they had a drooped look to them, like the flowers around him.

He peered closer and was startled. In spite of the rising chill in the wind, he saw many of the young men were sweating heavily. They looked sick.

FOURTEEN

Mears Park in the lowertown area of St. Paul is one of the most beautiful urban parks in the country. It occupies an entire city block and is surrounded by restaurants, jazz clubs, and theatres. The buildings above the sidewalks date back to before the turn of the century, updated with modern touches and facilities.

Through the middle of the park, a stream of fresh water bounces over small waterfalls, twisting its way down under the streets to empty into the Mississippi River at the foot of the bluffs below St. Paul, where tugboats groan to push heavy barges south to New Orleans.

A gray bank of rain clouds hovered above the park, and the air smelled metallic with ozone. A storm was coming for sure.

Paul remembered to grab his umbrella, because a May rain in Minnesota could be a gusher. He cut across the park to find the coffee shop Joan had recommended. At the door, two hanging baskets bent low, full of flowers that gushed over the edges.

Knowing about the intense competition that existed between government agencies, he was sure that any work or investigation he did with Joan would never get back to Conway. Whichever agency solved this case, would reap the rewards: bigger budgets, promotions and higher salaries. He needed her help badly.

Still, he knew he'd have to be extremely careful. Just that morning, Paul had walked by his secretary's vacant desk. He'd glanced at her computer screen to find his emails on the screen. Conway must have ordered her to shadow his mail. That scared him.

Ten minutes later, Joan interrupted his thoughts as she walked in the door, blinked at the bright lights, and spotted him. Although she had a Latin name, she was pure Scandinavian all the way. A tight red dress clung to her shapely body as she wobbled toward him on high heels.

"I'm like, never getting used to these damn things," she complained. "Gotta wear 'em for the office."

"You look great, Joan." Paul stood and hugged her a little too long. She didn't seem to mind.

"I need something stronger than coffee," she wheezed as she plopped into the chair next to him. "Talk about pressure! These disappearing kids have got all of us on high alert."

"I know."

"Immigration and Customs Enforcement is the first line of defense. The boss is whipping us day and night, and since I'm second in command, you can imagine the shit I'm getting." She squinted up at the menu, written in chalk on the wall. "They write too small to see from here. Maybe they should have fewer choices so they don't have to squish everything on the board so tight."

Paul smiled, knowing the real problem was that she was just a tad vain. "Wear your glasses. You look good in them."

She huffed but dug in her purse for the glasses case. "Well . . . listen," She glanced from right to left, "You gotta keep quiet about this case. If this ever gets back to the boss, I'm toast."

In the background, Paul could hear someone grinding coffee beans. It smelled rich and heavy. "Same here. I think Conway hates everyone at ICE."

"Screw him! Most of your agents think they're on TV." Joan bounced up and headed to the counter. She came back with a skim-milk latte. "Here's the skinny. I told you El-Amin is connected."

Paul nodded.

"Well, he's part of a larger criminal network," she said, her arms swinging wide. "We think he's a 'snakehead.'"

"A what?"

"Snakehead. It's a term that means . . . like we used to call 'em coyotes . . . the ones who do the dirty work—recruiting, transporting—stuff like that. But, now, they're a lot more sophisticated. A guy like El-Amin is trained and well-financed."

"Who do you think he works for?"

Joan shrugged, and her tightly bound breasts rose and fell with her shoulders. She sipped her latte and licked a strip of foam off her upper lip, slowly from left to right. "Who the hell knows? These are international networks, kind of like on the Web. They plug-in people as they need 'em from all over. Like, let's say you need financing to transport kidneys into the U.S. If you know where to look, you offer the deal to a select group of money guys. They bid on the job to see who gets it. Then, when you've got the money you're looking for, you offer jobs to others for procurement, warehousing, labor, and bribes to get by customs in the countries you'll take the stuff through."

"How can they trust each other?"

"Shit! They don't trust anyone. If you take a job and rip your boss off, everyone finds out, and you'll never, ever get another job. Besides that, you might get killed by yet another web of hired muscle. It's like the purest form of capitalism."

"They didn't teach *that* in my Econ classes in college."

"You're too old." When Joan laughed, it crinkled the corners of her eyes. "I guess a better example is Facebook. Criminals anywhere in the world can invite 'friends' to join their network. Each of them has different skill sets."

"Yeah, unlike the old criminal organizations, these guys can hook-up, do the crime, split, and disappear in a few days." He leaned forward, smelled her musky perfume. "And from what I've seen, these guys are really smart."

Joan raised her shoulders. "You do what you can."

"How does El-Amin fit in?"

She paused and moved her eyes over him. "Like I said, he's a snakehead—lower level labor. Today, its stolen kidneys a customer wants, maybe nuclear materials. Tomorrow, it's young Somali men." She sighed and looked at him closely. "I don't know how much . . ."

"Okay, I get it."

"We have to trade intel or this won't work."

Paul nodded. "But why'd he kill the boy?"

She took another sip of her latte. Another slow lick of her lips. "Don't know. But here's what concerns ICE: the network behind him must be bigger than we thought originally, highly organized, and full of loyal people. To pull-off 'disappearing' these young men . . . and getting away with it . . . is damn hard."

"They're sure drawing a lot of attention from law enforcement. Every agency in the local and federal government's involved. Say, that reminds me, have you ever heard of something called the Army Medical Research agency?"

Joan shook her head. "No. Now what can you tell me?"

"The network you're talking about's recruiting here. To have these guys fight for the Al-Shabaab. That's what everyone at the Bureau thinks."

"I can get that from the news junkies. Give me more meat, Buddy."

"Look Joan, I'm risking my career . . ."

"Bullshit. I've snitched to you. Give me something in return."

"All right. El-Amin's defense team has found an alibi witness."

"How do you know that?"

Paul leaned closer. "I'm in tight with the defense lawyer. She can't reveal anything confidential from her client, of course, but there's always more."

"Hey, ICE should check him out."

"Sorry, Joan. If I have to, I'll invoke the Patriot Act and get this guy off the radar." Paul opened his palms toward her. "Best thing to happen for the Bureau."

"Oh?"

"Patriot Act. Gave us new tools for investigation and interrogation like we've never had before."

She looked closely at him. "I can't imagine you water-boarding anyone."

"No. These are advanced techniques. Now, we can also pick up suspects and hold 'em for questioning a lot easier than before. I can't say more, but we've got places here where we work on these guys. National security is protected."

"What else?"

"Uh . . . we got an asset in the Somali community. Guy works at a local deli. He's given us good stuff in the past."

"Who is he?"

Paul smiled and remained silent.

Joan sat back in her chair and crossed her arms over her stomach. She watched Paul. "So . . . you're putting your neck on the line for this?"

"Well, at least my job."

She leaned forward. Her eyes softened. "It's because of the problem you had in Milwaukee? You wanna try to make up for that?"

Paul puffed out a small breath of air. "Could be."

"I remember when we met at the training at Quantico. Remember the rifle training and, oh, don't forget the self-defense course." A smile squirreled its way across her mouth.

Paul laughed at the memory. "Your fingernails, they just about recycled you because you wouldn't trim your nails."

"They were worried I couldn't get my finger into the trigger guard of the 9-mm fast enough. And then . . ." Her arms flew out to the side like an umbrella popping open. "The vest, the damn Kevlar vest. It was so bulky, I couldn't fasten it over my boobs. I'm like, tryin' to tell those old instructors with the crew-cuts."

"I suppose they wanted you to demonstrate the problem."

"No shit! I could almost hear 'em grunting while they drooled."

They both laughed hard.

Joan wiped an eye. "That . . . that was before your case that . . ."

"Yeah. I was on a fast track then. Two years later, I got a career break and was ordered out on a case for investigation of a serial killer in Milwaukee. Young girls. Grabbed, raped, and killed. Really stinky case. I worked my ass off on that one. Felt sorry for the families."

"Did you bust 'em?"

"Damn right. With the help from the Milwaukee PD, we got the son-of-a-bitch. I was told to hold him, don't do anything until the big shots from Washington got there."

"But . . ." she drew-out the word, "you didn't."

Paul shook his head, felt a shudder in his chest even after all these years. "No. I was gonna do a General George Custer—wrap it all up before the rest of the army got there. If I could pull that off, I'd be promoted to Washington within a week. So, I talked to him, and he told me a few things. When the Washington guys got there, they finished his full confession. Month later, the dude comes up for trial. The defense lawyer successfully suppressed the whole confession because of the way they said I 'forced' him to talk without his lawyer. Entire case was tossed."

Joan didn't say anything for a while.

Paul took a deep breath. "I ended up here, answering telephones on Sunday afternoons."

Joan reached for Paul's right hand. Her fingers felt warm and slightly moist. "Be careful, Paul. ICE is all over it. I'm gonna blow the lid off this and uncover whatever's underneath. Let us take the shots. We've been using some private contractors—don't you breathe a word—that are great. How about the murder case? Will this slug El-Amin be convicted?"

"Don't know. Our read is he's the guy. DNA matched. We want him taken out. And the alibi witness . . . that'll be taken care of."

She urged Paul, "You should back-off. If Conway's after your ass, don't make it easy for him."

He looked at her face, her hair and the brown color of roots peeking out from underneath the blonde. "It's personal, Joan."

"I can imagine. You want to prove yourself."

"It's more than that. It's the families of the victims in Milwaukee. The victims here. I let them down, and I wanna make it right in some way." He changed the subject. "How are your kids?"

"Kid. Just the one. Mark is ten. He's great. Can't say the same for his 'bio-dad,' who's usually never around. He never helps with the tough stuff, like when Mark's sick or has problems at school or with friends. Dad shows up for the fun things, like . . . sorry." Joan stopped, blinked. "Sorry, they don't let me out much anymore. I hardly date now—no time, and they're so many losers out there."

"It's tough trying to do it all," Paul paused. "I'd like children some day, but I have to sift through all those same 'loser' women out there."

Joan said, "If we weren't friends, I'd never be meeting like this. Be careful. Not only because of your boss, but this network has a long, well-financed reach. El-Amin may be in custody, but we don't know how many others are out in the community with an interest in the case."

"Yeah?"

"Who got the murdered kid back *into* the country? I mean, when you come through Customs and they ask you, 'What was the nature of your visit to Somalia? They can't say: 'Terrorist training.'"

"El-Amin?"

"He's too low-level. There are people higher up here in the Cities. People smarter and more connected than he is—that's who scare us. Who are they? And what will they do next?"

Paul sat back in his chair. Joan had echoed his fears.

She sighed, "Well, I'll keep you in the loop as much as I can, but you're on your own." She leaned close to him. "If these guys think we're getting too close to them, they'll do anything to protect themselves."

"If I get anything on this imam, the alibi witness, I'll let you know. Some of these imams are real cooperative, but others smell like terrorists. This one smells to me."

"Oh?"

"We're getting a lot more traffic all of a sudden. Phone intercepts. It means something's going on, but I don't know what."

Paul's eyes dropped to the table, to their empty cups and Joan's crumpled napkin stained with her ruby lipstick. It wasn't himself he worried about. He thought of Zehra.

FIFTEEN

At eight-thirty, Zehra sat at the edge of the counsel table in Judge Palmer's courtroom, as far from her client as she could. Jackie sat on the other side of their client, Mr. James Carlson.

She prayed this client woudn't freak out and cause her trouble. She had enough stress from the murder case. But knowing Judge Palmer, Zehra was sure something-would blow-up.

Jackie looked at Carlson. "We think the trial went well. What'd you think?"

Zehra felt her face twist tightly. *Wrong question, Jackie. Well, she'd learn.*

Mr. Carlson complained, "I don't think I got a chance to really explain to the judge."

"But you testified . . ." Jackie reminded him. She put on her dark glasses that almost hid her little nose.

"My daughter is making this all up because my former wife, the bitch, told her to blame me for touching her. I asked both of you to investigate that, but you haven't done shit."

Zehra held out her hand, palm down to him. "Sshh here comes the judge."

They all rose and sat to the rhythm of the coming and going of the judge. Palmer wore his robe, but Zehra could see the lavender collar of a cotton golf shirt poking out from the top of the black cloth. He looked amused and smiled at things no one else thought funny.

Carlson had been charged with having sexual relations with his teenage daughter. After hearing all the evidence, Zehra knew he was guilty. During the pre-trial hearings, one of the court clerks, a good friend of Zehra's, had approached her in the hallway of the courthouse to serve some papers on her client. Zehra smiled at the memory.

"Yo, Z," the clerk asked, "I have these papers to serve. Can you point out your client?"

"This is all you need to know, Henry. He's accused of having sex with his daughter."

Henry blinked and waited for a description. When Zehra smiled at him, he nodded and disappeared around the corner. In three minutes, he returned. "Found him," Henry said and, without cracking a smile, grinned with his eyes at Zehra. "Spotted him right away. You can always tell those kiddie sex offenders."

At the counsel table, Zehra looked at Mr. Carlson. He was white, thin, had scraggly blonde hair, and was so pale, she could see blue veins streaked down his arms. He twitched constantly. He insisted on sucking throat lozenges because he said he had asthma. During the entire trial, Zehra heard him next to her, sucking and coughing over the lozenges. He sneezed on her shoulder.

Judge Palmer finally stopped grinning, looked at the file before him, peered up into the ceiling, looked down and spied Zehra, Jackie, and their alleged sex offender client. The prosecutor sat quietly at the other table. She was winning and knew enough to keep her mouth shut.

The judge stuck his head out like a chicken plucking for food and bobbed up and down. "Ready, counsel?" he said to both sides.

Suddenly, the judge ducked down behind the raised bench and disappeared. He remained submerged for a while. Two arms popped up. On each hand, he had a puppet. A green and a purple one wiggled back and forth.

Zehra had seen it before. She wondered how Carlson would react and how much calming down it'd take to keep him from bolting out of the courtroom. Maybe Jackie could tackle him.

Judge Palmer finally sat up and looked down at Mr. Carlson. "Sir, you see these?"

Carlson crunched a lozenge and choked it down. "Uh . . . yeah?"

"These are the people who'll decide your case. This one," he lifted his left hand, "is Not Guilty. This one is Guilty." Judge Palmer wiggled his right hand. "After your lawyer's argument, one of these will decide the verdict. So, you watch because when I duck down, one of these will come up and pronounce the verdict."

Carlson jerked his head back and forth between Jackie and Zehra. He started to gag on his words.

"You got it, son?"

Carlson nodded slowly. "I . . . I guess," he coughed something onto Zehra's shoulder.

"Proceed, Counsel," Judge Palmer ordered. He lowered his arms.

After both sides made their final arguments, they sat down. The judge looked up to the ceiling and twisted his lips in concentration. "Okay let me think about the evidence . . ." He rotated his head, nodded, and then looked down at this notes. "Okay." He ducked below the bench.

The right hand puppet came up. From below the bench, a high-pitched voice said, "Guilty." And the puppet wiggled.

Zehra turned to Carlson. He looked sick to his stomach. She wasn't sure if it was the verdict or the bizarre proceedings. "Get used to it," she whispered. "We always appeal this guy. Don't worry, I'll file it tomorrow."

"But . . . but . . ."

"I said, don't worry. We'll get it straightened out." She sighed at the extra work this judge created for her.

Carlson staggered to his feet. Suddenly, he started flapping his arms. He jumped up and down like a chicken. He gurgled something unintelligible. The deputies had to assist him away because he couldn't walk very well. In a way, maybe this was true justice for him.

As she and Jackie left the courtroom, Zehra's phone vibrated. She glanced at it and sighed—her mother. "Yes, Mom."

"Have you got time for lunch today?"

"To meet another wonderful Muslim? I don't know, Mom, I'm really busy. The trial's coming up."

"Just lunch, Zehra. You've got to learn to let go and relax. 'Go with the flow,' they say. Now, this man is handsome and so nice. I know you'll love him."

"Is he another doorknob, like the last one—functional but pretty boring?"

"You want a Greek salad at Christo's?"

"Can I say no?"

"No."

"When?"

"Twelve-thirty. And, Zehra, comb your hair. It's your best asset."

At twelve-thirty, Zehra sat alone at Christo's Greek restaurant on Nicollet Avenue salivating for a very large glass of red wine and waiting for her mother. In front of the floor-to-ceiling windows that looked out on the busy street, a half-dozen ancient begonias in big green pots crowded out the sun.

Zehra loved the deep colors and thick leaves. White walls surrounded the window with sky-blue trim. She felt like escaping to Greece. It looked so relaxed and sunny and far away from her mother. And the best part—their growing season lasted all year long.

"There you are!" shouted her mother.

Zehra turned from the serenity of the window to see her mother steaming toward her with a small man following behind. *Here we go*, she thought.

At the table, her mother sat quickly and slipped her head covering off, to rest on her shoulders. Martha could be selective as to when she wore it. "I want you to meet Mr. Jamison Raza." She held out her hand as if she were delivering the original text of the Qur'an. "He's a doctor at Fairview. Thoracic surgery, I understand. A very lucrative practice." Martha smiled, her work almost done.

Zehra nodded and reached across the small table to shake Raza's limp hand. *Can't imagine those could crack open a chest*, she thought. He looked very Semitic.

Long nose, dark skin, and black curly hair. The only attractive thing about him was the hair—any woman would kill for it. He looked down at the table all the time except to glance up at her when he spoke.

"I'm pleased to meet you." He folded his hands, prayer-like, before him on the table.

Zehra felt a rumbling low in her stomach. Hunger? Fear? "Uh . . . yeah. Me, too."

"Your mother tells me your whole family is very observant."

"Huh?"

"You pray five times a day, attend mosque, and are faithful during Ramadan."

The rumbling in her stomach became shaking. "Uh . . . well, I don't know."

"I've taken my hajj twice, now. It is a profoundly moving experience. Have you made yours?"

"It's coming up next year . . . after I go to Greece." She looked hard at her mother. "Can I talk to you?"

Martha giggled. "I've got to run and freshen-up. You two get acquainted." Her mother left in a puff of old-fashioned cologne.

"I'm Pakistani. My parents are related to the Bhutto family, the former Prime Minister? Benazir Bhutto?" he said. "We own much land near Lahore."

"Bhutto was just killed, right?"

"The liberals did it."

"Who?" Zehra felt afloat without a life raft.

"She tried to change the laws of the Prophet. There's a reason order has prevailed for hundreds of years it's because people were faithful to the Prophet."

"What kind of surgery do you do, Jamison?"

"Thank Allah, I have an education and could provide for any woman. She would not have to work but could be faithful and bear children."

What an exciting thought. "Maybe you forget we're in America?"

"That's the problem here. Too many Muslim women have forgotten the True Way. Your mother told me that you're faithful."

"I am," Zehra asserted. "But in a more progressive way . . ."

"Let me remind you of what the Qur'an says . . ."

"I can read the Qur'an. And I don't need you to interpret it for me."

Jamison sat back and blinked. "But . . . but I thought you understood that Muhammad had clearly told us what Allah expects of a faithful woman?"

"And the Prophet gave many equal rights to women, also. That was about fifteen hundred years ago." She longed for a bite of a chocolate cupcake. Zerha's phone buzzed. Thank Allah! She looked. Jackie. Zehra clicked it on.

Jackie spoke fast, "Zehra, Mr. Peterson's called five times already. I didn't think the deputies allowed them that many phone calls. What should I do?"

"I'll be there in thirty minutes." She snapped the phone off. Looked back at the doctor. Zehra counted to ten. He represented many of the things she fought against—the intolerant attitude toward women and the ultra-conservative interpretation of Islam.

When she felt calmer, she said, "I've got an emergency. I'm sure you know how it is." She stood and hurried out so quickly, she forgot to look at the begonias. Besides her frustration, these dead-end men her mother brought all reminded Zehra of her loneliness.

In her car, driving back downtown to meet Jackie, Zehra's mother called.

"All right, make this quick," Zehra demanded, still mad.

"I'm sorry. He seemed like such a nice man."

"Oh, that's okay, I guess. Look, I'm busy, gotta run."

"Oh, there's something that's bothering me. I don't know if I should bother you with it."

"What's wrong, Mom."

"Well, I've noticed a car parked outside our house a lot lately. A gold one. You know how quiet our street is. Even your father commented on it. I can't imagine who it could be. But it, well, it makes me feel creepy."

Zehra gripped the leather covered wheel harder. "How often is it there?"

"Almost every day."

Zehra took a deep breath to calm her racing thoughts. A gold car had followed her on several occasions also. It couldn't be a coincidence. She didn't want her mother upset. "I'm sure it's just an admirer looking at your gardens. "If it'll make you feel better, I'll have my friend BJ Washington check things out. Or maybe you should call the police."

"Good idea. I'll call the police."

Zehra's fear rose up through her arms. She had to concentrate on driving. "Gotta run, Mom."

"I know you won't like this now, but this time your father has a man for you to meet."

"No!"

"Now, just calm down. He's an engineer or some scientist who works with your father. Originally from Egypt. We'll talk about it later."

SIXTEEN

Michael declined a glass of wine for the sixth time.

He weaved his way among the guests at the Health Tech party. Ostensibly held to celebrate the break-through in genetic engineering they'd made to the cold virus, it was really an excuse for the employees to get drunk at company expense.

He was anxious to meet Zehra Hassan. He had to win her over and gain her trust. Trying to avoid Posten, he bumped into Michael at the food trough.

"Mikey-boy," Posten lurched to the side. He balanced three small plates heaped with fried chicken wings in his hands. One almost flipped over onto Michael's Armani sweater. "How ya doin'?"

"Fine, John. Just fine," Michael said. He glanced at his Patek Philippe watch. He'd suffered through enough time to be polite. "Look, I have to run. Keep eating." Posten's smile broke through his reddened cheeks. He didn't realize that Michael was mocking him.

"Great wings." Posten smiled to show grease covered teeth with bits of chicken in the corners.

Michael made a point of greeting the CEO and the vice-president of his division. The social aspects of the party appealed to him. But he detested the drunken, gorging excesses. These Americans couldn't seem to get enough. Especially if it was free.

He'd promised his co-worker, Joseph Hassan, that he'd stay long enough to meet his daughter. Joseph obviously liked Michael and was anxious to have her meet Muslim men.

This woman could be the key he needed for information. Probably dumpy like most Muslim American women, Michael was still anxious to meet her. He sipped a Diet Coke and waited for Joseph.

From across the noisy room, Michael spied him.

Next to him walked a beautiful woman. She looked Semitic—black hair, long nose, darker skin but, at the same time, thoroughly American. *Maybe this will be worthwhile*, Michael thought.

"Ah . . . Michael. There you are," Joseph pushed through the crowd, pulling his daughter behind him. When she stood next to him, he said, "This is Zehra. I've told you about her. Now I know this is awkward, but I just wanted you two to meet."

She gave Michael a tentative smile.

He didn't hide his attraction and looked into her eyes. "Nice to meet you."

Her eyes darted around. She was obviously uneasy.

"Would you like pop, tea?" he offered.

"I really could use a big glass of wine," she laughed.

"I don't drink alcohol."

"Well, I do." She led him to the bar and ordered a glass of white wine. When it came, she sipped it carefully. "My father says you're a doctor here."

"I have a doctorate in molecular biology."

"Impressive."

"No it isn't. Not to you," he insisted.

She laughed out loud. "Okay, you got me. I'm really not too impressed to be here but to keep my father happy . . ."

"I understand." He turned on his warm, big smile. "Tell me about you."

"Huh? You really want to know?"

"I do."

"Well I'm a criminal defense lawyer. Uh, I like to garden." She paused and looked into the air. "I guess I'm excited about my work and like it."

"What cases are you working on?"

She frowned. "I've got a murder case I'm working . . . struggling through. Maybe you've heard about these Somali boys who have disappeared from the Twin Cities?"

He pretended to think about it. "Yes, I heard from people I know in the Somali community."

"I've been forced to represent the guy accused of killing one of the boys."

"Is that hard?"

"This guy is because . . . well, maybe you'd understand this better than these other people. The defendant is an extremist Muslim, a terrorist really. That's opposite to everything I believe as a Muslim. So, it's just torture to try and defend someone who thinks that way."

Michael nodded. "It must be hard. I find it hard just living in America. So many people don't know anything about Islam except what they see in the biased media."

Her face brightened. "Absolutely. If Christians only knew how close our religions were, they'd be shocked. And most of us aren't making bombs in our garages at night."

He laughed. "No . . ."

"Instead of making bombs, what do you do?"

"My work? I'm trying to alter the genetic make-up of viruses. When I have time, I do a lot of volunteer work in the community."

"Like what?"

"I try to give time to the poor people in the Somali community, even though they don't accept outsiders, even Muslims. I also host science fairs in several of the schools."

When Zehra nodded and looked at his eyes, Michael could tell she was interested. It usually worked this way. He could smell her perfume. Thank Allah it wasn't floral like so many American women It smelled like sandalwood. She had a full figure and thick hair. And what a stroke of luck—Allah be praised—she was the defense lawyer in the murder case. That interested him.

The noise from the party rose higher. Both of them squeezed to a corner to avoid the wilder dancers who had just erupted from somewhere. It was difficult to talk. Michael had to leave. "I'd like to meet you again," he said.

"So would I, Michael."

SEVENTEEN

On Tuesday, Zehra trudged into Courtroom Two for the pre-trial on El-Amin's case. She dreaded the confrontation. *Why couldn't I have a simple job like a corporate counsel?* she thought. Sitting at a desk. Reading five-inch-thick contracts all day long.

When she arrived, Steve Harmon was already there. He nodded at Zehra as he unpacked several files from a metal cart on wheels.

Zehra walked down the middle aisle, pushed through the swinging gate that separated the public area from the judge's bench and the lawyer's area. Judge Gordon Smith listened to another case from up on the bench. She looked bored. To her left, was where prisoners stood, a small area enclosed by a low wooden rail and topped by a partial glass wall.

Jackie came down the main aisle, caught her eye. Zehra watched as she made her way into the lawyer's area. Zehra envied Jackie's beautiful hair. Straight and shiny, it always looked good.

"Thought I'd be late," Jackie whispered.

"For what? Not much will happen today. Since we don't have any plea negotiation, this is pretty much a meaningless hearing."

"Josh made me breakfast today because he knows I'm working so hard on the case. I'm so like, impressed with this guy. I'm worried it's gonna be permanent," Jackie laughed. "What will I tell all the others?"

You're self-absorbed, was all Zehra could think. Jackie rarely asked Zehra how she was or what guy she was with—not that there were many. Jackie's full relationship contrasted with Zehra's lack of one.

"Who'd we get for a trial judge?" Jackie asked.

"Don't know, yet." Zehra turned her back to the judge and spoke softly. "'Hottub's' too lazy to actually try it, so she'll pass it to one of the five judges scheduled to hear trials in the next two weeks. Besides, I'm so damn mad at her for calling Mao."

In ten minutes, deputies led El-Amin into the holding area. He stopped and stood straight. Without moving his head, his eyes traveled over the entire courtroom. He spied Zehra and glared at her.

It always amazed Zehra that defendants took out their wrath on the defense lawyers, not the judges, nor the county attorneys—who were actually the ones prosecuting them.

"State versus Ibrahim El-Amin," the clerk read from the far side of the bench.

The defendant swiveled his head toward the judge.

Both Zehra and Harmon stepped up to a wooden podium directly before the raised bench. The judge asked them if the case had been settled.

"I don't think so, Judge," said Steve. "With a crime of this nature, we won't offer anything but a straight plea."

Zehra started to speak, "My client has . . ."

"I am not her client," El-Amin thundered from his side. "I represent myself. I do not accept the work of a woman, including the judge in this courtroom."

"Is that so?" Gordon Smith responded. Her eyes became small.

"I am in charge of my own fate and will make my own decisions. This infidel will not speak for me."

The judge turned toward him. "You're right. You can represent yourself, but I've appointed Ms. Hassan as back-up counsel, just in case. She's good and experienced. I'd recommend that in light of the charges against you, you take advantage of her services."

"I do not want this infidel to have anything to do with my case."

Gorden Smith yelled, "You're not in charge of this courtroom. I am." She spoke to the lawyers. "Ms. Hassan, I expect that you will vigorously prepare this case for trial because you're going to try it."

"As the court knows, many times in these situations, counsel is allowed to be in the courtroom but doesn't actually sit at counsel table with the defendant. I'm asking the court to relieve me of that duty."

"No. You'll be present for all appearances and will sit at counsel table, even if you don't participate in the actual trial. The defendant may, at any time, decide he needs your assistance to answer questions or give advice. I want you available for that."

Zehra felt warm anger cross her face and hoped it showed.

The judge flipped a few papers, leaned over to whisper to the clerk, and straightened up again. "I'll block this case to Judge Goldberg for trial in two weeks."

El-Amin exploded. "What? A Jew? I refuse. My fate will not be in the hands of a Jew!" He pounded the wooden wall with his raised fist.

"Quiet, or I'll have the deputies take you out," the judge warned him.

"It's your fault," El-Amin screamed at Zehra as the deputies reacted and stood to push him out the back door. "I will get my vengeance!"

After he'd been removed, the courtroom fell into an unnatural silence, like the air quivering without sound.

Zehra and Jackie loaded up their files and left the courtroom.

"I so like, hate that son-of-a bitch," Jackie said.

"I loathe him and everything he stands for. He's the reason Islam has such a bad name in our country. How can you expect people to see the liberal, progressive side of the religion with jerks like him?"

"So, what are we gonna do?"

"You heard the judge," she shot the words at Jackie. "We prepare the case as if we're actually trying it. I'll be damned if this guy wins an appeal based on incompetency of counsel because we haven't prepared well."

Zehra's cell phone buzzed. She answered and heard Paul Schmidt's voice.

"I'm glad I caught you. Uh, have you got a minute to talk?" He sounded out of breath.

"Sure. Just got done with our bronco client, El-Amin. It's going to be a long, hard trial." She threw her briefcase and files on a chair.

"Don't trust him."

"Paul, it's safe to say we hate each other. I don't trust him or anything he says."

Paul explained El-Amin's part in the criminal network that Joan told him about. "This case is a small part of something much larger and probably international."

"So, what can I do? All I can focus on is the trial."

"Are you investigating the case for him?"

"Of course. I have to be ready for trial."

"Are you going to talk more with the alibi witness?"

Zehra stopped, and her brain twitched. Had she told him about the alibi? Except for Harmon and her announcement in court today, she'd told no one. "Paul, how do you know about that?"

"Uh . . . oh, I happened to talk to BJ Washington."

"Yeah, we're talking to the guy this afternoon."

Paul took a deep breath. "I think I should help you."

"What? How can you help? The FBI helping the murder suspect?"

"No, I mean help you personally. Your client is financed and controlled by people we don't know, who are probably in the community now. I'm worried about you."

Zerha sat down and waved Jackie into the chair next to her. "What're you talking about?"

Paul coughed. "Are you still there?"

"Yeah, I'm here."

At the tone of his voice, she felt her stomach tighten. The gold car her mother talked about popped into her mind. The email.

"We can't find out anything about your client. People always leave some trail, but not this guy. We're not even sure if Ibrahim El-Amin is his true name."

She didn't answer for a moment as she digested the facts.

"Here's what worries me. Your client couldn't have done this alone. It's too expensive, too complicated. How did he manage to keep the boy from calling his parents once he got to Minneapolis? And if someone went to all the work to bring him back here, why turn around and kill him? This network is still out there and active."

"Active in what?"

"A cell. And I don't know if the murder of the boy was the end. There probably is more."

Zehra took a deep breath and stood up. "I'll be careful, but what could they possibly want with me?"

"Don't you understand? Anyone associated with this case, me included, could be a target for them. Who knows what they'll do to keep their secrets."

Zehra thought briefly of telling Paul about the gold car. Changed her mind. "Okay, thanks, Paul. Thanks for the warning." She clicked the phone off and sat still for a long time.

B Y THAT AFTERNOON, BJ, JACKIE, AND ZEHRA stopped in front of the mosque on Riverside Avenue, next to the University of Minnesota complex of buildings.

Zehra answered her buzzing cell phone. "Hi, Dad."

"Zehra, I know you don't want us to interfere, but I had to introduce you to Michael at the party," Joseph said.

She sighed. "Don't worry. He seemed nice. Tell me a little about him."

"He's got a doctorate in bio-medical engineering. He always dresses beautifully. He's very intelligent, modern. I've gotten to know him somewhat at the office. He seems kind. Of course, his real name is Mustafa, but he's Americanized totally. Maybe you should . . . see him again."

"I probably will." Zehra could never turn down her father. "But I won't meet him at home with Mom hanging around. If he calls, I'll meet him."

As the three approached the front door of the mosque, several men sat around it, dressed in colorful African clothing. Two women walked by, covered from head to toe, even in the warmth of the afternoon, in long, dark skirts that ended just above their sandaled feet. Over the robes, they wore shawls of red, green, purple, and yellow that covered their entire heads.

Zehra noticed that across the street there was a bar—the Nomad Bar. *How appropriate*, she laughed to herself.

She desperately needed the testimony of the Imam, the alibi witness. Had to make sure he'd cooperate.

At the door of the mosque, she reminded the others to remove their shoes and set them next to a pile of over twenty other pairs of shoes, mostly sandals. As they moved past the front entryway, the mosque opened into a large, quiet room.

Zehra brought a scarf with her, and, in respect, she flipped it over her hair.

Jackie lifted the back of her sweater up on her head. She glanced back and forth. "Don't I look beautiful?"

As they started into the open area, a man in a long tan robe came from the left and stepped in front of them. "I'm sorry, but it is not permitted to have women in the main prayer area." He nodded at a small balcony on the second floor to the right. "That is reserved for women."

Zehra bristled. On one hand, she wanted to remain respectful and get the information they needed, but this discrimination made her furious. Images of El-Amin yelling at her crowded into her mind. She tried to ignore them. Zehra stood in front of the man in the robe. "We have an appointment with the Imam, Hussein Moalim."

The man searched Zehra's face, only glancing at the others. "Wait here," he said.

Zehra looked into the open area. Many detailed Persian rugs covered the area. It was designed for prayer, and all faithful Muslims prayed from their knees on the floor if at all possible. BJ and Jackie moved to either side of her.

"I've never been in a mosque," Jackie whispered. "Who are those guys over in the corner? They look like they're sleeping."

"They're praying or meditating," Zehra explained. "A mosque is a place of worship of course but also for meditation and learning. The back side of this is probably a community center." She pointed to an ornamental arched niche set in the wall on the eastern end of the big room. "That's called a *mihrab* and reminds the faithful of the direction of Mecca. And that bench on top of the wooden steps next to it is the *minbar*. It's like a pulpit in Christian churches. The imam will deliver sermons from it on Fridays. As we have to perform ablutions, cleansings, before prayer, there have to be areas near here with water to perform the acts."

"It's so peaceful," BJ said in a hushed voice. "Tranquil. I can understand why people like it. It's actually relaxing."

"That's the idea. You have access to Allah here." She turned to him. "Remember why we're here. We've got to focus."

Jackie said, "I've been in Jewish synagogues before, and, you know, it's funny, but they look similar in many ways."

"Yeah?"

"Well, I mean my Catholic church looks like a circus with tons ornamentation.

The mosque and synagogue are really pretty plain inside."

She turned to Zehra. "By the way, is an 'imam' a priest?"

"No. Islam doesn't have a priestly class. Every believer has direct access to Allah. We don't need anyone to intercede for us. Imams are people specially trained in the religion and act as leaders and teachers."

"Welcome to our mosque," a voice said from the left.

They all turned to a man walking toward them. He wore a white robe from his shoulders to the floor. A gray beard hung over his chest, and he wore a pair of modern, stylish plastic glasses. He smiled to show huge white teeth.

"I am Imam Moalim." He bowed slightly.

In response, they bowed also.

"Let us go outside, It's a glorious day." He led them out the front door and down the sidewalk to a small patch of grass. "What may I help you with?"

BJ said, "We talked on the phone. Ms. Hassan here is defending Ibrahim El-Amin. You told me he was here the night of the boy's murder, right?"

The imam bowed, his head covered by a red skullcap. Then he said, "Yes, that is true. As you know, the mosque also serves as a community center, and Mr. El-Amin came here often for social purposes. I knew him, not well, but I saw him several times." His black face shone in the sun.

Zehra asked, "You definitely remember that on March nineteenth—a Thursday—he was with you?" She smelled the fragrance of flowers on the breeze.

The imam looked at her with his soft eyes for a long time. He said, "Yes. He arrived shortly after sunset, and we had tea in the community room. We talked of many things until late into the evening."

"You understand the murder occurred just around the corner from here?" BJ said.

"Unfortunately, yes. But Mr. El-Amin was here."

"He never left until the early morning?" Zehra asked while she thought of the DNA proof. "Because other evidence in the case points to him as the murderer."

"He never left," he said in a gentle voice.

They talked for ten minutes but the imam never wavered in his insistence of El-Amin's presence at the mosque. Later, he told them about the community he served. "We are poor, as you can see. Most are from Somalia and have suffered unbelievably. We offer religious training for everyone, especially the children, to keep them law abiding and faithful. We provide food, money, and homes for new immigrants. So many of the Somali people are misunderstood. The worst thing for us was the American movie, *Blackhawk Down*. It detailed the battle in Mogadishu between U.S. forces and a minority of crazy Somali fighters."

He raised his arm and swept it over the street before them. "Look at these people. They only want to live peacefully. They love America and everything it offers them. Although we miss our homeland, this is our new homeland." He smiled at each of them.

BACK AT HIS CAR, BJ SAID, "Seems believable to me. I watched his facial movements, and this guy seems like the real deal."

"I know. But what about the DNA? And the fact the murder was just a few blocks away. El-Amin could've slipped out for a minute."

"If he did, he'd have returned covered in blood. The killer hit both of the arteries in the boy's neck. Even if he jumped back at the right instant, there'd still be buckets of blood flying all over."

Zehra's training as a trial lawyer came forward. "Well, he'll make a great witness. Totally believable to a jury." She let BJ hold open the door of his Chevy Bronco for her.

BJ popped in his jazz group's new CD. "I got a friend hooked up with a company in Israel. They do testing on DNA results. Check them for accuracy. Maybe we should do our own, independent test."

"Why?" Zehra asked. "Our BCA is one of the best in the country."

"I know. But what would it hurt?" He turned to Zehra. "Can you get the money for a test?" He smiled that beautiful smile that always melted Zehra.

"Aw . . . Denzel, for you, baby, anything. How soon can your friend do it?"

"As soon as he gets a sample from the BCA—maybe a day. I'll tell him to rush."

"Get on it," Zehra said. She thought of Paul. "BJ, did you ever tell Paul Schmidt from the FBI about the alibi witness?"

"Huh? About Imam Moalim? No, why would I talk to them about anything?"

EIGHTEEN

Carolyn Bechter cruised the Seward neighborhood of Minneapolis in her Mercedes, feeling completely out of place.

Although the area showed many sign of revitalization, it wasn't rich by any means, and her car attracted way too much attention. She turned a corner, parked it and got out, careful to make sure it was locked.

A warm breeze blew up the street carrying the smells of spices and cooking meats. Dressed in a baseball cap, loose sweater, and running shoes, Carolyn wished she'd changed the tight jeans for something more modest. She put on a pair of sunglasses and started up the street.

She purposely came alone. If her instincts were right, this story was big enough to save her career, and she didn't want to share it with anyone else. Her editor thought she was at the Government Center, covering the court appearance of the guy charged with the murder, El-Amin. Carolyn knew she could get that information from any of the other media sources and feed it back to her editor. He'd never know. In the meantime, she could pursue this lead.

When she saw the Johnson Deli on the corner, it made her laugh. The Scandinavian name didn't fit, because now it served Somalis and other immigrants in the neighborhood. Probably owned by new people, too. Ben Mohammad worked part time there, and Carolyn meant to interview him.

She stood across the street for a long time, looking at the people in the street—a mixture of white and colored. The whites looked poor, and the colored looked Middle Eastern or African. Carolyn marveled at the difference in clothing. The whites dressed in faded blue jeans and gray or tan sweatshirts for the most part. The other people looked like walking rainbows. Every imaginable color of cloth covered them.

The women, especially, reveled in bright greens, yellow, blues, deep purple. Most wore the head covering but not the young girls.

Many of the men wore beards and small white skull caps.

Carolyn crossed the busy street and walked to the deli. She looked through the large plate-glass windows. A sign inside offered *halal* meat—whatever that was. She didn't like spicy food much, but the odors of the store drew her in the door.

Carolyn didn't understand any of the babbling people at the counter. The deli sold an interesting collection of American junk food, organic food, and foreign things she didn't recognize.

Several women stood at the counter arguing with one of the clerks. A few glanced over their shoulders at her. Some white women came in and ordered sliced beef from the second clerk.

Where was Ben Mohammad?

Carolyn waited until the American women left. She approached the clerk and removed her sunglasses. "Hi. I'm looking for Ben Mohammad. Is he here?"

The clerk frowned. "Ben . . . ? No one here named—"

"That's probably the name he uses at school."

"Oh, you mean Moses Mohammad. Yeah, he works at a school."

"Is he here?"

"He'll be back in a minute."

Twenty minutes later, Carolyn still waited. She looked at her watch. Put her shades back on and pulled the strap of her purse up on her shoulder.

Ben came through the front door.

She intended to cut him off before he had a chance to get to the back and avoid her. Carolyn stepped in front of him. His head jerked up when he saw her. "Hi, Ben. I'd like to talk with you some more." She spread her legs the width of her shoulders and stared at him. That usually worked with most people. Surprise was a good weapon also.

"Uh . . . what do you want?" he stammered.

"Just to talk with you. The people I met at the school speak highly of you."

He didn't seem to understand what she said. "I don't have anything . . ."

"This won't take long. If you talk to me now, I'll go away."

"What do you want?" He had a puffy black face that looked soft, unlike his eyes that were hard, like black marble.

Carolyn heard a shuffling behind her. "I want to know what you do with the young Somali boys at the school. What's your job there?"

His eyes darted back and forth like they had when she'd met him at the school. "I'm an outreach worker to the Somali community."

"But you take these young boys on trips, don't you?" Suddenly, she noticed the store had gone quiet. She sensed more movement behind her. Saw the reaction in Ben's face. Then the clerk was at her back, shoving her toward the door.

"You're not welcome in our store," he shouted.

Carolyn jerked back. No one treated her like this. "You don't know who I am, do you? I'm from Channel Six TV, and I could have twenty cameras and reporters down here in ten seconds to investigate your shitty little dump," she shouted.

"You will leave now." A second clerk moved beside the first one. Two of the African women crowded her on the left.

Carolyn realized the odds were bad. She wasn't scared and knew she wouldn't get any more information now. She sniffed at them and turned to leave.

She took her time walking back to the Benz, laughing by the time she clicked the locks open. That little scene proved that her instincts were right. There was something going on with Ben and the school. Otherwise, why would he and his pals react the way they did? She tingled with excitement.

What next?

She thought of texting her contact at the Department of Motor Vehicles to check on the driver's license for Moses Mohammad but decided he was probably illegal and didn't have a legit ID, anyway.

Instead, she'd follow him. Just like when she was a new reporter on a beat. Her cell rang. Carolyn looked at the caller ID, saw it was her producer, and answered.

"Reggie, how wonderful to hear from you," she said with faked enthusiasm.

"Bullshit. If you never heard from me again, you'd be happier than a whore at the end of the night. Where the fuck are you?"

"Covering the murder case."

"You're lying."

"To you . . . ? Never."

"What've you got?"

"I'm not sure yet, but it'll be good. Trust me."

Carolyn saw Ben hurry out of the store and run to an older car. "Hey, Reggie, gotta run, sweetheart. Keep it in your pants." She clicked off.

Ben pulled away from the curb and drove north. Carolyn threw the phone on the seat beside her and swerved away from the curb to follow him.

He meandered through the neighborhood until he came to the Riverside Avenue bridge over I-94. He crossed it and followed Riverside west. Near Augsburg College, he turned onto Cushing Street and parked near the end.

Carolyn slowed at the opposite end of the block so he wouldn't become suspicious. She watched him get out and hurry into a small, frame house with an open porch.

She felt uneasy but not from fear. What did she know about this street? Had she ever been here before? Carolyn tried to remember. After Ben went into the house, she pulled up beside his car and read the number of the house—657.

Carolyn backed up, parked, and waited. An hour later, and Ben still had not come back out. Even with the car windows open, the sun baked her. Sweat threatened to smear her make-up. Then, it struck her.

Six-fifty-seven Cushing Street was the same address where the murderer Ibrahim El-Amin was living when he was arrested.

Suddenly, the clues came together and made sense to her. Mohammed worked with young Somali men, young men disappeared, the FBI thought they left to fight in Somalia, and one came back to be killed by a guy named El-Amin who lived with Mohammed.

Another thought caused her stomach to tighten. Paul Schmidt.

Several years ago, they'd had a wild, short affair when she covered one of his cases. He'd dumped her hard. A cold, introverted pig, Carolyn remembered. Now, he was working on the case of the disappearing Somali boys. If she could break this story, maybe she could embarrass the hell out of him. He deserved it.

NINETEEN

Nervous about her meeting with Michael, Zehra treated herself to a latté. Normally, the calorie count deterred her, but tonight, Friday, Zehra waited at the Caribou Coffee shop in Northeast Minneapolis for him. She had to admit he'd impressed her at the party, but she was still cautious.

But the caution came from the left side of her brain, calculated from past experience. The right side, instead, longed for a relationship. For someone to have fun with, talk about her work, hold her, and ease the loneliness.

Northeast, one of the earliest areas to be settled in the city, rose up from the banks of the Mississippi River. At the highest point above the river stood the old church of Our Lady of Lourdes, topped by a steeple visible from the entire neighborhood. Jackie attended mass there. She said the church still had a hint of its old French heritage, which reminded her of services in Vietnam.

Zehra glanced at her watch. She thought of the mountains of work waiting for her. They had less than two weeks to pull together the defense. If this new guy, the Egyptian dude, didn't show in five minutes, she'd bail.

She took a deep, calming breath. At least, she had a small table outside on the sidewalk. To Zehra's left, stretched a garden of peonies, red, yellow, almost purple, and shades of colors she couldn't even name. And hanging beside her, almost touching her hair was a pot of begonias, one of her favorite plants because they were easy to grow and produced big flowers of such lush intensity.

When she looked back, he walked up to the door of the shop.

Zehra remembered dark skin, the tall, thin, athletic body that moved with an unusual grace compared to most Americans. He looked European. She noticed the long nose, like hers, that moved back and forth as he searched the shop for her. Zehra ran both hands through her hair to make it bigger, then stood and waved.

He smiled immediately and came over.

She shook his outstretched hand. It felt strong and warm.

"Zehra." He started to sit.

"Michael? Nice to see you again." Dark, quick eyes were framed with the longest, most beautiful eyelashes she'd seen. Zehra felt jealous.

"Call me Mustafa. Your father always tells me how attractive you are—he's right."

Phony obviously, but it still sounded nice to hear. "Thanks. You work directly with him?"

"No. I'm in genetic engineering." He wore a black cotton t-shirt made with expensive material. When he twisted to see the counter, she noticed the muscles in his chest. "I'll be right back. Want anything?"

After he left, Zehra thought of her "checklist" for these dates her mother set up. *Let's see . . . no bad breath, good looking, not grossly overweight, not too short, seems intelligent . . . so far, so good.*

He returned in five minutes. "Busy tonight. Guess it's the nice weather." He leaned back. "It smells good." His head turned toward her and looked into her face. "You said you're a lawyer. Tell me more about your work."

"I'm a pubic defender. I used to work as a prosecutor but switched sides a few years ago."

"What do you like about it?"

"Uh well, I like the courtroom. I don't have to sit at a desk all day and read boring contracts. I work on real-life problems that affect people, like their freedom. It's meaningful, and I feel like I can do some good." She caught herself and stopped. Why was she blabbering like this?

"I don't know much about those things. Do you have any interesting cases?" He sipped his tea.

"Right now, I'm working on the murder case I told you about. The Somali boy who had his throat cut open." Zehra purposely emphasized the details because people seemed most interested in that part. "Maybe you saw it on the news? I'm defending the man accused of the murder. Trial starts in less than two weeks. The FBI is also involved." She looked to either side and said, "I'm trying to pump them for anything they know about the murder but won't reveal."

Mustafa frowned. "Yes. My Somali friends talk about the case. It sounds like hard work. How can you do it?"

Her cheeks bulged, and Zehra blew out a puff of air. "It's really tough."

"I'm curious, you said you think you can do some good, but how can you do that for a murderer?"

"Good question. Sometimes, the only thing I can do is make sure the people I represent get a fair trial and vigorous defense."

"I've done some work with the Somalis in the mosques. They're so poor. I try to help them."

"You have? I wouldn't think they'd accept you . . . I mean, educated and Egyptian."

He smiled. "I know. It took a long time to gain their trust. But I feel sorry for many of them and try to help when I can. I know some of the leaders in various communities. And it helps that I raise money for them."

"I'll keep that in mind," Zehra said. She stopped again. Unlike any of the other men she'd met, this one sounded genuinely interested in something other than himself. "But, let's talk about your work."

"Not much to talk about in comparison to yours. I work in genetic engineering research. For you, it would be boring by comparison."

"What's that mean?"

"Oh, we're working with viruses now. Trying to see if we can find a cure for the common cold." He laughed a little and showed pretty teeth. "It is, how do you say, 'a long shot,' but can you imagine the profits if we could actually figure it out? We try a variety of things like, manipulating the genes, enhancing them. Then, we expose them to various antibiotics to 'heat them up,' to see how they react." He paused. "That is what I'm trying to do for the good of the world." He pronounced "s" like "sh." It sounded lush to Zehra.

She shook her head. "Wow."

"I travel a lot . . . too much. It seems I'm always gone."

Zehra stole a glance at him sideways as he leaned back. He curved into the metal chair and, although relaxed, she could sense coiled energy resting in his body. She shook out her hair again. This "date" wasn't going as planned. She looked down at her watch and knew she should get back to the office. But she couldn't move.

Mustafa turned back to face her. "May I ask you a personal question?"

"Yeah, I guess."

"Do you find it hard to maintain your faith here in the U.S?"

"Well, I was born here, so I'm an American who happens to be a Muslim. I assume you weren't?"

"Egypt. My parents came to Dearborn, Michigan, At first, it was hard. Now, unfortunately, they're fully assimilated. They've lost much of their Muslim faith."

"Sometimes it's tough being Muslim in a Christian society, isn't it?"

"Yes. It is more than religion for me—it is the culture. The constant striving for money and luxuries here bothers me."

"Oh, I agree. For me, it's probably the feeling of separateness I have at times. Sometimes, I really feel lonely. I date Christians, but when it comes to long-range things, it's hard to fit together. I'm trying to be a good American and, at the same time, a good Muslim."

"You are faithful?"

"Kind of. I mean, I don't always pray five times a day. And during Ramadan, I'm so busy that I start to feel dizzy if I don't eat a snack during the day. I try to read the Qur'an, but I find I get more comfort from the old poets, like Rumi."

Mustafa's face brightened. "Ah . . . you like Rumi?" When Zehra nodded, he said,

> "You rave about the holy place
> and say you've visited God's garden
> but where is your bunch of flowers?
> . . . There is some merit
> in the suffering you have endured
> but what a pity you have not discovered
> the Mecca that's inside."

She tried to stop it, but her breath caught in the back of her mouth. She couldn't believe this guy. Was he for real? She said to him, "I love that verse. He combines gardens with God and Mecca and how they can all be inside of us . . . even here in Minnesota in the winter!" They both laughed.

"Are you glad you are Muslim?" he asked.

"I am and I'm proud. People don't realize that Muhammad was one of the first great religious leaders to give women significant rights and freedoms."

His face clouded. "Yes . . . I see what you mean."

"Don't you agree?"

"Yes, absolutely," he added quickly.

"Thirteen hundred years ago, he gave women the right to inherit money and keep it. As their own. As a lawyer, I know how important that kind of a right is for anyone. Because the ability to own property and money gives that person power."

"Uh, of course."

"The fanatics in Islam do so much damage to the progressive Muslims like us in America. People here assume we're all alike and we all agree that there should be a jihad against the U.S. or something crazy like that. It makes me furious. I guess that's one of the reasons I went to law school. To be able to help empower Muslim women and Muslims in general." A damp breeze blew up from the river a few blocks below them carrying the cooking smells from the restaurants along the river.

Mustafa remained silent for a while. Then, he asked her, "Have you been on your hajj?"

"Not yet. When work slows down, if ever, I'd love to go. But, I'd also like to go with someone who's important to me. A husband, for instance."

"Ah, yes. I have been twice and it is a meaningful, moving experience. By all means, participate with someone you love."

She sipped the last of her latté. "What do you do for fun, Mustafa?"

"Not enough. I work hard, travel too much, and am very disciplined. But I love to bike. How about you?"

"Biking's great. I'm a gardener. That's why the Rumi verse means so much to me. He wrote often of gardens. My garden's my sanctuary, my refuge. I live to watch the plants come up in the spring. After a Minnesota winter, that renews my hope."

"Then, I should buy you a gift."

"Huh?"

"Around the corner, there is a garden store. You know of it?"

"Never noticed it before."

"Come on, I will buy you something."

They stood. As she passed in front of him, he rested his hand on the bare skin of her forearm. She couldn't miss it. On the sidewalk, they turned left and walked a little too closely side by side around the corner.

Nestled into a restored brick building stood a narrow garden store. The front door was propped open with a copper watering can. The scent of new flowers and damp earth drew them inside. Zehra loved the cute tools and unusual collection of plants they offered. All of it very expensive.

"Do you like orchids?" Mustafa asked her.

"Sure. I've even wintered over a few at home."

"Come here." He moved her as if he'd been in the store before.

Near the back of the shop was a partially enclosed area devoted entirely to orchids. When they stepped into the cramped area, Zehra felt moist warmth. A mister wheezed clouds in the corner, behind the various pots. Other than that noise, it was quiet.

They stood before a display of the most unique orchids she'd ever seen. But then, there were probably hundreds she'd never seen. For a long time, they studied each plant, looked at it from different angles, and leaned back to get perspective. Finally, Mustafa pointed. "This one. I want you to have this one."

Zehra moved closer to study it better. She gasped.

From a clay pot, a long narrow green stalk rose as if it were a cobra swaying to the piping rhythm of a trainer. At the top, it tipped over to explode into several leaves, open and vulnerable. The outer leaves, dull yellow and striped in purple, bent back to reveal a second set of tiny, perfectly formed openings like little mouths. On the bottom, hung little blood-red "slippers." She could almost imagine the plant breathing.

Zehra loved orchids but, at the same time, they were so creepy. She didn't even know this man and already he offered her a beautiful flower. Zehra felt dizzy, and the longer she stared at the plant, the more it seemed to sway to the sound of silent piping.

She pushed out of the room. Took a deep breath of cool air in the shop. Smelled the familiar roses next to the check-out counter.

Mustafa followed behind her. "I noticed you seemed to favor this one." He set it on the counter and paid quickly.

Zehra mumbled thanks and carried the thing outside. She didn't know what to think. It was weird, for sure. But other than a few $3.99 clumps of dandelions from Costco that other men had given her as an afterthought, this was the most exquisite plant anyone ever gave her. After all, there were roses and then there were orchids—a whole different level, if you knew anything about flowers.

She decided to accept it.

"I would like to see your garden some time," he said.

"Sure . . . sure." This was moving way out of control, too fast. Her cell phone buzzed. She answered it. BJ. The other world jarred her awake.

"Zehra, I've been trying to call you for an hour!"

"Huh? I . . . I've been busy. What's up, Denzel?"

"My friend, the scientist with the testing company. He just called me and said the DNA tests run by the BCA are faked."

"What?" She clung to the orchid for fear she'd drop it.

"Yeah. Someone doctored the sample, so the BCA got a false reading."

"What the hell does that mean?"

"El-Amin, they got the wrong guy."

TWENTY

T he Yemeni left Turkmenbashi with the briefcase, by ship. It didn't rain, but heavy winds heaved the ship up and down as it plowed westward into the storm. He hated traveling by ship, but in this case, the route across the Caspian Sea was the quickest. He'd secured the case under a bunk below deck. Whenever he moved, it came with him.

All he had to do now, was get to Cairo. He'd get his money when he handed over the package. He grinned when he thought of how he'd squeeze for a little more.

He thought briefly of the stupid Russian. All these Christian kafirs were so willing to endanger their people for the gain of a little money. He thought of them as being lower than dogs.

Once on the western shore of the Caspian Sea, the Yemeni would transfer to a train and continue his journey. The train system, some if left from the European construction in the late nineteenth century, was patchwork and worn out. Riding it required patience for the constant break downs and transfers. Flying would be easier of course, but the security on the train system was lax, and he could move without many questions. By early morning, they approached the rich city of Baku on the western shore.

Before the American crusaders invaded Iraq, the Yemeni would have turned south, in his journey, to Tehran, then crossed into Baghdad for the final leg to Cairo. Now, he had to take the northern, longer route through Baku and across Syria.

He'd travel in Muslim countries to make it easier.

The sun rose behind the Yemeni while he stood on deck and watched the city come closer. Before World War II, the Baku oilfield had been one of the largest in the world. The city boasted many rich, cultural adornments. He could see the minarets of mosques built in the old Walled City by the harbor. The dawning sun lit them up in coral and orange.

He felt the hot wind off the shore.

The ship passed next to the yacht club, then turned to the north for its own berth. Baku huddled under the southern side of a peninsula that jutted into the sea.

He was off the ship quickly and walked down the pier to a clump of palm trees. Several taxis waited in the shade under them. He called for one, and when the driver offered to put the briefcase in the trunk, the Yemeni refused. He set it on the back seat. When he climbed in, he clutched it next to himself. They left for the train station.

The journey to Cairo exhausted him.

Though a young man, the Yemeni struggled through endless waiting, transfers, currency exchanges, different languages, and old train cars that stopped often, but he finally arrived in Cairo. He'd been in such a hurry that he forgot to bring food with him. Luckily, in Damascus, there'd been a long delay, so he was able to get off, find a market, and buy food and water before continuing on his journey.

Before eating, he boarded the train and washed thoroughly. Along with dozens of other passengers, he knelt on the floor as the train rocked along on its way out of Damascus. He prayed, facing south, toward Mecca. After his prayers were finished, he ate slowly and read sections of the Qur'an. The lovely words of the Prophet strengthened him, reminded him of why he made this arduous effort for the greater glory of Allah.

From Damascus, he was forced to turn west again toward the sea. The direct route would go south through Israel, but security in that country was the toughest in the region. The Yemeni would have to travel through Lebanon and, once again, board a ship for Alexandria, Egypt.

From there, he'd make his way to Cairo, to meet the agent planted in America who would take the transfer from him. They had scheduled a time and safe place for the meeting. The Yemeni wasn't sure of all the details of the plan and really didn't care, so long as he was paid and the work was for Allah.

And he'd be happy to get rid of the briefcase, turning it over to the other man's care. It made him uneasy to handle it. They'd emphasized again and again, to carry it carefully, not to drop it or let it be slammed around. And he was never, never to open it. He didn't know what the contents were but had been assured it wouldn't blow-up or anything like that if it remained sealed.

It didn't weigh much, and many times his curiosity almost overwhelmed him. Two locks, with two different keys he'd been told, prevented access. What was in it? He longed to find out, as a child wanted to open a secret gift. But the fear of what would happen should he open the case stopped him. It was obviously valuable. He wondered it he could squeeze the rich American for a little more money

He reached Cairo in the evening, feeling tired and dirty. Long before they stopped at the station, the train trundled through the outskirts of the city, miles of small, drab huts and houses. For as far as the Yemeni could see in the dusky light, the city stretched in all directions. Even inside the train, he could feel the pulsing lives of millions of people around him.

He heard the chanting call to prayer from loud speakers in the mosques, the bawl of donkeys, and horns of hundreds of cars. He smelled the dust and heat. He saw groups of well-dressed school children walking together, going home probably. Women grilled fish for dinner in the narrow alleys. Bearded men huddled in small groups, talking and gesturing wildly. Some were playing chess.

The eruption of life around him made the Yemeni proud. *Let the imperialists in Europe and America have their luxuries. We have people and life and energy in our Islamic countries*, he thought. And considering his role as a warrior for Allah, he felt even more proud.

TWENTY-ONE

The next morning, Zehra and BJ waited for his friend, Dr. Malcolm Stein at the doctor's office.

Last night, after the call from BJ, she'd explained to Michael what happened. They had hurried to her car. After putting the orchid on the floor of the backseat to make sure it couldn't fall over, she turned to him to say good-bye.

"Thanks so much for a great time," Zehra said. She could feel herself blushing. "And thanks for the beautiful plant. No one has ever . . ."

"Dont worry. I enjoy you, and the orchid is a gift in appreciation of that pleasure I've had with you. Would you call me by my real name, Mustafa?"

"Of course, if you'd like."

He smiled. "May I see you again?"

Every nerve in her brain told her to be careful. This was just too good to be true. She hardly knew him. She'd tried to discourage him. Slow down. As the thoughts ran through her mind, her mouth opened and words came from somewhere inside her, "Sure. I'm gonna be swamped with the trial, especially now, but let's try to fit some time in." She smiled into his face. His skin looked flawless.

"Well . . . thank you again." He twisted from left to right. "You better get to work on the trial." He leaned forward and kissed her quickly on the cheek.

She could feel the warmth of his skin, and she felt herself blush like a teenaged girl.

"Yo, Z . . . you still here?" BJ's voice boomed around the conference room of Dr. Stein's office. His big hand rested on her shoulder and calmed her.

"Yeah . . ."

"Dr. Stein usually works on Saturday mornings, so he agreed to meet us. I want you to hear this directly from him."

In ten minutes, a large man with a moustache and a halo of curly gray hair came into the conference room where they sat. He wore a pink golf shirt and khaki pants. "Hey, BJ," he called. "What's shakin'?"

BJ introduced Zehra to Dr. Stein

"This dude can't be all bad, 'cause he's a fan of jazz."

"Even more, a fan of yours," Stein grinned.

"Can you tell us what you found?" she said.

"Sure. You guys want water? Coffee?" He sat awkwardly at the head of the table. A huge gold watch dangled from his wrist and tapped on the table when he gestured with his hand. "My brother in Tel Aviv has a company that developed a test that can distinguish real DNA samples from the fake ones. I've started the U.S. outpost of his company. We hope to sell the test to labs all over the country." He leaned back.

"Is it complicated?" Zehra asked.

"You have to know the techniques of DNA sampling and how to run the tests. Once trained, anyone could do this, I suppose. Probably, the average criminal doesn't have the brains or training, but an undergrad biology major might be able to pull it off."

"So, the DNA sample tested by the BCA for the El-Amin murder case is fake? What does that mean?" she said.

"It means someone planted false evidence at the crime scene. It's really easier than planting false fingerprints. When the BCA took their samples of saliva from the face mask, they did all the correct tests and determined the donor was Ibrahim El-Amin, but we discovered it's all faked. The sample doesn't ID him."

"Who does it identify?"

"Can't say unless we had a sample from the true donor on file. All I can tell you is that El-Amin is not the true donor."

"How does your test work?" BJ said. He leaned forward and rested his big arms on the table.

"You need a real DNA sample from the suspect. It could be a strand of hair or saliva off a drinking cup. It doesn't need to be large. Then, you amplify the sample into a large quantity of DNA, using a standard technique called whole genome amplification. Of course, you could use a strand of hair, but blood or saliva left at a crime scene is more convincing—which is what they did here."

"Anything else needed to fake it?"

"You could also take a small blood sample from anyone and centrifuge it to remove the white cells, which contain DNA. Then, we'd take those remaining red cells and add DNA that's been amplified from the person you want to frame. Since red cells don't contain DNA, all the genetic material in the 'new' blood sample would be from the other person."

"And the real person's white cells, with the DNA, are thrown out?"

"Sure." Dr. Stein lifted off his glasses and wiped the lenses with his shirt.

"They used saliva and a little blood in the face mask, here?" Zehra said.

"Right. The BCA did nothing wrong. In fact, they're one of the best labs in the country. But if you give them a phony sample, they're going to come up with phony results."

"And you can prove this?" Zehra looked at Dr. Stein.

"Simple. Our test is accepted by many scientists."

"Why doesn't the BCA do the same test?"

"They don't have the test. Why should they? Ninety-nine-point-nine percent of their samples are legit. We're working with a pretty sophisticated group of criminals in this case. Highly unusual."

Zehra sat back and looked up at the ceiling. Now what? She looked back at Dr. Stein. "I thought DNA was so reliable?"

He smiled through gray teeth. "Oh, it is. But what's happened is that, it's so good, everyone depends entirely on DNA testing. We're creating a criminal justice system that increasingly relies on this technology. It was only a matter of time before smart criminals figured out a way to beat it."

BJ drummed his fingers onto the table in a syncopated rhythm. "You gotta keep one step ahead of 'em all the time."

Dr. Stein looked at his big watch. "Have to run, guys. Anything else I can help you with? I'm available to testify at trial. I charge mileage and courtroom time from the minute I walk into the building. That okay?"

"Sure," said Zehra. She rose with BJ. They both shook the doctor's hand. After they left, riding in the car, she sighed and slumped into the seat.

"Wha's up? We caught a home run, girl."

She looked out the window as BJ drove out of the parking lot. Without turning around, she said, "Now what?"

"Well . . . we tell Harmon. He should dismiss."

"Doubt it. Not with a case this big. They'll fight it all the way, including Dr. Stein's test."

"But you heard him tell us the test's accepted."

"Hey, Denzel. Too much publicity. They're not going to dump it. They'll give it to a jury, so if El-Amin's acquitted, the prosecutor can blame it on the jury."

"Yeah . . . you're right."

After a long moment of quiet, Zehra said, "So, if it's not El-Amin, who killed the Ahmed boy? And can we find him in time before the trial starts?"

BJ drove slowly toward her condo. Twenty minutes later, they arrived.

"Want a cup of coffee?" she offered.

"Sure. You still got that stuff from Costa Rica?"

In her third-floor unit, she pushed her bike out of the way and told BJ to relax. She started the coffee. He walked in and seemed to fill the place entirely. He stepped out onto her deck, hanging from the sliding door in the living room, and took a deep breath. "The Garden of Eden," he kidded her.

"You like it?" she called from the kitchen.

"Love it. Put on some music, would you. We need music with this beauty."

Zehra put a copy of BJ's CD he'd given her, into the player. She heard two horns start up. "I like it," she told him.

"One of our guys wrote it. He calls it 'Ben's Trumpet.'" When his cell buzzed, he took the call. In ten minutes, he came back inside. His face drooped.

"What? What's the matter?" she asked.

BJ sighed. "My momma. She's on dialysis twice a week. She's having trouble. I may have to go to Chicago. I'm the only family she's got this close."

"Hey, anytime. Don't worry about this. Go anytime."

He nodded and wandered back outside. "Hey, what's this, Z?" BJ's voice carried into the kitchen.

Zehra came out with two steaming mugs. Handed one to him. "Careful," she said. "What're you talking about?"

"Uh . . . this thing." BJ pointed to the new orchid.

"Don't you even know what an orchid is? A friend gave it to me. Michael's his name."

BJ bent over and peered at it. He stood and laughed. "I know what he's got on his mind." His eyes darted up to hers. "You tight with this dude?"

"None of your snoopy business. But, the answer is, no. Just a friend."

"I could always check him out."

"Butt out, BJ." She wagged her finger in his face. "Let's talk about something important. What're we gonna do?"

BJ sipped and nodded. "The mask . . . remember Dr. McWhorter said the mask was commonly used in hospitals? It's an unusual one. A perfect disguise to hide the real killer's face. Maybe he works in a hospital."

"Yeah, and no one could get access to this kid without arousing suspicions unless the killer were Somali, or at least Middle Eastern. There can't be too many Somalis working in hospitals, are there?" She looked out from the deck and could see the corner of the new bridge crossing the river, replacement of the one that had collapsed two summers ago.

BJ sighed. "Don't know. And we don't have a lot of time to run this all down."

"Wait a minute! I've got my friend Paul Schmidt with the FBI. They've got the resources. I'll check with him. See if I can get any info, or if he's willing to look into it. You'd think they'd want to find the real killer as much as we do."

She stopped talking. Remembered the odd fact that Paul knew about the alibi witness before anyone else. Maybe she shouldn't trust him.

BJ left.

Jackie called ten minutes later. She sounded out of breath. "Hey, Z. I think I got something."

"What's up?"

"I was going over the autopsy line by line." She paused. "Gruesome stuff. And the photos . . . anyway, there's a note from Chopsticks in the report about something odd she found."

"What?"

"The victim had these red-like things on his hands and feet."

"Did Chopsticks say what they were?"

"Nope. But it was unusual enough that she noted it and photographed them."

Zehra thought for a moment. "We could get second opinion. Go to the Ramsey County ME. I'll get on it. We'll have to email all the reports and photos to him right away."

TWENTY-TWO

The next morning, knowing she had a more than full day, Zehra left the condo early. She dropped down the elevator to the underground parking lot. From inside the complex, she had access. Otherwise, the lot was secured.

She found her old heap of a car in the corner where she'd left it. Long ago, the remote lock had broken so Zehra started to reach for the key. She stopped.

She found the back window cracked open an inch. She never left her windows open. Panicked, she pulled on the door handle. It popped open, unlocked. After working with criminals, she never left her doors unlocked. Could she have forgotten last night, with all the stress on her?

She bent down slowly to look inside the car. Every part of it had been trashed.

Seats pulled up, glove compartment opened, contents scattered across the floor like a bomb had exploded. Files she had left in the back seat were gone.

Zehra backed away and started to shake. Her mind tried to assert that it was only vandals who'd trashed the car. A random act so common in urban areas. No. She knew that wasn't true.

Paul's warning clanged through her mind. Zehra stood still and looked around the deserted lot. Were they still here? Were they watching her right now? She fought to keep breathing, to suppress the panic that threatened to overtake her. Fumbling in her purse, she clutched her cell phone. Her fingers stumbled to dial 911.

Two hours later in her office, Zehra had calmed down. Of course, it had taken the police over an hour to arrive. She was scared but knew that a vandalized car was low on the list of emergencies for them. They promised to look into things, warned her to lock the car, and to be careful. Blah, blah, blah.

A cup of tea helped her to focus on what she had to do.

She called the prosecutor, Steve Harmon. She'd tell him about Dr. Stein's test and ask to have the case dismissed against her client. With all the weird, scary things going on, Zehra wanted out badly.

When he answered, Harmon panted, out of breath. "I started walking up the last ten flights of stairs to the office." He paused. "Trying to stay in better shape. I spend so much time chained to this damn desk."

"Steve, are you familiar with a test done to determine if DNA testing is accurate?"

"Never heard of it."

Zehra explained what she knew and how Dr. Stein had tested the DNA sample, supposedly from Ibrahim El-Amin. "He said it's not that hard to plant phony DNA evidence at a crime scene."

"I know this is part of your job, but I can't throw it out. Reason one is I think your guy is guilty as hell. Reason two is my boss, the elected county attorney. How do you think he'd look going in front of the cameras to dump the murder charges—the only break we've had in all these disappearing Somali cases. And reason three is, I ain't gonna lose this one."

"I know and it's not because I feel sorry for my client, believe me. I can't stand the guy, but think about this: what if you've got the wrong guy? This new testing procedure looks pretty impressive. And you combine that with the alibi witness we've found . . . don't you see, Steve? You've got the wrong guy. You have a duty to let him go." Zehra's voice rose.

"If you were any one of a dozen other defense lawyers, I'd hang up now. But, here's what I can do. Let me see the test results you've got, and I'll check it out. If the test is legit, we can look at the DNA samples that match your guy. I still know it's gonna be damn tough to get my boss to back-off on this case."

"I can understand but think about justice. You can't prosecute the wrong guy just because it's politically easier." She started to shout at him. "You just—can't."

Harmon didn't respond for a few minutes. "Look, Zehra, don't give me that crap," he said. "I've also got the FBI and some federal agencies breathing down my neck, too. Everyone's looking to wrap this whole mess up with a conviction. You've worked here. You know what it's like." Harmon paused and spoke again in a softer voice. "If the DNA was faked, we'll deal with that. But for now, I say he's guilty."

She sputtered some more, then gave up. "Okay, okay. I'll get the info on the test to you right away and contacts for the doctor." After she hung up, Zehra looked out her window. It wasn't like her to blow up, but the pressure, the threat, all of it had just exploded out of control. It scared her.

Zehra's next step would be harder. She'd have to tell her client.

Before she could go to the jail, Zehra had to appear at ten o'clock in court for the sentencing of another client. She planned to go from that hearing to the jail. If she were lucky, she could meet El-Amin before lunch, when the entire jail was shut-down for two hours.

Zehra left her office, carrying her briefcase and purse. The air felt thick and humid. She looked up to the heavy, dark clouds moving overhead, followed by low rumbles from the west. She smelled an electric freshness that confirmed coming rain.

Good—her oasis on the balcony needed rain badly. With her busier-than-usual work schedule, she hadn't been able to water as much as they required.

She thought of El-Amin. Would she be able to convince Harmon before the trial started? She had about a week. Maybe, considering the new evidence of the phony DNA, the judge would give her a continuance. Of course, El-Amin would have to agree to that.

Zehra shook out her hair, trying to shake out all the conflicting ideas. Just another day in the life of a public defender, trying to juggle a dozen balls in the air at one time.

When she thought of Mustafa, Zehra felt a little lighter on her feet. Of course, it was too early to say, but compared to all the other guys she'd met lately, he shone like a prize. He was a bright spot among all the heavy problems that pressed in and her loneliness lifted a little.

AT HIAWATHA HIGH SCHOOL, Dr. Michael Ammar met with the principal, Robert Sandford, who was squeezing hand springs for exercise. His feet rested on the desk before him. "The left hand's the most important, because you grab the shaft of the golf club with that one. The left's gotta be the strongest."

Michael nodded, bored and anxious to see the students. With the launch coming up in a few days, he didn't have time for this waste. He felt a dribble of sweat work its way down the side of his chest. There were so many things left to be done. In spite of all his meticulous planning, certain events threatened the entire launch. He'd had to protect the network. Take care of loose ends. Make sure people didn't talk. And, of course, there was the room in the school he had to prepare immediately. That's where the glorious jihad would begin.

"Thanks so much for your help with the projects for the science fair. As you know, we've had a longstanding agreement with Health Tech to send their scientists here. It's worked out great. We really appreciate it."

"I enjoy it, and I want to help these young people understand the importance and excitement of science." He glanced at his watch. "I should get into the lab now."

"Yeah, of course. Well, thanks again, Doc."

Michael left and hurried across the high school complex to the lab room on the far west end. Jim Miller, the head engineer who ran the physical plant, almost collided with Michael as they both rounded a corner.

"Hey, Doc, what's the rush?"

"I'm late for the class."

"I s'pose with the fair coming up, you're all working overtime."

"Right. Well, I have to run." They liked him and appreciated his work, but he didn't want to get too friendly with any of them. Besides, he had lots of work to get done before he left tonight—for the science fair and the other, final preparations.

When he reached the lab, the usual teacher, Ms. Hall, was wrapping up her class. She brightened when Michael entered the back of the room. Hall stopped talking. "Here he is now."

All twenty-two students turned and applauded for Michael. He half raised his hand and felt slightly embarrassed.

Ms. Hall said, "So, I want the last four chapters finished by next Monday. I'll give you extra time because I know so many of you are presenting for the fair. Dr. Ammar," she looked up at him, "are you ready to handle this crew?" She laughed.

"I'll take them all on," Michael said.

After she left, he assigned each student who was participating in the fair to show him their progress. The students scraped out of their desks, pushed and shoved each other in fun, and went to the lockers on the side of the room. They started to remove their projects.

One of the most intense kids, Sergio, came up to Michael. "Do you want to see the heart sections I've displayed?"

"Sure. Where is it?"

Sergio pulled him to a table in the far corner. Lifting a box off the floor, Sergio removed a remarkably life-like model of the human heart. "It's plastic material I can mold by hand. When it sets, it looks pretty real, doesn't it?"

Michael marveled at the model. All the chambers, muscled walls, and arteries looked accurate.

"See," Sergio explained, "this first model shows the heart with the arteries blocked." He pointed to an area in the upper chamber. Turning around, Sergio lifted another model out of the box. "This one here's been surgically repaired. And in between each model, I'm gonna put up the videos I got off the web that show the actual surgery. Lots of blood and guts," he laughed.

"That should cause people to stop smoking," Michael said. He pulled back his cuff to see the time. There was so much work to do down stairs, he couldn't spend a lot of time with the students today.

One by one, Michael hurried around the room to check each project. He offered advice to many, congratulated others, and pointed out problems in projects that didn't look complete.

He had come to like the young people to a degree, but they all had been corrupted by the materialistic culture around them. None of them understood how privileged they were. Although he suspected they professed a number of different religions, none of them took any of that seriously. They were spoiled and selfish.

"I have something to do myself," he announced. "I'll be back in a while. In the meantime, continue working or cleaning up if you're done." He left them in the room while he hurried down the hall, found the door to the basement, and stepped down into the dark stairway.

TWENTY-THREE

P aul Schmidt punched the button on the elevator in the Government Center repeatedly, as if that would make it move faster. He'd just come from a meeting
with Steve Harmon, who told him of the testing Zehra Hassan had done on
the DNA sample.

Paul knew of the new test and thought it was reliable. That proved what he'd
told Conway, but it also scared him.

If El-Amin wasn't the killer, who was? It also proved the network was larger and
more sophisticated than he'd imagined. What were they planning? Questions and problems churned in his mind like the beginning of a tornado. Why'd they want El-Amin
to take the fall? Paul felt he'd been right all along.

At some point, he had to tell Conway but wasn't sure what reaction he'd get. Especially after the stormy meeting earlier this morning.

Conway called him into his office. He shut the door, something very unusual.

Before Paul could sit, Conway launched into him. "God damn it, Paul. I warned
you."

Paul remained quiet, waiting to see how much Conway actually knew.

"I told you to cease and desist." A red tinge came up from Conway's neck and spread
across his wrinkled face. "And what the hell do you do? You fuckin' disobey an order
from me. I'm mad as hell about this, boy. I stuck my neck out for you after your fuck-up
in Milwaukee and this is how you re-pay me?"

"But—"

"Shut up for now. You got nothing to say, as far as I can tell. I know what you're
doing behind my back and I am about one inch from firing your ass."

Paul knew him well enough to just let the storm pass.

"I told you in front of all the other agents, at the meeting, to stop your investigation.
Don't 'bogart' this thing by yourself. I got witnesses. If what you've done blows up in my
face, not only will I fire your ass, I'll get you charged criminally." His breath came in short
gasps. "You got the picture clear this time?"

"Yes, sir." He slinked out of the office.

He stepped into the open elevator at the Government Center. Before he told anything more to his boss, Paul had other actions to be taken. He'd have to make damn sure his information was tight before he risked a firing from Conway. And he didn't have much time left.

After riding the elevator to the second floor, he looked up. Outside, across the plaza, he could see the old, hulking pile of stones called City Hall. It reminded him of a castle topped with a bell tower. Rain splattered over the ornamental stones, giving the building a fuzzy edge.

Paul decided to take the underground tunnel through City Hall, to come out closer to his office. Down two floors, he hurried past the cafeteria and turned into the basement of City Hall, underneath the Minneapolis Police Department offices.

As he rounded the last corner, he bumped into Lieutenant Patrick O'Brien of the Minneapolis police.

"Hey, Father O'Brien," Paul said. He worked with O'Brien on the kidnapping cases and knew the old cop had a reputation for getting more confessions out of suspects than anyone else. The name fit.

"Schmitty. How're the feds treatin' ya?"

"Busy. The killer of the Ahmed boy goes on trial in a week."

"Hope they nail that son-of-a-bitch." O'Brien slouched against the wall. Unlike the younger cops, who all shaved their heads or had short hair, he wore his gray hair longer than usual.

"Ah . . ." Paul didn't know how much to reveal about the DNA sample.

"Only problem left is the jury. Worst damn thing we ever invented. They can take a perfectly good case and turn it into a failed wet-dream. I don't know how, but I've seen it enough."

"I know what you mean. I remember a case in federal court. We all knew the sucker was guilty as hell, even the judge knew it, but the jury found him not guilty. The judge was so pissed-off, he wouldn't even talk to them. Just left the courtroom in a huff." He peered at O'Brien. "But don't worry. We've got 'advanced techniques' of investigation we're going to use on this case."

O'Brien frowned and shifted his weight to the other leg. "Say, Schmitty, running into ya, makes me think of something I wanted to ask."

"What's that?"

"You know I was one of the first cops at the crime scene on the Ahmed case?"

"I remember."

"Now, I don't do the forensic investigation, but I gotta protect the scene, keep people outta there, and generally run the show." He looked to the side and back to Paul. "There was something strange. A guy was there."

"Who?"

"Damned if I know, for sure. He showed up soon after the Minneapolis coppers did. Older guy, dark-blue windbreaker that said USAMRD, or something like that, on the back in yellow letters. Might have been with some woman, too. Of course, I stopped him, asked for ID. He said you guys gave him the okay."

"What'd we give?"

"I mean, the FBI gave him the okay to be there. He even showed me some kinda ID, looks like yours but not the same. Some federal ID."

"Did you get the name? Or where he was from?"

"Naw. You know how crazy a crime scene is, especially that one with all the press and gawkers. I had my hands full just keeping the civilians out. You wouldn't believe some of 'em. You put the tape up, plain as day, and they fuckin' crawl under it! Right in fronta me."

"Who do you think this guy was?"

"Don't know. That's why I thought to ask you now. See if you knew something." He used a fingernail to pick something from between his teeth.

Paul shook his head. "What'd he do?"

"Well . . . let's see." O'Brien looked at the floor while he thought. "Walked around but didn't wander. Know what I mean? Like he knew what he was doing, was familiar with a crime scene. Didn't seem to disturb anything—that was my main worry."

"Anything else?"

"Yeah. Kinda weird. He did pick up something. Some gloves, I think. Off to the side, near the sidewalk away from the fence and the parking lot. Know where I mean?"

"Think so. To the south of where the body was found?"

"Right."

"That's the way the killer left, according to the witness on the porch."

O'Brien pursed his lips. "At the time, I didn't think much about it. There's lots of junk laying around that neighborhood anyway. Kinda trashy."

"How'd you let him get away with evidence like that?" Paul felt his face flush hot.

"Outside the tape. He picked 'em up outside the tape. I was plenty busy with trying to maintain the integrity of the scene *inside* the tape."

"Sure. Where'd he go?"

"Don't know. Until I saw you, I'd forgotten about it. Maybe it's nothing, anyway."

"Remember what kind of gloves? Winter gloves?"

"Naw. These looked like latex gloves. Like you'd use in a hospital or something."

"Wait a minute. The mask . . . do you think the killer wore both as a disguise?"

O'Brien smiled and showed crooked teeth. He coughed with a smoker's bark. "Well, the glasses and the mask, yeah. The ID from the guy on the porch wasn't great. If it hadn't been for the snitch who heard the killer braggin' about it, I don't know . . ."

Paul started to move toward the door. "But gloves as part of a disguise? Sounds odd."

"What're you gonna do?"

Paul shrugged. "The gloves and mask, maybe we got someone who works in a hospital or a medical facility."

"But Schmitty, we got the killer already."

BACK AT HIS OFFICE, PAUL PACED around his desk, wondering what to do next. He felt like time was running out. Should he go to Conway with the DNA and glove information? Paul worried he would be fired if Conway found out he was investigating the murder. No, he'd wait a little longer. Put together a tighter case before presenting it to Conway. Paul took a deep breath. One more screw-up and he knew he'd end up doing security work at power plants for a living—if he didn't go to prison.

His cell phone rang.

"Hey, it's Zehra."

"I just heard about the DNA test. Quite a knock-out punch, Counselor."

"We haven't knocked out anything yet. The prosecutor won't bail on the case until he's checked it out completely. Can't blame him for that. At least I can trust Harmon to be honest about things." Her words came out in a jerky fashion.

"Then, you've got the alibi witness. Where'd you say he was?"

"Oh, the imam at the mosque on the West Bank, Mr. Moalim. Yeah, he's cool. I think the combination of his testimony and the faked DNA, should give us a great defense."

"Zehra, remember I told you to be careful? The real killer's still out there, and someone is protecting him."

TWENTY-FOUR

arolyn Bechter watched with growing horror.

She had just mixed a third Mojito in her tenth floor condo overlooking the Mississippi River and the Stone Arch Bridge. High white clouds puffed up on the northern horizon. Shoes off, air conditioning on high, chilled glass sweating in her hand, she clicked on the Channel Six news.

After following Ben Mohammad, she'd kept searching but hit stone walls. No matter which source or friend she contacted, Carolyn couldn't shake anything loose. She knew she was on the trail of something big, which caused even more frustration.

She understood the Somali community was hard to crack, that they didn't trust many people outside their individual clans. But Carolyn had pushed on her contacts in the police department, FBI, snitches, and even a few seedy, self-appointed "spokesmen" from the Somali community who were always willing to talk to the press. Not a damn thing.

On her couch before the TV, Carolyn had put her feet up on the ottoman and crossed her legs. She had been thinking of the last time she'd been laid--too long ago, when the news show had started.

Watching her employer try to deliver the news—especially since she was rarely a part of it anymore, always frustrated her. To Carolyn, the holes and weaknesses were so obvious. Did they really think the public would buy the shit they called "news" anymore? Ratings were down, and Carolyn knew why.

The familiar pounding rock music cued up, and the graphics started flashing on and off to create a sense of something happening, even if the lead story was just a suburban art fair.

This show was different.

Out from the studio, Reggie had cut immediately to a street scene. The usual young blonde with a quivering voice stood with a strained face. Suddenly, the scene looked familiar to Carolyn. She reached for the remote to turn up the sound.

"Antoine," the reporter said to the anchor as if they were intimate friends— which they were, but the public didn't know that, "I'm here in the Seward neighborhood of south Minneapolis. It looks beautiful and serene but don't let that fool you."

She stretched out her hand in a practiced manner. "There's apparently been a robbery gone bad—very bad."

Carolyn recognized the Johnson Deli. *Sure, that's it*, she thought. She sat up.

The camera man, probably Ray for this shot, moved to the front of the deli. Sure enough, Carolyn could see the large dirty windows. The door was propped open.

"Witnesses tell us that about four-thirty this afternoon two men came into this small deli and tried to rob it at gun point." The camera traveled in through the open door. "The two men working inside were cooperative. When a customer came in behind the robbers, something went wrong. Wrong because it caused the death of the two workers and the customer." A breeze pulled the reporter's hair up on the left side.

Carolyn couldn't believe her eyes. She had stood right there a couple days earlier.

The reporter made a nice move between the camera and the open door to get inside. "All three men are dead, shot to death. We don't have information as to why they were killed. Two of the victims, the workers, are identified as Jason McMillian and Ben Mohammad . . ."

Carolyn stood unsteadily. It couldn't be true. She'd seen plenty of death and violence in her career but this frightened her for another reason.

"Police are searching this normally quiet, integrated family community for other witnesses. As of now, they don't have any suspects and are baffled as to how this could happen in broad daylight."

A creepy feeling worked its way over Carolyn. She'd sensed a big story and every step of her investigation confirmed that. This killing couldn't just be a random robbery gone bad. That was bullshit. This was a hit, a hit on Ben Mohammad.

But why?

Where was the FBI in this? They missed it and missed it big. That is, Paul Schmidt missed it. And Carolyn would make sure the public knew all about him.

TWENTY-FIVE

Back in her office, Zehra shut the door in order to pray. Christians often asked her why Muslims prayed so often. Although she never managed to fit in five times daily, she tried for a few. It was a wonderful way to remind her of the blessings of the day, and it also brought her peace in the midst of a hectic job. With all the problems facing her, it helped. The past day's events had shaken her badly.

She faced northeast, looked out her window to St. Paul on the horizon, and started her prayers.

In fifteen minutes she was finished and refreshed. Better than meditation, she thought and she didn't even need a bite of chocolate cupcake. Zehra called for Jackie to stop by the office.

Ricky from forensic IT had left her an email. He'd never seen an email like hers before. The sender had used a series of anonymous servers and mirror sites. Very sophisticated stuff. He'd keep searching, but so far, he'd come up empty.

Zehra thought she should call Paul. He'd know how to handle this. She started to dial his cell and then stopped. Was this serious enough to involve him and the FBI? Zehra didn't know what to do. Pulling open her lower drawer, she reached in for a bite of a chocolate cupcake. *Guilty . . . you bad girl*, she worried.

In another fifteen minutes, Jackie arrived and looked at the chairs pushed to the edges of the floor. "Praying again?" She looked up at Zehra. "Is the case that bad?"

Zehra laughed. "No. One of the 'Five Pillars of Wisdom' of Islam is to pray five times a day."

Jackie pursed her lips. "That'd be a good practice for a lot of Christians I know."

Soon, she had the El-Amin file spread over the small conference table that they pulled from the corner. Jackie knew of the faked DNA sample and Harmon's response.

"So, what do we do? Prepare as if trial will like, start on time?" she asked Zehra.

"We have to. I want you to prepare a motion for the judge, asking him to delay the trial because of new evidence we just discovered that's crucial to the case. If he won't grant that—he probably won't—we'll have to demand a hearing. I can tell him more about Stein's test results. That should be enough to delay things."

"I can't believe he wouldn't do it."

"You know these judges—they're always concerned about the case loads and how long it takes to get a trial out, which make their stats look bad."

"I suppose, but in this case . . . I'll get that drafted today so you can check it out. I'll get it filed as soon as you give me the green light."

"Cool. Have you finished the research to challenge the search of El-Amin's apartment? I think it's clearly illegal. Just in case we have to start the trial, we need to be ready to argue it at the Omnibus hearing before we get to the jury selection."

"I'm all over it. It'll need a little polish," Jackie said.

"Damn! I forgot to get the jury questionnaire. Even though our 'client' may not let us participate in the jury selection, we've got to be prepared for that, too. We may get involved. I'm really concerned since he's Somali, there's probably going to be a lot of strong feelings against him on the panel of jurors. I want them all biased—for us, not against us."

Jackie stopped and looked at Zehra. "Have you experienced much prejudice against you in court?"

Zehra stopped. Jackie finally asked her something about herself. Zehra shrugged. "I suppose, but I don't pay any attention. I figure if I'm professional and prepared, what else can I do? When I first started trying cases as a prosecutor, jurors would come up to me after the verdict and tell me how surprised they were with me. Like, they couldn't believe anyone who looks like me could handle it."

Jackie shook her head. "I'm like, go figure."

"I've found the tough part in representing someone like El-Amin is that jurors want to sound unbiased, because it's not cool to admit you're a racist in public. Underneath, those people really hate all black Muslim Somalis. We need to find out the truth about each juror as best we can."

Jackie sighed. "I'd forgotten how much work a trial can be."

"It's like a marathon—lots of training and prep, then as a reward for all that work, you get to try the thing for a few weeks."

"What a prize." Jackie gathered the loose papers on the table into brown file folders. She powered-down her laptop, folded it, and tucked it under arm. "I'm really dragging. I thought private practice was hard. This is tough. Okay, boss. I'm back at it."

Zehra thought of Mustafa. He had told her he had some connections in the Somali community. Maybe he could help her. Zehra caught herself. Was she thinking this way because it could help her prepare for trial or because she felt attracted to him? The truth involved both reasons.

While she tapped out a text to Mustafa's Blackberry, she thought of his long eyelashes, the quick eyes that sparkled when he talked about his work. So worldly.

Zehra sensed passion in him and intelligence and discipline. They'd discussed their faith and how committed Mustafa was to Islam—like Zehra. Crazy as it seemed, maybe this arranged date would lead to something, although she wouldn't hold her breath.

She asked if he were willing to help in some investigation for the case.

Within ten minutes, to her surprise, Mustafa replied. He was just leaving for a couple days in Cairo, returning to a two-week vacation, didn't think he'd be of much help, but was willing to try.

Zehra keyed back she was going to talk with the imam first thing tomorrow. After that, she'd contact Mustafa.

The next morning, she dragged herself into the office. She hadn't slept well, dreaming weird things: orchids growing all over her condo, up from under her bed, and finally taking it over. Those images had faded when she looked out at the serene beauty of her plants and remembered the thoughtfulness of Mustafa.

Zehra was anxious to see Mr. Moalim. She called BJ's cell but couldn't reach him. Jackie hadn't come into the office yet. Zehra looked at her Casio, felt time slipping by, and decided to go over to the mosque herself. She had to make sure the imam stuck to his story.

Caroly Bechter from Channel Six had called to ask for an interview. Against her better judgment, Zehra agreed to do a short one in the next few days.

She parked the Audi around the corner and walked to the mosque. The sun peeked over the tall classrooms of the University of Minnesota to the east. Bright green leaves stretched up to meet the promise of warmth and life. The cool fog of the night still hovered under bushes that Zehra felt on her legs as she walked.

The mosque looked deserted. The front door was shut, no one stood outside like before, and a silence surrounded it. Maybe it was too early. Since she never attended mosque here—most were filled with Middle Eastern or African Muslims that she had little in common with—maybe things didn't get going until later in the day.

Zehra knocked on the front door and heard a hollow boom from the big prayer area inside. No one answered. She knocked again.

She pushed on the door, and it creaked open.

Inside, the sun hadn't penetrated yet, leaving the cavernous main hall in shadows and quiet, settling dust. She stepped one foot in the door and waited. She heard nothing and put the second foot in. Without shutting the door, she moved deeper into the dark interior.

A squeal startled her until she realized it was a mouse, as startled as she was. She heard it scurry away. Tingling feelings rose up her back. She didn't like mice.

Zehra remembered to flip up the back of her jacket, over her head. She called out, "Mr. Moalim? Is anybody here?" Her words echoed throughout the prayer area.

She started to work her way to the side, toward a door that might lead to the back area. Usually, every mosque had a community center nearby. Maybe someone would be there.

The door was locked. She turned around and walked back to the front. She jerked when the door she'd just found locked, creaked open. She spun back to face it.

A small man approached her. Dressed in a black robe with a black skull cap, he had a long beard that reached almost to his waist. He didn't look Somali. He came to her quickly. "What do you want?" he shouted. He grasped at something near his stomach that looked like it might be a ceremonial knife.

At first, Zehra felt like an invader, as if she'd done something wrong, until she remembered this was a mosque and she was Muslim. She took a deep breath, spread her feet, and prepared to deal with another chauvinistic male. "Zehra Hassan. I'm looking for the imam, Hussein Moalim."

The fierce eyes of the new man softened. "Why do you want him?"

"He met with us several days ago. He has information about my client, Ibrahim El-Amin. I want to talk with Mr. Moalim again."

He squinted at her. "Why now? And why do you want to talk to him?"

"Where is he? It's very important that I meet with him."

The man stopped talking and looked into the open, deserted area of prayer. He looked back at her. "He is missing."

"What?"

"I am sorry. He is not here and did not come in this morning. We have checked at his home and at the hospital where he works. He has disappeared."

Zehra felt an electric shock jolt through her. "When . . ." she mumbled.

The man circled her. "Why do you ask these questions? Why do you seek him?"

"I already told you. You're sure he's missing?"

"He is our imam. I would not joke about such a matter."

Zehra handed him her business card. "I really need to see him. He was supposed to testify in our trial. If you find him, please have him call me." She turned to leave. "I'll investigate it too."

The man studied the card for a long time. "This is where we can locate you?"

"Huh? Yeah, that's my office." She didn't like the way he looked at her. The air became thick and cloying. Zehra had to leave. She backed to the door, felt it still open, and jumped through it. Outside, she turned and hurried back to the Audi. She breathed deeply and felt the warm touch of the sun, slanting down at a sharper angle.

The sweet smell of jasmine carried on the breeze from someone's garden.

Zehra paused to look in the windows of the small shops on Cedar Avenue. Out of the corner of her eye, she thought she saw the man from the mosque coming toward her. She spun around but didn't see him. Her breathing came harder. Zehra hurried toward the car, parked around the corner.

As she passed the corner of a brick building, shouldered next to a vacant lot with high bushes along the sidewalk, the man from the mosque popped out. He must have ducked around the back to ambush her. He lunged for her.

Zehra screamed and stopped.

Of all the things she shouldn't do, she stopped. Shocked. He reached for her again, trying to pull her behind the bushes. She threw-off his grip and launched herself down the sidewalk. He came after her.

Suddenly, the sidewalk was deserted of people. Where had they gone? Zehra ran for the corner, then thought that even if she reached the car, he'd be able to grab her before she could get the door open.

Around the corner was an old frame building that housed the West Bank School of Music. Surely, someone would be in there.

When Zehra rounded the corner, she saw the house a block away. She sprinted for it.

The man yelled at her and crossed the street to cut her off.

Zehra's lungs hurt and her legs felt like lead. She pushed on, cutting left to avoid him. She faked turning down the street to the left. The man changed course and leaped back across the street. Zehra saw a swirl of black robes as he increased his speed in order to intercept her.

At the last moment, she faked right and, with a shrug of her shoulders, let him pass off to her side. Zehra clambered up the steps to the school and tugged at the door.

Luckily, it popped open and she dove inside, slamming it behind her.

Sweat poured from her face and she gasped to gain her breath. Zehra remembered to turn around and lock the door. The school remained quiet except for her bellowing lungs.

TWENTY-SIX

The phone rang.

A breathy voice asked, "Mr. Schmidt? I don't know if you remember me but . . . well, I didn't know who else to call. This is Gennifer Simmons and you were so good."

"Who's this?" Paul sat at his desk watching the sun rise higher over the sky-scrapers to the east, burning off the last fog.

"Gennifer Simmons. Remember? Gennifer, with a 'G.' I'm the school teacher at Hiawatha High School. We talked a few years ago, and you were kind and listened to me."

"You're the one who called about that 'Pied Piper' guy who disappeared with the Somali kids?"

"That's right. Well, I hate to make this call. You know, as a teacher we are hard-wired to protect our kids but . . ."

"What happened?" He was wide awake.

"I . . . I talked to a student. Well, he came to me, actually. A Somali boy, about seventeen. He's one of my favorites, and I'm really worried about him."

"Tell me."

"His name is Ibrahim, but he's taken the American name, Abraham, and he's the sweetest boy."

"What happened?" Paul shouted.

"Oh. Well, he caught me after school one day as I was walking to my car. He obviously didn't want anyone else around. He told me he was scared, because some of the other boys had talked him into a meeting at the community center in his mosque. In fact, they'd met several times. Each meeting was attended by one of the elders from Abraham's tribe and another younger, Middle Eastern looking man who was Muslim. The other man must've been some kind of a scientist, Abraham thought, because he talked to Abraham about his math and chemistry courses." She cleared her throat.

"Did the scientist try to kidnap your boy?"

"No. That's the strange part."

"He didn't talk about leaving for Somalia?"

127

"Just the opposite. The man talked to him about doing something great for Allah in the mosque."

"What?"

"I don't know. Abraham hasn't been back to the mosque because he's afraid."

"Tell his parents?"

"No, he's afraid the elder from their tribe will find out. Mr. Schmidt, what should I do?" Her words tore at Paul.

"Nothing. Give me your address. I want to meet with the boy and yourself. Just us. And don't say anything to anyone. Is the boy there today?"

"Yes, for regular classes. I could have him meet you."

"I can be there in thirty minutes." He hung up and called Conway. Paul knew on one level Conway would be upset, but the teacher called Paul. He had to follow-up. His boss didn't answer. Paul left a voice mail and ran out of the office to his car.

A HALF HOUR LATER, on his way to the school, Paul's cell rang.

"All right, what are you doing?" Joan Cortez asked.

"What do you mean?"

"Don't bullshit me. I just called your office and your secretary said you shot out of there like from a cannon. What's up?"

Paul took a deep breath. How much should he tell her? Since he was already on his way to meet the kid, ICE could never keep up. "I'm meeting a high school boy who says someone's recruiting him to go to a mosque in Burnsville." It sounded stupid, so he explained some of what he'd learned.

"Doesn't make sense. Did you say the recruiter wants him to go back to school?

"Think so."

Without saying good-bye, she clicked off.

In ten minutes, he met with Ms. Simmons in the teacher's lounge at the high school. A small woman with brown hair, she hopped around the room like a nervous bird.

"We can meet Abraham in the classroom next to mine. No one's in there for this hour," she told Paul.

He followed her to the classroom, and, within a few minutes, Abraham entered. Paul looked at the slender boy with dark skin. He had short, shiny black hair and immense coal-black eyes and perfectly white teeth. No wonder Ms. Simmons liked him. The boy's eyes darted from Paul to the teacher. She smiled and put her arm around him while she introduced Paul.

"Abraham, I won't tell anyone that we met so whatever you can tell me will not get out of this room. Okay?" When the boy bobbed his head, Paul continued. "Your teacher told me you said a man, a scientist, talked to you at the mosque?"

Abraham looked at Simmons again then turned toward Paul. "Yeah. A couple of times with Mr. Kamal."

"When were these meetings?"

"In the past year or so. One of the elders of my tribe was there, and he seemed to be friendly with the scientist."

"Why do you call him a scientist?" Paul said.

"He told us he was some kind of scientist and that Islam had an ancient history of the best scientists in the world, but that it's been lost. It's up to people like him and younger people like us to regain that spot."

"What kind of scientist?"

"He never said."

"Did he want you to do something?"

"Yeah. He wants us to volunteer for a special mission for Allah."

"What?"

"He didn't say exactly, but it would involve a great and important sacrifice, he said. He wanted us to meet at the mosque."

Paul shook his head. "He didn't ask you to go to Somalia?"

"No. He told us we must attend our schools. That was the most important thing," Abraham said.

"Are you sure he didn't talk to you about becoming a freedom fighter in Somalia?"

"Nope."

Paul looked at Simmons. She shrugged her shoulders. He asked the boy, "What are you supposed to do at the school?"

"I don't know, but it's something very important for Allah. We were instructed not to tell our parents about anything."

"Did you?"

"No, because the scientist isn't Somali and my parents don't trust many people outside of their tribe." He glanced at the teacher. "I didn't know what to do, so I told Ms. Simmons." Tiny drops of sweat popped out over the boy's forehead.

"You did the right thing, Abraham," she told him.

Paul asked, "So, you were supposed to go to the mosque. When?"

"At the end of the week. Then, we'd have to go to school every day without missing any classes. The end of the week, Friday, is the holy day for Muslims."

"Sure" Paul said. "What were you going to do at the mosque?"

Abraham shook his head. They all stood in silence. Paul wrestled with the facts. They were thin—some scientist told the boys to go to school. So what? Was this connected to the other missing Somali boys?

"But I know where he works," Abraham said.

"Huh?" Paul looked at him.

"Well, I saw his briefcase that he always brought with him. It had the initials, 'M.A.' on the top and the name of his company on it too."

"You remember the name?"

"Sure, Health Technologies."

A grin burst across Paul's face. "Great work! I should recruit you for the FBI. You remember anything else? What'd he look like?"

"Uh . . . tall, skinny dude. Wasn't Somali. He looked Arab. Big nose, smooth skin, good looking. I don't know."

"That's okay. Are you scheduled to meet him again?"

"Only if I want to participate. I'd like to."

"In the next few days?"

"Yeah."

Paul thought for a moment about using the boy as bait to lure the scientist in, but decided it was too risky. "Health Technologies, huh? I can follow up on that." He thanked both of them, left the school, and climbed into his car. He pulled out his Blackberry and keyed in Health Technologies. He found their website and address in Arden Hills, a suburb on the north side of the Twin Cities. He checked to make sure he had FBI identification, and left the school. There probably weren't too many Middle Eastern men employed there. It should be easy to find Mr. A, the scientist.

He tried Conway's number again and received his gruff voice mail. Depending on what Paul found when he arrived at the company, he'd call for back-up if necessary.

TWENTY-SEVEN

At the elevator in the basement of her building, Zehra pounded on the button to retrieve it. She rode it up, rushed inside her condo, and locked and chained the door.

She tried to calm herself. Gasped for breath but couldn't seem to get enough. She felt as if she were choking. This was too close. What should she do?

To distract herself and calm down, she filled the old copper watering can her parents had given her when she first moved in. Her condo had an unusually large deck, which she'd crammed full of pots. Gardening had always given her a respite, a spiritual retreat.

Zehra sprinkled the spinach and chives then watered the begonias. It was easy because her hands shook. Gardening magazines urged her to buy worms for the soil. They created a richer environment for the plants and even disposed of garbage.

They were right of course, but the thought of all those worms crawling around her deck made her queasy.

The missing imam.

Zehra punched BJ's number on her cell in speed dial. He answered. She told him everything as fast as she could get the words out.

"Chill, girl. I'll be over."

"But, BJ, we lost our main witness."

The trial was scheduled to start next Monday. Now, what would they do for the defense? The fake DNA test might not be enough to win, depending on the other witnesses and evidence.

Like a dog sensing things before humans could, Zehra felt a gathering storm. Someone had to fake the DNA . . . who? And why? Now, the imam was missing. Who were the people recruiting the young Somali boys? Paul had been right—this was bigger than the murder case. She felt alone and vulnerable.

She thought of Mustafa and emailed him. Since BJ wasn't able to make headway with these people, after Mustafa's work in the community, maybe he could help. Zehra explained how she'd gone to the mosque and found the alibi witness missing. Did he think he could open any doors for her? To her surprise, he responded immediately. Maybe, he told her. He agreed to meet her later.

Zehra unlocked the lobby door downstairs to let BJ come in. He couldn't do much and Zehra knew that, but just having him with her for a few hours helped. He assured her he'd stick around. He hugged her so close that she could hear his heart thumping and that made her feel relieved.

"What really spooks me was the guy from the mosque. He kept asking if he could find me." Zehra's voice didn't sound like her own. "Do you think he'll come after me again? Here?" She started to shake.

"I'll be here as much as you need me," BJ said. "I'll call my old partner and get him to have a squad hang around here."

Zehra felt like crying. BJ's presence calmed her. She sniffed back a few tears.

In TEN MINUTES, MUSTAFA arrived, and Zehra was happy to leave the condo She introduced the two men. BJ said he'd let himself out. Zehra climbed into the front seat of his Mercedes. He turned off the air and opened the windows to let warm summer air surround them. It felt good, and Zehra relaxed a little. His car had a manual transmission, and she watched his strong hand maneuver the stick, shifting with confidence. They must find the imam

"I have done some work for the Somali community at Cedar-Riverside but they are closed to outsiders, even other Muslims. I don't know if I can help much."

She told him of the faked DNA evidence.

"I have never heard of that. It is true?"

"Yeah, and the research I've done says it's not too hard. Someone would have to prepare it ahead of time. Luckily, most criminals get caught because they aren't too bright. It's the ones who are smart who worry me. Obviously, someone thought about the murder ahead of time and prepared the fake sample to frame El-Amin."

"You think he is innocent?"

She turned in the seat to face him. "After a few years of defending criminals, I've come to distrust most of what they tell me. But the evidence here sure makes him look innocent." She paused, wanted to tell him so much more. "Sorry, I have a lawyer's duty to not reveal confidential info from my client."

Mustafa nodded, and the sun glistened off his shiny hair. "I'm always honest about everything. It is written in the Qur'an."

"I know. But why would someone want to frame El-Amin? What's going on that I don't see?"

"Do you think your client will be found guilty?"

"I don't know. The faked DNA helps the defense, but so far, the prosecutor won't dismiss."

Mustafa turned onto Cedar Avenue a few blocks from the mosque. He hummed quietly to himself. "What do you think the federal agents will do when they find out the DNA was faked?"

"I'm sure they know. Agent Paul Schmidt is an old friend of mine. He knows by now."

"So, what action will they take? Will they look for someone else as the killer?"

Zehra was flattered that Mustafa asked as many questions as he did. Few of the men in her life were as interested. "I know from my friend that he doesn't believe the Somali men were used just to fight in their country. Although the local FBI isn't backing him, he thinks there's something behind the disappearances and the killing. He's still digging into it a lot deeper. After what I've seen in the case, I agree."

He turned and faced her. "What do you think is going on?"

His eyes stared into hers, making her feel a combination of unease and excitement at the same time. This man was certainly different from many others. She found herself attracted to his intensity and passion.

Zehra said, "I don't know. It scares me to think what I may be getting into, but if it'll help with my case, I've got to follow up."

"What do you think this agent . . . uh, Mr. Schmidt, will do?"

"He's determined to crack the case. I know he'll be relentless, and I don't trust him."

"Why not?"

"He knew about our alibi witness almost before we did. And now, the witness has disappeared. Maybe the feds grabbed him and will interrogate him."

Mustafa stopped talking and pulled up in front of the mosque. Several robed men slouched at the door. Every set of eyes watched him get out of the Benz.

"*As-salaam alaykum*," Mustafa called to them.

One of the men finally called back, "*Wa-alaykum as-salaam*." No one moved in front of the mosque.

Zerha stood by the car while Mustafa approached. The men stood up and surrounded him.

"I am a friend of your imam, Mr. Moalim," Mustafa said. "I have worked with him. Is he around to meet with us?"

No one spoke. Then, a younger man from the back stepped forward. "I know you. You are Mustafa Ammar. You have worked with some of the young people before, in the schools."

"Yes." Mustafa cleared his throat. "Is the imam here?"

"He has not come in today. We are worried since this is not like him to fail in his responsibilities here."

"Has anyone checked his home?"

"He has not been there for two days," the young man replied.

Mustafa asked, "He worked at a hospital, didn't he? Have you checked there?"

The man turned to his right and pointed down the street. "He works at that hospital, down there. In the kitchen. No, we have not been over there to look for him. He would come here first."

Thanking the group, Mustafa and Zehra got back into the car and drove five blocks to the hospital.

Zehra noticed the new flowers standing in the window boxes of the coop food store. The petals looked like they opened themselves to worship the sun. "Do you know gardens were first recorded in ancient Persia?" When he nodded, she continued, "You can imagine how magical and wonderful they must've been in the middle of a desert. Cool, fragrant, shaded, and with running water usually. Maybe that's where I get my love of gardens."

"Probably." He turned sharply into the parking lot of the hospital. "You must show me your gardens at home some day soon."

"Are you really interested?" She looked at him.

"Of course. I am interested in them because you are. I want to understand your love for flowers."

"They're spiritual for me. Allah has given us many blessings, Nature being one of the greatest."

"I agree that Allah has given us many blessings. It is too bad most people do not see them." His voice had a sharp edge to it.

"Should we check the kitchen first?" Zehra said. "I think the HR people would be better."

Inside, they identified themselves and were led into the Human Resources offices. After waiting ten minutes, a small man came into the lobby to greet them. "I'm Roger Weber, director of Human Resources." He wore a stiff white shirt with red suspenders. Blond hair spiked over the top of his head. He shook each of their hands and offered them seats in his small office.

"You say you're looking for Mr. Moalim." His eyebrows furrowed. "That's interesting, because we're looking for him also. He hasn't been at work in two days."

"Has he done this before?" Zehra asked.

"No. He's one of our most reliable workers. We employ many of the Somali community here. They're so good with the patients. They're very warm, kind people."

"He worked in the kitchen?" she said.

"Yes, and he also worked in the supply room."

"What's that involve?"

"Oh, you know, keeping inventory, stocking, things like that," Mr. Weber said.

A thought poked into Zehra's mind. "Does the supply room contain face masks?"

"Of course. In a hospital, we have to be particularly careful. We only use the 3M N95, 8000 model respirator here. It's the best on the market for screening most of the nasty things we don't want to breathe."

Zehra felt her chest tingle. The same type found at the crime scene. She didn't say anything else.

After they left, Mustafa drove Zehra back to her condo.

At the door she hesitated, then invited him in. She walked into the kitchen and marveled at the way he seemed to glide as he walked, so graceful. "Would you like something to drink?"

"Do you have tea? I don't drink alcohol, of course."

"Of course." She pulled out a box of green tea and heated water. "I try to be faithful, but once in a while I'll have wine."

His face clouded. "That is not good. You should try to be more faithful."

She felt flustered. "Well . . . of course, but here in America most people drink a little. I don't think it affects my faith."

"Zehra, do you not understand how all the little transgressions can add up?"

"Transgressions?"

"It is against Islamic law."

"I think that's a matter of interpretation."

He frowned, and Zehra could tell he was thinking. Had she offended him? "But it's not that important to me, I mean, to drink. Let's have our tea."

"What do you think your friend, the FBI agent, will do about the witness missing?" He shifted the cup from hand to hand.

"Huh?" The shift in conversation surprised her. "I'm sure it'll support his idea that something larger and more sinister is going on. I don't know." She looked at him. "Why do you ask?"

"I'm thinking about our talk in the car. I am trying to help you."

"My part is only the murder case. What does the FBI have to do with that?"

Mustafa stood. "I am trying to think of anything to help you." He looked at his watch and started to walk to the door. "I will be very busy in the next week but will try to help you as I can."

"Are you going out of town on business, again?"

"I'm going to Cairo for a very short trip."

"Maybe we can get together again soon."

He stopped and his eyes focused somewhere outside the deck. "Yes . . . yes, that would be wonderful." His attention came back to Zehra and he reached for her. His eyes roamed over her face, he smiled, and squeezed her arm gently.

He pulled her toward him and leaned down. He stared into her eyes and, at the last minute, turned his head to reach her lips. With any other man, the long stare would've made Zehra think she was kissing a weirdo, but not this exotic man.

Zehra's mind swirled. She smelled the lingering hint of his cologne and still sensed his powerful presence. Zehra longed to touch him, to feel his strong muscles. They kissed long and deeply. Then he left

She walked to the sink to clean the cups. Thoughts pressed into her mind about him. She was still cautious but found herself drifting toward him anyway.

Zehra felt a shudder of desire low in her body.

Her cell phone buzzed. A text from Jackie. Zehra called immediately.

"I've got great news," Jackie said. "Dr. Portman's got a window of time and can meet us in this afternoon."

In two hours, they sat in the Ramsey County Medical Examiner's office in St. Paul. A tall man with long white hair that hung over his shoulders, Dr. Portman moved slowly. He sat deliberately in his leather chair, leaned back, crossed his legs slowly, and steepled his hands across the bulge in his middle. "It's a pleasure to meet you young ladies."

He made Zehra think of an old hippie. "Thanks for your time. We needed a second opinion on Dr. Wong's examination."

"Yes, Helen's a friend." He smiled and revealed small teeth. "I found two things that are of interest to me." His head pushed back and he sucked in a dry breath. "The unusual red markings on the body that Dr. Wong noted . . . very unusual. Without actually seeing the body itself, I can only make my observations from the photos you emailed me from the autopsy."

"Of course," Zehra said.

"Looks to be a rash of some sort. Something like you might think of with eczema but different. Discounting any skin disease, which Dr. Wong didn't observe, and therefore I won't speculate, this rash could only mean one thing."

"What?"

"The young man was sick."

"Sick?" Jackie looked at Zehra. "Are you sure?"

Dr. Portman's head came back down to rest on his chest. "I don't think I could testify under oath, but I'm telling you what I suspect. Yes, he was sick and whatever he had caused the slight swelling and red rash that covered his palms. It's also interesting the rash was on the palms."

"Anything else?" Zehra asked.

Portman grinned. "The other evidence even you could see."

Jackie frowned. "Huh?"

"The contents of the stomach. Alone, it wouldn't mean much to me—as it didn't for Dr. Wong. And, it certainly wouldn't be the cause of death. But together with the rash, it suggests the victim was sick."

"What was in the stomach?"

"Undigested pills. Ibuprofen, Advil, and what I think were aspirin."

TWENTY-EIGHT

W hen Joan Cortez hung-up the phone after talking to Paul, she quivered with excitement. But she forced herself to sit and think. The scientist insisted the boys go back to school, he'd said. She didn't want to go off in the wrong direction, but this sounded like the plot they feared. Should she call the Army now?

On the one hand, she wanted to break the case and uncover the plot herself. This one by itself would insure her career forever. Still, she knew she couldn't do it alone. ICE had the manpower but not the technical expertise.

Poor Paul, so far over his head. By the time he figured out what was going on, she'd have it wrapped up. A nice guy, but business was business. He would complain to her after she'd taken it down. She'd simply tell him, "homeland security." If it was even half as big as they suspected, she'd be a national hero. Her grubby little life would change forever. She could give her son all he deserved. And no need for the dead-beat ex-husband and the pennies he offered. In fact, she may have a lot of interested men in her future.

What scared her was the time table. In a few days, the boy had said. That was a lot faster than expected. Joan calculated. They would have less than a week and a half to head things off. They wouldn't have much time.

Ribbons of sweat coursed down the sides of her chest. Joan took a deep breath. This wasn't the same as chasing a bogey across the Mexican border; this would challenge everything they had to combat it. How far had the enemy gotten? Was it here yet? How would they deliver it? If they all missed the small window of time to stop everything, they may as well give up. It'd be too late.

With all the pressure, her mind seemed to slow down until Joan could feel her thoughts struggling to organize themselves, to make some sense of it all, to decide how to proceed. What should she do next? Joan glanced at her watch.

She had to pull a piece of paper across her desk and pick up a pen to try to calculate the timing. *Let's see . . .* she thought. *On Friday . . . the boy said.*

Fear crept up from behind her, causing her to lose her concentration.

Joan sat back and shook her hands out, leaned forward, and started calculating again. She pulled her jacket closer around her shoulders. Joan ran the numbers three times. Finally convinced, she knew what had to be done.

Should she email them?

Too slow. That's why he'd given her his cell phone number.

Joan picked up her cell and tried to dial the number, but her fingers couldn't hit the small keys. She started again. This time, it worked.

The phone rang, kept ringing. Finally, someone said, "Yes?"

"It's Agent Joan Cortez from ICE."

"Yes . . . ?" The voice sounded hollow, almost bored.

She swallowed. "I have a message. Is this Dr. Samson?"

"What do you have, agent?"

"I think . . . tell him that it's already here."

TWENTY-NINE

C arolyn Bechter couldn't believe her good luck. The old mojo was back.
While covering the murder trial of the terrorist, she'd casually asked Zehra
Hassan for an on-camera interview. To Carolyn's surprise, she agreed.

Carolyn would film a killer interview that, combined with what facts she was
already gathering, would kick ass all over the country.

She took a deep breath. It was almost too good to be true. Only an old pro
like her could handle the whole story. She thought of Schmidt. She'd kick his ass
but good.

They met in the late afternoon in the common room of Hassan's condo building.

Luckily, Carolyn had been able to snag Ray for the camera work. The interview
started well, although nothing new was coming up. Hassan was dressed casually and
had beautiful eyes. She was photogenic, smart, and Carolyn could sense a toughness
underneath. A passionate young woman. Carolyn was confident Ray could pick that
all up on film.

She also sensed fear underneath Hassan's facade. Years of interviewing people
gave Carolyn the skill to read people perfectly.

As for herself, Carolyn was in Oscar-like form. She fluffed her blonde hair more
than usual, wore an off-white linen jacket with a teal blouse opened down the front as
far as she could without causing Reggie to pull the piece.

She was particularly good at pausing mid-sentence to keep the audience's attention until the end of the question.

As they worked, Carolyn knew parts of the interview would have to be cut. The
long statements Hassan made about how most Muslims weren't terrorists and were
totally opposed to people like the defendant and all the violence they used. That shit
wouldn't sell to Channel Six's audience. Ray got some nice close-ups of Hassan's face
when she was most passionate about those beliefs. Instead, they'd splice those shots
with her words about the rights of all accused people to have a fair trial. *This is fucking
America after all*, Carolyn thought. A little of the flag waving would sell better.

Because of her own suspicions, Carolyn pushed Hassan hard about what else
was really going on behind this murder. Hassan acted like she didn't know.

In twenty minutes, the interview was over. Hassan said she'd forgotten her car in the public lot so she walked out with everyone else. They all moved into the parking lot. Hassan told them she was driving to her office. Carolyn watched her get into the car. Ray started to pack the camera and tripods into the van. Hassan tried to start the old car. The engine just clicked.

Ray noticed too, set the camera down, and went over to help her. He opened the hood and ducked his head down. Poked around and came back up without an answer. Then, he stretched out on the ground to slither underneath the car. *Come on Ray*, Carolyn thought. *Reggie'll have my ass with all the time and money we're wasting.*

Ray shot out from under the car. His black skin was bleached white with fear. "Bomb!" he had yelled over and over.

They all turned to run when the clicking sound got louder and louder until a flat whump behind them and a blast of scalding wind knocked them all to the ground. Carolyn sprawled across grass, pissed that it probably stained her linen jacket. As she twisted around, she saw the front end of the car explode into an orange ball with black edges of smoke. Her head felt like it was squeezed by a pair of large, hot hands.

Ray, always the professional, was rolling toward his camera, still on the ground. He shot some footage of the flames from several angles as dead leaves fluttered down around all of them.

Black, stinky smoke billowed up into the sky.

Carolyn's ears rang, and she couldn't hear much. Suddenly, people started to gather, gawking. She struggled to stand up. Checked her jacket and smoothed the front, knowing she'd have to go back on camera soon. She steadied Ray and pointed to the shots she wanted. Great stuff. Shocked people. Scared. Now there were sirens wailing. Perfect.

Carolyn remembered to get Hassan's face also. Ray swung the camera on his shoulder to find her. The confident, controlled woman of ten minutes before was gone. She stood, leaning against the company van, motionless, her face blank with shock. She started to shake.

"The eyes, Ray," she screamed at Ray over the noise around them. "Get the eyes." Carolyn pushed Ray in for a closer shot. Yes . . . the perfect expression for the ten o'-clock news.

THIRTY

Paul drove to the Arden Hills campus of Health Technologies. He'd googled the company and found they were one of the largest bio-tech companies in the country, with offices all over the world.

He parked in the spacious lot surrounded by manicured bushes, bright green grass, and a fountain that shot a jet of water high into the air. He thought of calling Conway again. Then, he remembered his boss' order to stop any new investigation. The news from the boy at school would probably change that, but Paul didn't want to take any chances yet. He'd just do a little investigation. If it produced legitimate information, he'd call Conway with the results.

He worried. What if he couldn't find the mysterious Dr. A in time? Should he contact headquarters? No. For now, he'd run this alone.

The main lobby of the company soared three stories into a clear-glassed area above him. Sun danced off the steel supports and cascaded into the lobby so that no lights were required. It faced south to minimize energy use. Expensive plants fanned out from the front door like open arms.

Paul's' heels clicked over the polished granite as he walked toward a low, modern desk in the middle. A beautiful woman with dark-brown hair pulled back in a loose bun, looked up at him, smiling as brightly as the sun above.

He pulled out his FBI identification and told her what he was looking for.

"Oh. You should talk to the head of security, Mr. Crenshaw. Please take a seat, Agent Schmidt. Would you like coffee, tea, mineral water, a Coke?"

After she handed him a chilled bottle of water, he waited in a soft chair, so low he was worried it'd be hard to get back out.

In two minutes, Crenshaw appeared in the lobby. He was short, thick, and had an unusual hair style. Must be a rug, Paul thought to himself. He followed Crenshaw down a long, quiet hallway. His feet sank into the gray carpeting until he came to the office. They sat in seats at a small conference table.

"We've never had the FBI here before. Usually, we just deal with petty thefts and collisions in the employee's parking lot," he said, patting the back of his head as if the rug had slipped. "I hope we haven't done anything wrong." He grinned, but it quickly disappeared.

"No, of course not. I'd like to talk with someone I think is employed here. Do your people get briefcases with their initials and your company name on them?"

"Some do, yes. Who do you want to talk with?"

"I think he's a scientist, Middle Eastern probably, with the initials, M.A."

Crenshaw's eyes flicked over his face, then left to look around the room. "Our employee information is usually confidential and . . ."

"Listen, Ms. Crenshaw, I'll cut the bullshit."

He sat up and stopped patting his hair.

"This is a matter of homeland security. After we talk, I want you to call for your own security people. I'll need to talk with them before we approach the suspect."

"The suspect? What's going on?" His face flushed.

"We don't know all the answers, but I'm convinced this man could be very dangerous."

"He works here?"

Paul nodded. "Any ideas who M.A. could be?"

He didn't move, and Paul could tell his brain was whirling. He rose and moved behind a desk. "We have scientists from all over the world working here." He tapped on a computer for a few minutes. Frowned. "Here . . . here he is, I think. We have several employees in the science department. Malcom Alpers, Michael Ammar, Vicky Aniston, and of course, lots of Andersons. We are in Minnesota, you know." Crenshaw looked up from the screen with a grin from his own joke.

"This guy is Middle Eastern. What about the name Ammar?"

"Uh . . . worked here about three years. In our micro-biology labs." Crenshaw gave him a brief bio of the suspect.

"Tell me where he works and the physical lay-out."

Crenshaw frowned. "What do you mean?"

"Are there lots of people around him, or is he alone in an office?"

"He has his own office and shares a secretary. Should I call to see if he's in?"

"No," Paul shouted. "Call the secretary, but tell her not to say anything else."

Crenshaw called and found out that Ammar was out on vacation for two weeks.

Paul slapped his knee and swore. "Of course, he is. He wants the students back to school in the next few days . . ."

"There's something odd," he said, "His secretary said he' was scheduled to go to Cairo for a business conference. Normally, we don't allow people to take vacation immediately before a business trip."

"Cairo?" A hollow tension expanded in Paul's chest. "What's his home address?"

Crenshaw hesitated, "We're not supposed to give out that . . ."

Paul jumped from his seat and leaned over the desk, spinning the computer screen out of the way. "Look, what don't you get about national security? Do you want to be the one who stopped the FBI from catching a terrorist? Let's talk to your boss right now!"

Crenshaw gulped, it looked like his rug moved, and he turned the screen back again, and started to key. "Here . . . here it is." He printed it for Paul.

He tore it from Crenshaw's hand and raced out to his car. He called Conway and luckily, got a hold of him.

"Paul, goddamn it! I told you . . ."

"Bill, the teacher who called us five years ago called me. I just took the call and made a routine follow-up investigation at the school. Don't you see that we've got to move on this—yesterday!"

"What's your point?"

Paul heard a small *plup* as Conway talked, having taken a puff from a cigarette. Smoking was prohibited in his entire office. "Something's going to happen at a mosque in a day or two. I don't know what, but we've got to intercept this guy before anything goes down."

Conway was silent awhile. Then said, "You're sure about this?" he sighed. "These damn Somali cases . . . it just won't end. Okay, where are you now?"

"I'm just about to case the house. I need back-up."

"Right. I'll get the emergency response team scrambled to meet you there. Cruise the neighborhood to see the layout but don't stop for anything," Conway ordered. "Wait for us." He paused. "And if you screw-up this one . . ."

"Yes, sir."

A MMAR LIVED IN SOUTHWEST MINNEAPOLIS in a quiet neighborhood of single family homes. Minnehaha Creek twisted through the neighborhood, on its way to the Mississippi. Walking and biking trails hugged the small creek.

Large elms and ash trees stretched over the streets, creating a canopy of shadow in the front yards. He found Ammar's house, a tight bungalow made of stucco with brown wood trim on the edges. Green ivy snaked from the side and threatened to engulf the front door. The front lawn, speckled with yellow dandelions, needed mowing.

Paul slowed as he reached the house and tried to see in. Shades hid the interior. A rusted air conditioner stuck out of a window on the south side. There were no cars parked in the front on the street.

He turned at the end of the block and drove to the alley that separated the two rows of houses. Driving down the alley, each house had a garage. Many leaned to one side and needed paint. Trash cans guarded the sides of most garages, with their lids clamped on tightly.

When he reached the end of the alley and turned back onto the street, something bothered him. There weren't any trash cans behind Ammar's house.

Paul parked around the corner at an angle where he could watch the front of the house and waited for the FBI team. The hollow feeling returned to his chest, and he felt as if he had to piss badly.

At his ankle, he carried the little Glock 29, the subcompact. Under his arm, in the shoulder holster, he cradled the Glock 21, with the .45 caliber slugs in it.

He took a sip of water from the bottle he'd received at Health Technologies. It helped moisten his dry mouth. He sipped again—not too much or he'd really have to piss.

His Blackberry buzzed.

The assault team was near and asked for intelligence about the house. Paul told them everything including the details about the neighboring houses.

In five minutes, a dark van pulled up behind Paul's car. He looked in his rear-view mirror and then got out. Five agents, dressed in dark-blue jackets and pants, jumped from the van and huddled next to it on the sidewalk side. Large, yellow letters said FBI on their backs. Paul knew they were armed for any problem and vested also. One agent carried the "bunker buster," a light but protective shield carried before him when he burst through a door.

The leader, First Deputy Tony Valentini, came up to Paul. Without shaking, he said, "What's the intel, agent?"

Paul nodded. "The subject's around the corner up there," he pointed. "There's also the alley."

"We'll take both," Valentini said. "I'll take two agents with me, and I'd like two to ride with you up the alley. We'll be responsible for primary contact. You'll cover the escape route, if necessary. Description?"

"Middle Eastern, tall, thin. About thirty years old."

"Anyone else with him?"

"Probably not. He's not married and doesn't have a family."

"From what you say, he could have a bomb in there. Once we're in position, we've got to move." Valentini emphasized the word "move." He thought for a moment, and then said, "Conway wants us to wait for him, but he'll just get in the way." He grinned for a moment. "We can't let the suspect escape, can we?" They all agreed, so Valentini said, "Let's move out, men."

The agents separated into the two vehicles. Paul backed up and turned into the alley. He waited for the van to round the corner into the street and gave it a little time to reach the front of the house. He rolled up the alley and peered through the houses to keep pace with the van.

When he reached the house, he parked his car diagonally across the back to block the garage and the yard. The two agents fanned out to each side of the door and pulled out their weapons. One had a pistol and the other a shotgun.

Paul, who didn't have a vest, screened himself with his car by standing behind it. He leveled his Glock 21 over the roof, holding it with both hands. He pointed it directly at the back door and waited.

He forced himself to breathe slowly, to keep calm. The two agents, although experienced, fidgeted while in position. Paul strained to see into the dark windows for any hint of trouble. To be prepared. No matter how many take-downs a person went through, they were always tense. Anything could happen.

Five minutes later, Paul heard a crash from the front of the house. Probably the door breaking. Men shouted. His impulses told him to storm the back door, but they'd been trained to wait for a possible escape. No one appeared in the back until Valentini shouted to them before opening the door himself.

Paul shouted back and everyone holstered their weapons. "We're coming in," Paul yelled. Valentini agreed.

Inside, they all walked through the small home. It was obvious no one had lived there for many years. The refrigerator was clean and off, the toilet paper roller empty, the cupboards bare, and dust settled on every surface. Paul sniffed at the stale, closed-up smell that reminded him of his elderly grandmother who never got out.

"You got bad intel," Valentini said. "Nice work, agent," he scowled at Paul.

Paul raised his shoulders. "Hey . . . how did I know? This is the official address he gave his employer."

"What the hell's going on?" A hoarse voice from the front door shouted inside. Conway stepped into the living room. He huffed and looked around. "What'd we get?"

Conway looked from one agent to the other until he came to Paul. No one had to speak. Bill took a deep breath. "Can you explain this?"

"Of course not, Bill. You agreed to the grab."

"After you talked me into it."

"Chief," Valentini raised his hand between the two men. "Let's look around. Maybe we'll find something."

Everyone separated, and Paul walked to the front door. It stood with the frame splintered in two places. Sun flooded the area, making it uncomfortably warm. Paul noticed the mailbox and opened it. A bundle of mail tumbled out. He picked it up and scanned the addresses. "Hey," he shouted. "I've got something."

Conway and Valentini hurried to the front. Paul held out the letters and junk mail. All of them were addressed to Michael Ammar.

"Drop house," Valentini said. "Probably never spent one night here. I'm startin' to like this smell—we're definitely on to something now. Any idea where our man could be?" he asked Paul.

"I don't know."

Conway nodded. "Well . . . I guess you're right. This guy stinks, and I want him brought in," he ordered. He spun toward Paul and scowled. "As for you, I think I'm gonna fire you. Right now."

Too upset to go back to the office, Paul headed for home. He didn't want to face Conway. Besides being embarrassed, Paul worried that Conway really meant he was fired. At least Paul had proved one thing. Michael Ammar was somehow tied in with the Somali boys and could be dangerous.

At his home, Paul booted up his computer to check email. While waiting, he remembered to google USRAMID, one of the agencies that called Conway. When he keyed it in, the program didn't find any matches. He rearranged the letters and got a hit. What he found stopped his breath.

USAMRIID was an acronym for the U.S. Army Medical Research Institute of Infectious Diseases, located at Ft. Detrick, Maryland.

THIRTY-ONE

Outside of Minnesota, Michael could become Mustafa again. He looked out the window of the Egypt Air flight as it cruised over the vast city of Cairo. Even from this altitude, it stretched for as far as he could see in all directions. The plane circled the airport and landed at Terminal 3, the newest and largest one.

He carried only the company briefcase for his laptop and a small suitcase. He'd substitute the new laptop for his old one on the return flight.

Although the airport was only ten miles from central Cairo, it took a long time to reach his hotel, the Ramsses Hilton. A new freeway promised a quick entry into the city but, as most things in Cairo, corruption, crowding, and millions of people slowed progress. Piles of garbage stood everywhere. Mustafa didn't mind. He had plenty of time and from inside the air-conditioned cab, he could watch the unfolding of humanity on the streets in all its forms.

He'd forgotten the noise and the smell.

Car horns, scooters whining beside the cab, the bawling of donkeys, shouts of vendors, the crush of people everywhere, crying children, the dry wind from the western desert that whistled through the arches in the markets, the calling to the faithful to prayer by *muezzins*, and the tinkling of bells all assaulted Mustafa's ears.

Even in the spring, the sun beat down on everything, retarding time as if it were in slow motion. Sometimes, if you were out in it too long, your head could begin to ring until the cacophony of noise around you started to feel painful.

Finally, the cab pulled in front of the huge, dusky Ramsses Hilton. It rose all by itself above the east bank of the Nile. A modern square pyramid with flat sides and protruding corners. From its rooms, Mustafa could see up and down the length of the Nile, the city, and the ancient pyramids to the west. He liked that the sun, settling into the deserts beyond, infused an orange glow into the rooms in the early evening.

He also liked that the hotel staff kept beggars away from the front door, and he liked the feel of the clean, dust-free cold air that hit him as he walked through the automatic doors into the lobby. It refreshed him.

As he walked in, he saw a man plodding across the street, hunched under an immense stack of cardboard, bound in twine and perched on his curved back. With his pants legs rolled up, the man placed one sandaled foot in front of the other, careful to avoid the potholes in the street.

"What is that?" Mustafa asked the doorman.

"Zabaleen. Christians who've collected all the garbage in Cairo for hundreds of years. They used to have herds of goats to eat the organic things and the Zabaleen removed everything else on their backs to sell."

"What do you mean they 'used to have goats'?"

"Not one anymore. Since the government killed all the goats here to avoid the flu, no one collects the organic garbage. Stupidest decision ever, but it's usual for the government. Can't you smell it?" The doorman lifted his nose to the breeze.

Mustafa could detect the odor. He hurried into the hotel.

After leaving his bag and briefcase in the room, he retreated to the Terrace Café, which overlooked the Nile. Shaded with awnings from the afternoon sun, the breeze felt good. He ordered a Diet Coke and felt guilty. Try as hard as he could, some items of Western decadence still remained with him.

Cairo was hemmed in by deserts to the east and west, so the city crawled along the banks of the Nile to the north and south. He could see this easily from the terrace. Across the Nile, Gizera Island sat in the middle of the dirty waters. Beyond that, squatting at the exact edge of the city, were the pyramids. From the backyards of the homes, a child could almost throw a piece of camel dung and hit the monuments.

He planned to meet the shipment and the courier at one of the Cities of the Dead, the northern one, for the transfer.

In the meantime, the conference would only take one day. He must get back to the United States quickly.

Attended by scientists from all over the world, it would be mildly interesting. Presenting his paper provided a wonderful cover. The company paid for everything, and Mustafa had an excuse to return to the world of Islam for a short time.

Tomorrow, he would meet the courier and take possession of the briefcase. Because of his corporate credentials, he had special privileges to carry research items through customs. He'd practiced with other, non-threatening parcels on several occasions without ever having a problem. The test camps in Somalia had been a success. All his efforts in the United States to recruit the young men would pay off. Once he had the material back there, he'd have the young men meet for the launch.

He planned to buy a gift for Zehra to win her trust. Although she was corrupted like most Muslims born in America, Mustafa found her somewhat attractive. He would avoid any real personal relationship with her for the sake of the mission, but he couldn't deny how pretty she was.

He'd find a gift at the *souk*, or bazaar, at Khan el-Khalili, one of the oldest and largest in Cairo. Although it would be crowded with tourists, it was still a good place to find gifts, and he needed a good knife in case of trouble later on.

Mustafa smiled to himself and the thought of its history. In the late 1300s, the ruling family of Egypt had a stranglehold on Europe. All spices from the east came through this *souk* on their way to Europe. The family had a monopoly and made the kafirs pay and pay—much like the stranglehold on oil that the Islamic Middle East held around the throats of the world today.

He'd go in the coolness this evening, when the city came to life at a normal pace. The last time he'd been here, he'd noticed a beautiful jewelry box in the bazaar. It was handmade with the pieces of mother-of-pearl set into tight, traditional patterns, then polished to a high gloss. Inside the box, he would put a silk scarf for Zehra. In a tactful but forceful way, he could remind her she should wear *hijab*, the traditional head covering Muslim women were supposed to wear.

Mustafa worried about her. She didn't seem to accept him without question as most other American women did. He was convinced he could win her trust with these simple kinds of trinkets. It had worked before.

THE NEXT MORNING, THE LOUDSPEAKERS woke him with the call to prayer. Today, theses Islamic cities were much too large for human *muezzins* to call and be heard. Public-address systems with recorded calls amplified the message to reach everyone above the ceaseless noise of the city.

Mustafa rose, washed, stood facing east, and crossed his arms before his chest. He went through the normal chants to call to Allah and thank Him for the blessings. He knelt, bent forward, and touched the seven parts of his body—the forehead, palms, knees, and both big toes—to the carpeting in the room. It felt rough and reminded him to be humble before Allah. He rose again, continued the prayers, knelt and touched his forehead to the carpet once again.

When Mustafa finished, he dressed in tan robes and went down to the grill for a light breakfast. He took a cab across the 6 October Bridge to Gizera Island, the largest one bisecting the slow moving Nile. At the southern end of the island, the conference would be held in the Sheraton Hotel, as it had been in previous years.

At the lunch break, Mustafa took advantage of the charming, small Fine Arts Museum, just north of the conference hotel and visited it.

He started to become anxious at the thought of the transfer. So much rode upon his successful insertion of the shipment into the United States. The defense of Islam and the enormity of his task often overwhelmed Mustafa. At those times, he would slip away to a quiet spot and open the Qur'an to read. The flowing Arabic words of the Prophet calmed him.

How proud he felt to have been chosen to spearhead the destruction and eventual redemption of the infidels. After it was all over, depending on how many remained alive, how could they fail to see the True Way of Islam and Allah's laws?

At the end of the day, Mustafa prepared for the flight back to the United States and his meeting with the courier. He covered his Western clothing with a tan robe.

He carried the small suitcase and strapped the briefcase with the corporate logo over his shoulder. The new laptop would be sealed for protection. Mustafa erased his hard drive and would switch them after the transfer. The cab driver looked at him closely when he asked to be taken to the City of the Dead. Mustafa assured him it was okay. Back out on the Salah Salem Highway, the cab slowed to turn into the Northern City of the vast cemeteries clumped at the foot of the Moqattam Hills.

Mustafa told him to wait. He stepped out into a dusty wind. In the distance he could see, quivering from the heat in the beige and sandy landscape, the minarets of the Citadel. The smell of rotting garbage struck him, but this was the safest place to make the transfer, so he started to walk.

Five million people lived in the Cities of the Dead. Because of the chronic shortage of housing for the urban poor, they'd moved into these facilities over the years. Unlike Western cemeteries, Egyptians buried their dead in room-like sites so the family could live in them for the required forty days of mourning. Once the families left, the rooms remained vacant and available for the poor to move in.

Electric lines sagged from one roof to another to bring in power, illegally. The entire occupation was illegal but tolerated by the government as an easy way to house the poor and avoid violent protests. For his purposes, Mustafa knew the authorities ignored most of the activities in the Cities, and he wouldn't be bothered.

Mustafa started through the twisted, unplanned streets of the cemetery. Cockroaches and flies spread before him. An occasional car languished between the tightly packed buildings.

He made two left turns and avoided stepping into a pool of stinking liquid from the garbage pile. He looked up the street to see white laundry flapping in the dry wind, strung between two gravestones. To the side, a fat man sat in front of a grave marker turned sideways for his desk. Wrapped in a dirty robe, he scratched a pen across stained papers before him. The man looked up with large, bottomless black eyes at Mustafa. One eye was clouded over with a milky cataract. Mustafa felt for his new knife, hidden under the robes and continued.

Around one more corner in a narrow alley, Mustafa met him.

A swarthy man, carrying a briefcase stamped in big letters on the side which read, "ISTC, Moscow." Mustafa almost laughed at how ironic it looked—a briefcase of death in the middle of a city of dead people.

Mustafa approached him, looked him in the eye and said, "*As-salaam alaykum,* peace be with you."

"*Wa-alaykum as-salaam,* and peace be upon you also." The man returned, eyeing him with suspicion.

Mustafa waited for the handoff. No one moved. A puff of dry dust blew past them. Mustafa saw the stark contrast between the slanting white light and the shadows that still gripped the sides of walls and gravestones. He greeted the swarthy man again.

"WHAT IS THIS WORTH TO YOU, AMERICAN?" the man said.

"What?"

"You pay for this. I know it's valuable."

Mustafa felt blood rush up across his chest and into his face. His anger boiled out of control. His legs shook violently. He came closer and burned his eyes into the man. "Give it to me, you goat!"

Holding the briefcase behind him, the man backed up to the wall, shrouded in shadows.

Mustafa trembled, dropped what he carried, jerked the knife out and without taking his eyes off the man's eyes, stabbed him repeatedly in the torso. Mustafa worked his way up the midriff to reach under the ribs to find the heart. A last, deep plunge and the swarthy man jerked once, fell into the dust, and died.

Catching his breath, Mustafa stood back for a moment. The wind blew a greasy piece of paper across the dead body and down a dark alley.

Mustafa grabbed the new case, traded laptops from his corporate briefcase, removed his bloodied robe, dropped the knife and left. He made his way back to the cab. Setting the laptop carefully beside him on the seat, he told the driver to go to the airport.

In spite of the air conditioning in the cab, Mustafa found himself sweating.

THIRTY-TWO

Zehra fought desperately. The early spring heat threatened to kill her plants before they even had a chance to get going. Since the growing season in Minnesota was so short, she was determined to win the battle. They all needed as much water as she could give them.

As she always did when in trouble, she went to her garden. The beauty and peace calmed her, reminded her of larger things in the world, of hope.

The comfort of her extended family, the attention of the FBI, and lots of drugs helped also. The shaking had stopped. Zehra felt good enough to keep going.

The FBI had arrived in the parking lot quickly, promised to investigate, and had assigned an agent to stay close to her. He sat in the lobby downstairs.

She had brought home the parts of the El-Amin case that she wanted to work on, including the video the prosecutor's office had burned onto a DVD. She wanted to see exactly what the killer and the scene looked like.

Like a dumb ox, she just kept moving forward. Zehra didn't know what else to do. At least action took her mind off the fear that haunted her.

BJ was coming to watch it also.

In her mind, Zehra debated whether to call Mustafa. She had already told him about the car bomb. The video wouldn't be of any interest to him and his best help was in penetrating the Somali community. She held the cell phone in her hand, admitting to herself she'd like to see him. Zehra made the call. He said of course, he would come over.

After she clicked off, Zehra's phone buzzed, and she saw her parents' name on the caller ID. *I know what this is about,* she thought.

"Zehra, with all this horrible stuff going on, I forgot to ask how your time with Michael went the other night. How is he?"

Zehra sighed. "Actually, Mom, he's really great. I didn't expect this at all, to be honest, but he's pretty cool."

"How serious are you?"

"Aw, Mom . . . Let's just say, 'I'm interested.'"

"Isn't he smart? Your father likes him and says his reputation at the company is good."

"He is smart and, unlike all the others you've sent my way, he's actually interested in someone besides himself—me. He's even agreed to help me, since he's done work with the Somali people here. Hopefully, he can open some doors. What a coincidence, huh?" Zehra paused, knowing what her mother wanted to hear. "And we've talked about religion. He's a lot more conservative than I'm comfortable with, but he seems to be open to new ideas. So, we'll see."

"I'm so happy for you, Zehra. You deserve someone good. Don't scare him away with your feminist stuff."

"I can handle it. Gotta run, bye."

The security system rang. Zehra buzzed in BJ. In a few minutes, he walked through her door. "Gettin' hot out there," he whistled. He reached around her shoulders and gave her a tight squeeze. His presence was so peaceful. She really needed that now. "How are you, sister?"

Zehra slumped into his arms. "Okay . . . I guess. I'm coming back to some form of normal. In a way, the trial's a welcomed distraction. I can keep going."

"What do you think?"

"Who did it? It's got to be El-Amin's people. Who else?"

"Will you get pulled from the case now?"

"No, I won't be that lucky. I can't prove he was behind this, so I keep the case."

"What can I do?"

"Here, you can help." She handed him the big watering can. "You can start on the hibiscus over there, the big plant with the red flowers." He held the can as if it were radioactive.

Zehra noticed it and said, "Look, Denzel, just tip it and pour."

They worked their way around the deck. "How's Momma?" she asked.

"Holding her own for now. My papa was a cop in Gary. Momma worried every night while she raised the kids. They were both a lot tougher than I am."

"I know what you mean. So were my parents. Hey, when Mustafa gets here, we can take a look at the video," she said.

"Mustafa? He the dude your mother wants you to marry? I thought his name was Michael."

Zehra laughed. "Mustafa's his Arabic name. But don't worry. Right now, I'm just shopping." She told BJ of Mustafa's help at the mosque and the hospital.

"If it's cool for you, go for it but take your time."

"Hey, look who's talking, Mr. ADD," she joked.

The security rang again, and Zehra let Mustafa in. He wore tan slacks, perfectly pressed and a cotton shirt that once again, clung to his muscled body. A heavy silver watch glistened on his wrist when he stuck out his hand to shake with BJ.

He carried a package and set it on the table in the main room. When he came over to Zehra, he touched her shoulder. In spite of her reticence, she needed more than that now. Glancing at the package, he told her, "For later."

"How was Egypt?"

"Hot. The conference was boring and nothing interesting happened."

Zehra moved to the far side of the table and shuffled through the thick files. "I've got the DVD here. BJ, if there's anything you pick out, let me know." BJ sat in the wicker chair next to the TV, but he studied Mustafa instead of the screen.

Zehra pushed in the DVD and clicked the PLAY button. A scratchy, black-and-white scene came on the screen. She could see the edge of the deli, the parking lot below, and a fence. Nothing moved in the scene, but the picture jerked repeatedly.

"Cameras are usually programmed to take shots every two seconds," BJ explained. "Cheaper that way."

About five minutes into the film, the door on the fence opened out into the parking lot. The victim, a young black man, started into the screen. His jerky movements reminded Zehra of watching films from the early days of Hollywood. A bright light from the deli shone from the right side of the scene.

Suddenly, from the same door, another man jumped out. The young one didn't react, so maybe he was unaware of the second man behind him. The second man was dark, tall and wore glasses and a huge white mask over his lower face. He dressed in a colored robe. In one jerk, his left hand reached up to the boy's forehead, yanked it back. Simultaneously, he drew something across the boy's throat. It happened so fast, Zehra couldn't see the knife itself.

The killer wore what looked like latex surgical gloves. She hadn't seen any mention of them in the police reports and wondered why he'd worn them. Why hadn't the police noted their presence? Hadn't they been found at the crime scene?

She shifted in her chair and felt a horrid captivation with what happened on the screen. It sickened her, but she couldn't look away. Thankfully, the film didn't have any sound.

Even with the bad focus and jerking film, it was clear that the boy's head snapped back. The killer jumped out of the way. A black gush of blood exploded from the front of the boy. He staggered ahead one step, faltered, and dropped to the ground like a puppet whose strings had been cut.

The killer lurched out of view to the right.

No one moved in Zehra's room as they watched five more minutes. The boy sprawled on the ground, motionless while a black pool spread out from his head. Otherwise the scene remained completely still.

Zehra found herself breathing fast and deeply. Up until now, the killing had all been on paper. The description of the death, the autopsy, the witness statements, and the police reports of the crime scene—it had held little more emotion than a stack of paper.

The film showed the life and death of a real human being. Zehra couldn't talk for a few minutes.

BJ broke the silence. "What I wonder about are the gloves. Along with the surgical mask, it suggests someone who worked in a hospital or clinic."

"Like the imam?" Mustafa said.

BJ nodded and looked closely at him.

"Why the gloves?" Zehra finally spoke.

"Hide his fingerprints from the weapon, keep the blood off of him," BJ said. "Where are the gloves? Cops found the mask but didn't find any gloves. Curious."

Zehra turned to Mustafa. "I'm so sorry . . . you must think I have a horrible job. I didn't realize it'd be so . . . I didn't mean for you to have to watch."

Mustafa's eyes narrowed. "That's okay. The curved knife cutting the throat upset me." He sighed. "I do not like violence, but I will be okay," he told Zehra as he stood.

BJ cleared his throat. "Got a few clues, Z. I measured the height of the fence, and it looks like the killer was tall, about six feet. El-Amin's a lot shorter. 'Course at the angle of the camera, it's hard to tell, but I'd bet the killer was six feet. Since he wore a robe, hard to tell his body shape. Notice he didn't have African hair. The killer's hair was straight, although he had dark skin."

"Anything else we can pull out of this," Zehra said.

"The top of the killer's face was uncovered except for the glasses. In the film, we couldn't make out much, but the prosecutor's gonna stop each frame and enhance it," BJ said. "The lighting was good, so the still frame should give us a better ID on the killer."

"Your client?" Mustafa asked Zehra.

"No. The DNA doesn't match him, remember? The killer is someone else."

"So, that will solve the case for you?" Mustafa asked.

"Not exactly. That's the job of the police and prosecutor but of course, if we could find the real killer and give the info to them, we'd win our case," Zehra said.

"Does your trial start soon?"

"This Monday." Zehra dropped her shoulders. "We're running out of time."

Mustafa smiled faintly. "Pardon me, I don't understand. If your client's DNA does not match, will he not be released?"

"The prosecutor hasn't had enough time to check out our doctor and the new testing method. Besides, when the trial starts, I have the burden of convincing the judge to allow my test results into evidence before the jury."

"So, you think El-Amin will definitely be convicted?" Mustafa asked.

"Don't know. If our DNA test is admitted, I think he'll walk."

Zehra noticed a frown flashed across Mustafa's face. Maybe he still didn't understand how a trial worked. She started to explain more until he waved a hand to stop her.

"Well," BJ stood and stretched. "Gotta hit the bricks."

It surprised Zehra. "Don't you want to review some of the case now?"

"Naw. I'll be in touch. Not much more I can add here." He nodded at Mustafa, didn't shake his hand, and left.

Zehra slumped into the chair by the deck. "Sorry . . . I wasn't sure you should come over but I wanted to see you." She looked out at the traffic crossing the 35W bridge that had collapsed a couple years ago. Mustafa handed her his gift.

She felt funny about accepting something else from him, but he was so considerate. Most other men thought that giving her a free copy of the NFL schedule for fall was a wonderful gift.

She opened the wrapping paper and the carton. From inside, she lifted out a small, beautiful jewelry box. Dark, lacquered mother-of-pearl covered the outside. It felt smooth and cool in her hands. She opened it to find a silk scarf. Red, yellow, and green colors flowed through the exquisite material. It must have cost a fortune.

Zehra slipped the scarf around her neck and felt the softness of the silk on her skin. She looked up to find Mustafa watching her, his eyes big and alive. She didn't know what to say. "Thanks," she stammered. "It's so beautiful."

"Directly from Egypt. I know the markets and looked for something special for you."

Zehra felt her face redden as heat coursed up from low in her body. She stood slowly and wanted to kiss him in the worst way. As she moved toward him, she reached out, but he leaned back. Zehra opened her eyes and looked at him.

"Not yet. It is proper for a man and woman to get to know one another first."

"This is America, and I want to thank you—my way."

"Soon enough." He stepped away from her again.

She sighed. "Oh . . . all right. But you have to understand this is moving faster than I imagined." She took a deep breath. "Mustafa, these gifts are beautiful. They're some of the nicest things I've ever been given. How thoughtful of you."

He remained quiet awhile. Walked out onto the deck.

Zehra followed him. Felt the hot sun burning down through a clear sky. With their watering, her plants' leaves shone brightly. Those that had drooped and wilted before now stretched up to the life offered by the sun.

Mustafa turned to face her. He reached out to take hold of the ends of the scarf, still draped over Zehra's neck. "I thought this color would look good with your hair."

She sighed. "That's so kind of you."

"I know many American Muslims do not, but would you ever consider wearing this as *hijab*?"

She sighed. "My mother says the same thing." She looked up at him. "No, I can't."

His eyes focused on her and seemed to harden into black dots. "It is your choice, and I respect that."

Zehra raised her arms and dropped them at her sides. "Mustafa, I'm an American. I'm faithful in the way I think is proper. Traditionally, women wore *hijab* to 'protect' them from men. Actually, in my experience, I can handle most of them easily." Tension rose inside her until she looked up at his face and felt everything wilt within.

"I am sorry," he quickly explained. "I was carried away. Of course, American women have their own rights."

"No, that's not it exactly. I interpret the Qur'an the way Allah gives me understanding. In my opinion, that's a ritual determined long ago and really doesn't apply to me today. There are so many more important issues in Islam to focus on. Some that we can work on together." When he frowned, she continued, "Like, how do we get a basically Christian nation to see that we're different from the Muslim terrorists that get in the news so often."

Mustafa nodded and turned toward the condo. "I understand." He started to walk inside until he spotted the plant by the corner of the door. "Beautiful. Hibiscus, is it not?"

Zehra let her breath escape. She walked to the plant. "Yeah. Look at the deep green of the leaves."

"And those huge, red flowers. They are stunning. You should pick one and put it in your hair, then you would both look stunning."

"Do you want to know something weird and beautiful about them?"

"What?"

"Hibiscus flowers bloom once during the day and then every night, the spent blossoms fall off and die."

THIRTY-THREE

P aul forced the meeting with Conway. They crowded into his office at seven in the morning, along with the first deputy, Tony Valentini. Without drinking his coffee, Paul started, "I know you're pissed off at me, Bill."

With his arm propping up his wrinkled face, Conway scowled at Paul.

"Tony said it himself—'I like the smell of this.' We're onto to something." Paul looked at Valentini for support.

"That's right, Bill. You've gotta admit we're into it now. Something big."

When Conway dropped his eyes and sat motionless, Paul knew him well enough to stop talking. Conway's mind, always sharp, was probably clogged with facts, suspicions, pressures, and fears. He struggled to put them into a logical order. Reluctantly, he fought the obvious truth and Paul could imagine Conway testing the truth from various angles.

Conway sighed and looked up from Paul to Valentini. "You're right." He heaved his body up and shook his shoulders. "Shit! I thought we had this sucker wrapped-up. Okay, now what?"

Paul stood up from his chair with his finger extended toward Conway. "We need to find Ammar. Obviously, he's led a double life here."

Conway nodded. "How about the mosque? We'll carpet it with agents. What's our time frame again?"

"Friday. We should also follow-up on the interview I had with the kid at the school and his friends. Find out where Ammar was going to meet them. Stake it out and grab 'em when he shows."

"That'd be the high percentage play," Valentini said.

Conway turned to Paul. "You get back to the school and get that kid to tell you all about the next meeting. I see that as priority number one." He walked closer to Paul so that the smell of cigarettes wafted over him. "And I don't want you to Bogart this thing. You got that, agent?"

Paul started to laugh until he realized Conway was serious. "Right."

"No one talks to the press without approval from me. Tell that to your support, too. I'll fire anyone's ass that leaks one goddamn word." Conway scowled again. He let out a huge breath and ran his hands through his hair. "This is frightening enough for the public. For now, at least, they think we've got the bad guy in jail, waiting for trial. I don't want any possibility of a panic on our hands. This is probably the last big case of my career, and I'm not gonna screw it up."

When Conway turned, Paul knew the meeting was over. They reached for files and empty coffee cups. At the door, Paul stopped. "Bill, I got something I'm wondering about."

"Yeah?"

"What do you know about the U.S. Army Medical Research Institute for Infectious Disease?"

"Never heard of 'em."

"Someone from their agency was at the crime scene of the murder."

Conway's eyes opened wide. "What? Why didn't we know about that?"

"Not only that, they picked up some crime scene evidence."

"Son of a bitch! Who are these guys?"

"Can you get a meeting with them ASAP?"

Conway grabbed for his phone. "Damn right. I'll call now. If I have to, I'll call the director himself to move some asses." He fumbled with his phone. "What the hell's going on with this case? I don't know anything."

Paul called Gennifer Simmons at Hiawatha High School and asked her to have Abraham available for another talk—alone.

Within thirty minutes, he arrived at the school. Simmons and the boy waited in a lounge area at the entrance to the school. Paul hurried in and followed them to an empty room. He closed the door.

"Abraham, all the things you've told us are very important. I don't want you to be scared, but the FBI thinks this scientist who meets with you and your friends is someone we'd like to meet also. Could you tell me more about where you meet?"

Abraham looked at Simmons and back at Paul. He took a deep breath. "Well, it's the mosque in Burnsville, near the mall. There's a community room that people meet in and, well, our group meets back there once a week. He is going to meet us tomorrow." He was so thin, Paul worried that if the clothes draped around him were removed, Abraham would collapse.

"You sure?"

"Yeah. He's really a nice guy. Me and my friends like hanging with him. He talks to us about lots of stuff about being Muslim."

"Oh?"

"Yeah, maybe you wouldn't understand, but my parents work all the time. I never see them. Most of the kids at school, when they hear I'm Somali, they walk away. They don't like us. And the American blacks don't like us . . . so, it's kind of lonely. Mr. Kamal was nice to us. We talked about things like that."

"What were you going to do at your meeting?"

Abraham shrugged. "All my friends want to go, so I guess I want to go, too."

As Paul took notes, Abraham gave him the directions to the mosque. Satisfied he'd gotten all the information he could from Abraham, he said, "I don't think it'd be a good idea for you to go back."

Abraham's face twisted.

"I know you want to, and there may be times in the future you can but not this time, okay?"

Abraham's eyes came up to meet Paul's, but he didn't agree.

Simmons broke in. "Abraham's going to present his project at the Science Fair tomorrow night." She turned to him and smiled.

"What's that?" Paul asked.

"All the high schools in the area are having Science Day to promote math and the sciences. Hundreds of students participate, and it's open to the public."

Before Paul left the school, he pulled Gennifer Simmons aside. "Do you know his parents?"

"I've never met them. Most of the Somali parents work very hard and don't have much time to come to school conferences. That's why these kids are so lonely and cut-off. They're desperate to fit in somehow. These families are close and loving but the parents have to work two or three jobs to support them. I'll try to find Abraham's."

Paul gripped her arm. He looked at her. "Even if you have to take him home with you the next couple nights, you should do whatever you can to keep him away from the mosque. Trust me, it's dangerous."

Color flushed into her cheeks, and she took a sharp breath. "Okay."

Paul left the school and drove toward the mosque. While he turned onto the freeway, his cell rang. It was Zehra Hassan. She was crying. "What's up?" he said.

"Uh . . . my car . . . Paul . . . I can't believe it . . ."

"What?"

"They blew up my car!"

Paul had difficulty concentrating on his driving. He'd been so busy he hadn't heard about it. "Has the FBI been notified?"

"Yeah . . . everyone's been here . . ."

"Zehra, I'm right in the middle of something big. Do whatever the agents tell you."

"I have to keep going. The trial's still starting in a few days. You know anything else? Paul, what the hell's going on? I'm losing my mind." Her voice cracked with hysteria. "I was doing ok, then just collapsed. Can't help it, I'm scared."

"Zehra, I don't know any more than you do," he lied to her. "I always thought this was a lot bigger than your client. And now we've got some leads."

"What? What leads?"

Paul sighed and weighed the harm in telling her what he was doing. It didn't seem to be connected with the defense of her client. He said, "We're following up on a suspect, a Pied Piper, who's getting some Somali boys together at a mosque in Burnsville real soon. We're not sure why, but we're breaking it down right now."

"Good for you." She paused. "Maybe this guy is the real killer, not El-Amin."

He felt a rush of emotion flood into his body. How many times in the past had he longed to comfort her, to hold her? It hadn't worked out for them, but the longing still remained. He thrust the thoughts away. No time for that now.

"Don't know if there's any connection. Hey, Zehra, I'd like to talk more, but I gotta run." She agreed and hung up

Paul circled the block until he saw the small sign for the mosque. Like many Muslim groups in Minnesota, they didn't have the money for a fancy mosque. This one occupied the end unit of a one-story row of offices. From his drive around the back side, Paul found several cars parked there.

He stopped in the front, made sure he had his badge out, checked the Glock under his arm, and stepped out of the car. A tall ash tree covered the corner of the building and leaned over the roof. Bright green leaves dotted the branches. Cardinals flitted from branch to branch as Paul approached.

When he got to the door, he knocked.

Paul rapped harder. He peered in through the dirty window in the door. Finally, a lone man shuffled toward the front. When he reached the door, he pulled it open slowly. He wore a tan skull cap, had a long black beard, and a full-length brown robe.

Paul lifted his badge and stuck it in the man's face. "FBI. I'd like to talk to you."

The man squinted at the badge as if near sighted. "What do you want?"

"Anyone in charge. I'm looking for a man named Mr. Kamal or Ammar, a scientist, who'll have a group of boys here in a day or two."

The man stretched himself to his full height. His black skin glistened in the sunlight. Without speaking, he gazed at Paul. Finally, he said, "I do not know anyone. He is not here. Good-bye."

Before Paul could jam his foot into the open door, it slammed shut.

Paul realized he was breathing deeply. Frustrated, there was nothing more he could do at this point without a warrant. At least, the man's actions confirmed what they all suspected. Mr. Kamal was going to bring the boys here in two days. Paul felt elated.

Back in his car, Paul called Conway. "Bill, I'm at the mosque in Burnsville. This is the hot spot. We'll need a stake-out immediately, and we've got to move fast."

"Great work, Paul. I want you back here right now."

Something in Conway's voice bothered Paul. "Huh? I told you, I'm out here and I'll handle surveillance until the team arrives."

"Get back here now."

"What's going on?"

"I've got a meeting starting in ten minutes. I got through to the Army Medical Research Institute. They're meeting with us, along with ICE."

"But . . . the mosque . . ."

Conway dropped his voice and spoke slowly. "Paul, we'll get someone out there as soon as we can. In the meantime, you're gonna want to be here . . ."

THIRTY-FOUR

We haven't got a lot of time," Zehra reminded BJ while they sat in her office. "I've got a meeting with Harmon in ten minutes. Coming along?"

"I'm with you all the way, Z."

When they walked outside her office, they crumpled under the oppressive blast of wind and humidity. An FBI agent assigned to Zehra followed a few steps behind them.

"Something's wrong with this weather," BJ said. "Storm must be coming."

They crossed the street and took the elevator in the Government Center to the County Attorney's office. BJ didn't say anything during the ride.

"What's up? Out too late last night, listening to music?" Zehra asked him.

He shook his head. "Naw."

Her thoughts returned to Mustafa, to the feel of his smooth skin and the smell of it. She tried to place the fragrance . . . sandalwood cologne maybe. She wondered what he was doing right now and longed to see him again. Her loneliness lifted for a moment.

In a few minutes, they met with Steve Harmon in his office.

"Have a seat, guys." His face softened. "Hey, Zehra, sorry to hear about you. Are you okay?" He paused, then said, "Any last minute things we should cover?" He sat back and crossed his arms over his chest. "Judge Goldberg's anxious to get the trial started."

Zehra leaned forward. "Yeah, Steve, there is something. We watched the video of the crime scene yesterday and noticed the gloves. Have you seen it yet?"

"Uh . . . yeah, of course. Gloves? I guess I don't remember any gloves . . . heh, heh," he forced a laugh.

Zehra knew he hadn't seen the film. "The killer wore gloves. Latex from the look of them. Why? More critical, where are they? Are you holding out on us?"

Harmon's eyes opened wide. "Don't ever accuse me of anything unethical," he shouted. "I've given you all the Discovery material I have."

"Then, where did the gloves go?"

"Maybe El-Amin kept them and tossed 'em later."

"The killer dropped the mask, why not the gloves?"

Harmon stood and moved around his desk. "How the hell should I know? I don't need any gloves to get the conviction."

"You've got to admit," Zehra said, "this is an odd murder—the type of mask, gloves, glasses. It's more than a disguise."

"You can argue your case in court. To me, it's simple—a cold-blooded murder of an innocent young man."

No one spoke for a while.

Zehra said, "Can we get a look at the evidence in the property room?"

"Sure. I've already called ahead. Sergeant Miller's waiting for us."

In ten minutes, they'd all gone down the elevator to the second floor of the Government Center, crossed under the street in the tunnel past the cafeteria, and come up in the massive City Hall where the police department had its headquarters. In the basement, they stopped at a worn wooden door with a frosted glass window in the top half. Large letters stenciled on the window told them it was the property room.

As they walked through it, Sergeant Miller came out from a secured door and shook hands all around. He smiled broadly when he saw BJ. "Hey, dude, still on the wrong side, huh?"

"Pays better," BJ lied. "Everything's cool. By the way, nice threads," he joked about the officer's uniform with the frayed blue shirt cuffs.

"Budget cuts." Miller led them back into the large room. Rows of metal shelves towered around them as they worked their way deeper into the room. Each shelf held dozens of banker's boxes, numbered and marked with the name of the case they came from. They were filled with exhibits for hundreds of cases.

Other than the clopping of their shoes on the cement floor, silence hung in the air like old dust.

After four turns, Miller stopped and reached for the appropriate box. "Here it is," he grunted. Although a younger man, he looked like he'd been in the basement, alone with the boxes, a long time. His skin seemed as dry as the shelves, and his left eye twitched unnaturally every once in a while.

He carried the box to a small metal table at the end of the row. "I've almost got everything down here computerized now. We're getting some of that federal drug-bust money to help us upgrade things. It's a bitch to convert it all from those old files to computers, and no one appreciates all the work I've done."

Since forensics had already analyzed the evidence, they could touch it with bare hands. Miller lifted out various items. Most of the things had been taken from El-Amin's apartment or found at the crime scene. Some items, like the mask, had been sent to the BCA for testing. *It should have been back here, but the case loads were so heavy, no one had gotten around to returning it*, Zehra thought.

She watched as shirts, shoes, pants, a pair of glasses that resembled the ones in the video, and the curved knife were laid on the table.

The knife was unusual. From a long handle, the blade curved slightly, resembling a scimitar. It had been tested for blood samples, revealing the victim's blood type. Nothing else, including fingerprints, was found on it.

Zehra held it in her hands. A shiver ran through her when she thought of what had been done with this weapon. Who had held it? she wondered. As she turned it back and forth, the fluorescent lights from the ceiling glistened off the shiny blade. A similar light flashed across her mind. There was something . . . something she tried to remember. About the knife? After a few moments, Zehra gave up, hoping her memory would come clear later.

After rummaging through all the items, Zehra and BJ thanked Miller and left with Harmon.

Outside the door, Zehra asked, "Hey, Steve, got time for coffee?"

"Too busy fighting crime. Thanks anyway. At least you got Judge Goldberg."

"He'll do a good job."

"Aw . . . he hasn't got any balls." Steve walked away.

BJ said, "That offer of coffee good for me, Z?"

"As long as you're paying."

In fifteen minutes they sat in a Caribou Coffee shop on the second floor skyway. It connected the Government Center to most of the downtown area. With the brutal winters and steamy summers in Minnesota, the skyways bustled with life as the entire city flooded into them.

They reminded Zehra of the ant farm she had as a child. The ants scurried through the narrow passageways on their way to work or food. Similarly, people moved in lines through the skyways for the same reasons.

BJ licked the foam off his upper lip from his latte. His eyes flicked up to Zehra's. He cleared his throat. "Uh . . . Z, I got something to say to you."

Zehra could tell he was serious. He dropped his usual smile, and the brightness in his eyes dulled. She set down her cup. "What? What's up?"

"Well, it's none of my business of course, but like my momma always told me, 'If you got something to say, say it.'"

She waited.

"It's about your friend, Mustafa."

Zehra sucked in her breath. "Denzel, look, we got a lot to do in the next couple days. Can it wait?"

"Sure, but I gotta say it quick." He looked at the settling foam in his cup and then to Zehra. "He's lying to you."

She jerked back. "What do you mean?"

"I don't know what it's about, but you know my FACs training. At least I can tell when somebody's probably lying."

Zehra wrestled with her emotions. Sure, she didn't know Mustafa well, but so what? That was the whole purpose of dating. "Maybe because he's foreign, his way of talking and expressions are different than ours."

"Don't make any difference. The signals are universal." He leaned forward and reached out to her. "I know how you feel about him, but I have to warn you." His hand covered hers. "You don't know this guy, and, well, he's foreign, like you say. You know I got your back."

"Yeah, but I can't think about it now." She waved her hand in front of them. "Too much dropped on me . . ." She looked at BJ's eyes and found them wet and shiny again. "I'll be careful. Thanks for always thinking about me."

He shrugged and stood. "I got a few errands. I'm still gonna see if we can find the missing imam."

Zehra nodded as he left.

She sighed and tried to think straight. With the trial and all its problems, it was difficult to sort through her emotions. Maybe in her thrill of meeting such an attractive Muslim man, she'd missed things she'd normally spot. Of course, he was too conservative, and Zehra worried about his flexibility.

At times, he'd been patronizing toward BJ. Was it racism? Was BJ reacting to that without recognizing it himself? Was it the immense cultural differences between Americans and Egyptians?

Zehra had agreed to meet Mustafa for a quick dinner later. She looked forward to it and hoped things would work out. But BJ was good at what he did. She decided to at least look at Mustafa more critically.

HER PHONE RANG. It was BJ again.

"Zehra, girl. I'm picking you up in three minutes." He sounded out of breath.

"What?"

"Coppers found the missing imam. My pals called me and we're going to the crime scene."

In twenty minutes, they squealed into a three story parking ramp on the West Bank, near the hospital where the imam had worked in the supply room. They bounded out of BJ's car and ran to a circle of squad cars, Medical Examiner's van, yellow tape, and a few reporters.

Carolyn Bechter was there and waved to Zehra.

As she and BJ closed in on the activity, a cop in uniform came out to meet them. "BJ," he said. "Gotta stay back."

"Thanks for the call. What's shakin'?"

"A citizen saw the car parked here and thought there was an unusually big pool of oil underneath it. When he got closer, he saw it was blood. Looks like the killer backed the car over the pool after killing the victim. To hide it. They're tire tracks in the blood."

"Where's the imam?"

"Trunk. It's his own car. M.E. says he's been there a couple days."

"Leads?"

The cop shrugged his shoulders.

"Lemme take a quick look."

The cop looked back and forth. Sighed and said, "Okay. But just a minute. I'll get my ass whooped."

"Yeah."

BJ and Zehra moved slowly toward the car. As they got closer, Zehra saw the trunk standing open and a lumpy form stretched out inside. A pallid white hand with dirty fingernails hung over the edge. She started to shake.

BJ stopped and put his arm around her. "Okay, Z?"

Taking a deep breath, she nodded yes.

They came up from the side of the car. A tech bent over the body. She worked on something and then stood up. When she moved to the side, BJ squirmed to the end of the trunk. Zehra moved beside him. She forced herself to look at the body.

Just a glance was enough. She felt sick and her knees began to buckle. She gagged on the fear rising from within her body.

The imam's head flopped back at an unnatural angle. His neck had been sliced open from ear to ear, penetrating deeply into his throat. It was an identical wound like the one that killed the young Somali boy, the victim in her case.

SEVERAL HOURS LATER, Zehra met Mustafa at a small Thai restaurant across the street from the Guthrie Theatre. BJ had stayed with her for awhile until she felt calm again. She wanted to see Mustafa, to get away from all the blood and killings she'd seen lately. When he insisted on meeting, she readily agreed. Zehra walked the few blocks from her office and arrived sticky from the humidity.

As she stepped into the air conditioning, she fluffed her blouse and ran her hands through her hair to lift it off her shoulders. Zehra normally would have put it up but thought it looked better down for now.

Mustafa, handsome as ever, stood in the corner and came to her quickly. He opened his arms toward her.

Zehra paused, worried that she was a little sweaty.

When he touched her arms, for a moment, she wondered about him, hoping BJ was wrong.

As he pulled back, his eyes opened into a smile. "You look hot and starved." He caught himself. "I did not mean 'hot' like . . ."

"Of course, you didn't," she laughed and followed him to the table. It felt good to laugh, to have a man look at you and tell you he liked what he saw. She relaxed and tried to clear her mind of every horrible event of the past days.

He had already ordered chicken satay. They sat, and Zehra launched into the food, surprised at how hungry she was until she remembered she'd missed lunch.

While they ate, Mustafa asked dozens of questions. The waiter brought an order of vegetable curry and Pad Woon Sen, a noodle dish with shrimp that Mustafa had ordered previously for her. For a moment, this bothered her, but his formality was sweet, thoughtful. She let it slide.

Suddenly, BJ's words echoed in her head. Was Mustafa more interested than normal? Was he simply curious about her work? When she met people and told them what she did, they usually reacted with fascination. Maybe Mustafa was like them.

"You seem so interested in this trial. Is there a reason?" she asked.

His eyes dropped to the table for an instant and flicked back to her. "I am interested in anything you do. There are few Muslim women in my country who are like you."

Impressed, Zehra still pushed on. "But I'm wondering why."

"Why? There is nothing special. It is you."

Her thoughts twisted. Was BJ correct or was he too critical? To stall for time, she leaned over her plate and twirled some noodles around her chopsticks. When she looked up, her body shuddered. Mustafa's expression had changed to something Zehra'd never seen before. The look slipped away quickly, but it left her shaken. She leaned back in her chair.

His voice resumed the pleasant tone of before. "All right, if you insist. Let us talk about me for a while." He told her of his volunteer work at three mosques with younger people.

"As I have told you, Islamic scientists used to be the best in the world, many centuries ago. One of my missions in life is to resurrect that leadership. I work with younger Muslims to encourage them to go into the sciences. No one else does that for them."

"What do you do?"

"Science fairs are coming up tomorrow at many of the schools. In cooperation with my company, the schools let us scientists help the kids with their projects." He lifted his shoulders. "This is how I can help them."

"How wonderful."

His head tilted up. "Maybe you would be interested in visiting with them."

"When?"

"Tomorrow, Friday afternoon." He stopped. "I forgot. You are probably too busy for that. On the other hand, it may be interesting for you. I could pick you up."

Zehra paused. The work required for the trial grew larger, but in the back of her mind small suspicions, like the new weeds in her pots at home, poked their way out. She had to find out the truth about him. Zehra smiled. "Sure, I'd love to come."

But before she went, she'd call BJ with the details just in case.

THIRTY-FIVE

When Paul returned to the FBI office in downtown Minneapolis, he could feel humid hints of a coming storm. As he walked into the lobby, a similar sense of tension struck him. It wasn't so much the level of noise or activity as it was the lack of both.

Conway's voice had a panicky edge to it and this time, he hadn't yelled at Paul. Something was wrong.

He hurried to the conference room to find Conway pacing back and forth. Several people Paul didn't recognize surrounded Conway. Paul was surprised to see Joan Cortez, standing in the corner.

He walked up to her and said quietly, "What are you doing here?"

She didn't look him in the eye. "We've been pulled in, too. You better listen."

Nervous conversations rose from pods of people around the table until Conway cleared his throat. "Listen up, everybody." In a second, the crowd went silent. Paul could feel the electricity in the air.

"Folks," Conway began, "this is Dr. Stanley Samson from the USAMRIID."

"The what?" asked someone from the back.

A man who looked like a college professor stood up next to Conway. Short white hair bristled over his scalp. He wore a button-down shirt with a striped tie. He carried a coffee cup with stained brown edges from all the coffee it had held. Immense wire-rimmed glasses hid a small face with blue eyes. He moved slowly in contrast to Conway.

"I'm Dr. Samson from the U.S. Army Medical Research Institute for Infectious Disease." He lifted his eyes to look around the room. "Haven't heard of us, huh?" He grinned. "Just call us RID."

Dr. Samson lifted a thin arm and waved it toward a group of drab looking people who stood to the side of the conference table. "My team. We don't have much time, so I'll cut the crap and make this short. We've been in existence since 1969. Our mission is to research biological threats to the military and develop strategies for medical defense against the threats that require containment. Of course, our work usually includes the defense of the civilian population, also."

Conway, always needing attention, stepped forward. "You'd be surprised to learn they have over 200 scientists working in their labs at Ft. Detrick, in Maryland. We got involved in the wake of nine-eleven. Remember, there were several anthrax threats in the form of mailings to senators and people in Washington?"

When heads nodded, Dr. Samson continued, "As a result, we evaluated over 30,000 samples. We initiated Operation Noble Eagle, which required our country to expand its capacity for threat agent identification by tenfold." Dr. Samson's face lit-up. "And we did it."

Valentini spoke, "Is this about an anthrax scare? I haven't heard anything."

Dr. Samson furrowed his eyebrows and shook his head back and forth. "Not so simple, I'm afraid to say." He sipped coffee.

Paul felt his insides squeeze tighter. Something bad was coming.

Looking around him, Dr. Samson said, "Don't repeat this, but we were taken by surprise, frankly. Until the message came from our Russian counterparts at Vector, we would never have guessed . . ."

"Vector?" Conway asked.

"Sorry. I'll back up, but we don't have much time so keep your questions short," the doctor said. He shifted from one leg to the other and looked down into his coffee cup.

When he looked up, he spoke quickly. "Smallpox was eradicated from the planet in 1979 according to the World Health Organization. However, two repositories were established to contain the smallpox virus, called by its scientific name Variola, for future research purposes. One is located in Atlanta at the Center for Disease Control and the other is in eastern Russia. It's called Vector."

Paul glanced at the people around him. No one moved or sat down.

Dr. Samson continued, "Vector was chosen because the Soviets had established a top-secret biological warfare research lab there during the Cold War. It was only natural to continue to use the facilities. President Richard Nixon officially halted all biological warfare research in this country in 1969. The Soviets agreed to halt theirs also." He pursed his lips and shook his head. "They lied. In fact, as late at the 1980s, they were actively assembling biological weapons.

"Once the communists fell, our government moved into Vector and set up joint research projects, mostly to monitor their work. In fact, the complex is under military guard and has a security system built by the Bechtel Group and paid for by our government. Today, Vector stills conducts research as we do in our labs in Atlanta and Ft. Detrick."

Conway asked, "I thought you said only Atlanta has the small pox virus?"

"That's correct. We just do research. Atlanta and Vector are the only places on earth where the virus is kept in deep freeze storage. By the nineties, we learned the old

Soviet Union had a culture collection of extremely virulent Variola strains and they were manufacturing it by the ton."

"So, what's the problem?" Valentini said.

"I'm getting to that. Our defense department actually funds much of the present research at Vector in order to have access and to control it. We received word two weeks ago that a sample of the smallpox virus and the vaccine against it had been stolen from the secured facility."

"Where'd it go?"

Samson shrugged. "Disappeared. The Russians are questioning all employees but that's a lot of people. As of now, they don't have any answers."

"So . . . what's that mean for us?" Valentini asked slowly. "After being frozen, are these samples dangerous?"

"As a rule, the Soviet scientists preferred to manufacture their viruses in dry, powder form. That wasn't true of Variola because the liquid form retained its viability for months when deep frozen and would be extremely stable if converted to aerosol form. That means the stolen samples are probably extremely hot."

"Huh?"

"Dangerous, contagious," Dr. Samson said. "The Soviets had a three hundred gallon tank that looked like the hot water heater in your home. I've seen it. They filled it with live kidney cells from African green monkeys and pumped in smallpox. They ran it at warm temperatures and in a few days, the reactor became hot with amplified smallpox."

Paul could tell people still failed to catch on to the danger. When Dr. Samson looked around the room, he didn't get any reaction.

Dr. Samson continued, "A single run of the reactor could've produced one hundred trillion lethal doses of smallpox—enough to give everyone in the world about two thousand infective doses. It would be easy for someone to draw off samples that could've been freeze-dried in small vials and easily carried anywhere in the world. I'm sure you remember that smallpox invades the respiratory system from human to human. It's spread by coughing, sneezing, saliva, anything that can be airborne. So, it's easy to transmit and wouldn't take a lot of the sample to start a pandemic."

"And," Conway interrupted, "you think the samples are here."

Dr. Samson stopped to sip his coffee. He swallowed slowly. "Yes."

"What evidence do you have?" Valentini demanded.

"When the young Somali man was killed a few months ago, the local Immigration and Customs Enforcement agents were alerted, as they'd been tracking these young men for months. Agent Cortez," he nodded at Joan, "worried there may be something more to the murder since he returned to the country, rather than stay in Somalia to fight like the others. In turn, she alerted our contract scientist in Minneapolis to accompany her to the crime scene."

Paul stared at Joan. She refused to catch his eyes. He was furious. When they'd met, she hadn't lied exactly, but certainly left out big chunks of what she knew. Paul forced himself to calm down. He'd deal with that problem later.

Dr. Samson continued, "Several things struck us as odd—the use of the medical mask. Of course, it could've been a disguise, but the killer used a respirator designed to prevent the spread of air borne contaminants. He wore glasses. We also found latex gloves, worn by the killer, at the crime scene. To prevent fingerprints? Maybe, but could they have been worn as a further protection against a contagious disease?"

"I still don't see how this evidence is conclusive," Valentini said.

"We agreed. Up to that point, the evidence was curious but not much more. For a while we stopped our investigation. We really didn't know what else to do until we remembered an autopsy had been done on the victim. We contacted the Medical Examiner's office here and obtained the records and specimens from the autopsy. When we viewed the tissue remains, we clearly saw the results of a Variola invasion."

"What? You're saying the victim had smallpox?"

"That's exactly what I'm saying," Dr. Samson answered. "So, the question became—if small pox doesn't exist in the world, how did the young man contract it? Again, we were shocked but didn't know where to turn."

"Wouldn't the victim infect others?" Conway said.

"Depends on the incubation period. Normally, it's two weeks. It takes a while for the patient to be contagious. Maybe the young man was killed just before that point."

"So, Doctor, where the hell does this leave us? And what can we do to help?" Conway crossed his arms over his chest and spread his legs.

"Thanks to your agents, Bill, we just learned that some scientist was talking to young Somali men at the mosque."

"You think he's going to introduce smallpox?" Conway's eyes opened wider. "We're already tracking this guy and have the probable insertion point under constant surveillance. Well, it will be. But what I don't get, is how's he gonna do it?"

Dr. Samson shook his head. "We don't know. Smallpox is highly adaptable to the human body and is considered to be the worst human disease. It's estimated to have killed more people than any other infectious pathogen in history."

People around the table shifted uncomfortably. Some looked into their coffee cups and drank. Murmurs bubbled around the room. Finally, Valentini spoke, "I don't know . . . I mean, I'm not a doctor, but I remember the anthrax scare. Turned out to be a lot of fear and not much substance. How can this guy carry out such a plan?"

"You make an excellent point. Before an outbreak of smallpox could occur, two major problems must be overcome. One, the terrorist must get a hold of the Variola virus and be able to transport it. Until the theft in Russia, that hadn't been accomplished by anyone that we know of, although we suspect several other countries have secret stockpiles they've purchased on the black market. Second, the person must develop a delivery method. That's where we're at now. Would they dump the virus in drinking water, drop a bomb of it on New York? To make it harder, the Variola virus can live outside the human body for up to several months. We're wracking our brains trying to anticipate how a terrorist would deliver the virus."

Conway's assistant came into the room. He told her, "Get the director and notify the Strategic Information Operations Center in Washington." She nodded and left immediately. Conway held up his hands. "Folks, let's take a break to clear our heads. We need to all be at our best for this."

Paul's phone vibrated. "What's up, Zehra? I'm very busy."

"Sorry. I just wondered if you knew anything about a pair of latex gloves at the crime scene?"

"Uh . . . no," he lied. "I've got lots of other problems. I can't tell you much, but I want you to be careful. Stay away from Burnsville for the next few days."

"What are you talking about?"

"We suspect uh . . . uh a problem may occur at the mosque there. Gotta run." He clicked off.

As people wandered out of the room, Paul approached Joan. He cornered her near the window that looked out over downtown Minneapolis. He asked her, "Why? I realize you've got your secrets, stuff you can't tell me, but this wasn't a small item."

"Paul, most of this is so highly classified. I couldn't even write it in my own diary."

"I don't believe that."

"Well, whatever you believe, I was instructed to be careful with the intel."

"But you were at the crime scene. Why didn't you tell me that?"

"Because of the evidence we found."

"Joan, this is bullshit."

She interrupted him. "National security is all I can say."

"I work for the god damn FBI! National security's what we do, or did you forget? You knew how serious this case is to all of us."

Joan sighed. "I've got my career to think of. If ICE busts this, I'm golden. I gave you the things I could give you." She looked up at him. For a moment, her eyes softened. "Sorry. Shit happens."

"I don't . . ." Paul shook his head and turned away. Once again, ambition trumped cooperation and unfortunately, national security. Maybe now that everyone was literally in the same room, they could operate together. He walked away without saying another word.

Back at the conference table, many people had returned and sat in the chairs or stood. Valentini said, "I get how this works, Doc. But, do you really think it's gonna be a problem? I mean, if smallpox has been eradicated, we can just snuff this out and we're done, right?"

Dr. Samson's eyes lifted slowly. He unwrapped a Snickers candy bar and took a big bite. He looked at his team grouped into one corner. He looked back at Valentini. "Agent, I don't think you understand the gravity of the threat. You'd better sit down for this."

THIRTY-SIX

Friday morning, Mustafa rushed from his second house to the mosque in the northern suburb. He knew the drop house had been discovered. He must move quickly now before the FBI found out any more.

Luckily, he had access to information through Zehra. He paused to think about her. In a different time and a different place, maybe she could have . . . he dismissed the thought abruptly. She would never submit to him as a faithful Muslim woman should.

For now, he must keep that channel open and pretend to be interested in her. He knew she had become suspicious. Mustafa planned to keep her fooled until the end. He'd dispose of her like the rest, a sacrifice she would make for Allah.

She had called him a few minutes ago with more valuable information. For some reason, Zehra also wanted the exact location of the school where they would go for the science fair tonight. Mustafa assured her that he would drive and return her home early. Her brazen questioning bothered him, but he'd been smart enough to let her talk. She revealed that she'd contacted the FBI. Mustafa learned they had discovered the southern mosque. If they had not already flooded the area, they would soon. Since Mustafa had worked at three mosques with three different groups of kids, it didn't make any difference anyway. He wouldn't be there.

Instead, the science fair would be crowded with hundreds of people.

Would Zehra inadvertently tell the FBI? Mustafa worried about the possibility, but she still did not connect him with anything of interest to the FBI. He was probably safe for now. That was why he had to keep her with him tonight—so he could control her movements and communication.

It would work perfectly.

He ran over the details. Because many of the private companies had such good relations with the schools, he was given free access to the building anytime he wanted it. Mustafa had purposely spent time wandering in the basement of his school to the point the maintenance people ignored him.

In twenty minutes, Mustafa pulled his Benz up to the faculty parking lot of Hiawatha High School. He got out, locked up, and hurried into the school. It was between classes, so the halls were full of students. Mustafa walked to the main office and checked in. The receptionist recognized him.

"Hey, Dr. A. Nice to see you again. Ready for tonight? I'm like, so excited to see all these projects."

He nodded at the stupid woman and hurried past her with the ID she handed him. She deserved to be one of the first to go, he thought.

He had already made precautions to avoid exposure during the release. In addition, he'd already taken the vaccine that came with the package in order to immunize himself, just in case.

He walked to a long hallway at the end of the building and let himself through a door that led downstairs to the extensive spaces underneath the school. The area was used for storage mostly. Mustafa looked for the air ducts he'd found earlier. Although he'd gone over this many times, he would inspect it all again.

He reached a corner of the lower level directly below the classroom where he and his students would present their projects. He looked at the vents on the outer walls to make certain they were open and clear, as he did also with the return vents in the center walls.

Next, he went over to the air pump attached to the return vents. He flicked it on and went back upstairs. Today the room was not used, which was why Mustafa picked that one to have his students occupy tonight. He had unencumbered access now. Lighting a match, he held it in front of the vent and watched as the air pulled the flame down toward the basement. It would create a negative pressure condition in the room to assure the process worked efficiently and quickly.

Back in the basement, he shut off that pump and inspected the aerosolization device attached to the inflow air ducts from the air conditioning. He also turned on that pump. It hummed quietly. Mustafa repeated the match test upstairs and found air blowing hard out of the vents in the room.

He decided to launch it at precisely eight o'clock when he calculated the maximum number of visitors would be present.

He had personally devised the special equipment that would take the dried sample and vaporize it with just enough moisture to adhere to the respiratory tracts of the boys and every single one of the hundreds who would trudge through the classroom. Mustafa had designed it to release a prescribed amount for two hours—plenty of time and quantity to infect them all easily. And with the high concentrations, the incubation period in people would be considerably shortened.

The unsuspecting people would not smell anything or feel anything until the symptoms showed up in a few days. Even then, it would seem like the flu, and Mustafa doubted any doctor would know enough to make an accurate diagnosis—at least not quickly enough.

Back in their homes and schools, the people would be unbelievably hot and lethal. That was the key to the plan. By the time the authorities figured out what happened and where the epicenter was, the second transmission would have occurred. The supply of vaccine in the United States was inadequate for that stage of an epidemic, and it would be impossible for them to contain the spread. The multiplier effect would take care of everything else. Nothing devised by mankind could stop the explosion.

Mustafa felt his groin tighten at the prospect. To further protect himself, he would leave the country to view the carnage from afar. He detested suicide bombers as crude and limited in their effect. His way would shock the entire world. The casualties would be immense and would lead to mass chaos. It would bring about the kingdom of Allah in the heartland of the infidel.

He stopped and sat on a stool in the classroom to savor the moment. All the years, the planning, study, the double life he had led, the fools he had to pretend to enjoy, the enormous costs to obtain the samples, and the risks weighed on him. He felt sweat moisten his forehead. When he reached up to wipe it off, his hand trembled.

Almost all alone, he would bring the victory for Allah and revenge!

THIRTY-SEVEN

While Valentini trudged back and forth in the conference room at FBI headquarters, Dr. Samson sat on the opposite side of the large table. He invited others to sit. Paul was too nervous. He wanted to catch every word. What was unfolding shocked him beyond anything he'd imagined. He hoped to God the scientists had some answers.

Dr. Samson had filled his coffee mug from the carafe in the corner. "We were talking about the technical difficulties facing a criminal. First, they'd have to obtain the virus, and they'd need the help of a scientist who understood how to deal with it. We assume that's already been accomplished. Next, they'd need a vaccine to protect themselves and they'd need a delivery system."

"Why not just drop a bomb?" Valentini asked.

"Maybe. In 1965 Army experts conducted secret field experiments to asses the country's vulnerability to a smallpox attack. They ran the test at Washington's National Airport where they fitted briefcases with small aerosol generators that sprayed a harmless fake, like the release from a bomb that had the same properties as smallpox. The results were disturbing—one out of every twelve people passing through the airport would have become infected, rapidly dispersing the contagious disease around the country." He crumpled another Snickers wrapper and set in on the table. "It would be almost as bad as eating candy bars all the time," he chuckled until he realized no one responded.

"Today, it's much different. Security's tighter," Paul added. He wanted to be convinced the problem with Michael Ammar was as bad as it seemed.

"True. But since then, the world has grown more vulnerable to the disease. Considering that routine vaccination of Americans ended in 1972 and the rest of the world in 1984, and the fact the immunity of those who were vaccinated decays in about eight to ten years, we have a nation that is totally vulnerable to the virus."

"How much of a spread are we talking about here, Doc?" Valentini said.

"Given the technical problems a terrorist faces, the risk of reintroduction of Variola remains quite low—but it's not zero. If they were able to deliver the virus, and I repeat 'if,' the results would be catastrophic."

"Why's that?" Conway spoke up. He took deep breaths, and Paul could tell he needed a cigarette badly.

Dr. Samson stood and paced to the window. He turned and said, "When epidemiologists study the spread of diseases, they have models that can tell them how fast a disease will spread. The main figure they concentrate on is the number of people who will contract the disease from an infected person. It's called 'R-zero' or the multiplier of the disease. It tells them how fast the disease will spread.

"In a modern country like the U.S. with mass transportation, shopping malls, public schools, a mobile population, the multiplier is between three and twenty. Meaning an infected person could give it to three or as many as twenty people. We don't know for sure." Dr. Samson moved to a white board near the table. He picked up a red marker and started to write.

No one interrupted him.

"Let's say smallpox has a multiplier of five, which may be low. The spread of the disease will be explosive because five multiplied by itself every two weeks—the incubation period—can reach millions of cases in a few months without any control." He drew the figures on the board. "It's like a forest fire that expands faster and faster as it feeds on itself in an explosive transmission through a population of people with no immunity." After he finished the numbers on the board he sat down.

Paul felt a growing panic. He looked around the room at all the pale faces.

"But as I understand these things," Conway said, "wouldn't you put up a fire ring around the outbreak and vaccinate everyone possible? Kind of like how we fight forest fires?"

Samson nodded. "Classic response. The CDC has stockpiled millions of doses of vaccine, but since they haven't really been tested, we don't know how effective it would be. And the vaccine is actually a type of pox. That means it could have adverse effects on the recipients, including death from the vaccine itself." He poked the air with his finger. "Can you imagine quarantining everyone in the Twin Cities to their homes for two weeks or more while the medical teams vaccinated everyone? That's how we'd build the ring around the outbreak."

Heads around the table started to nod.

"If we can't contain it quickly enough, we lose and the virus takes off. You see, smallpox isn't like a cannon shooting one shell and doing limited damage. The virus is designed to go out of control, to kill as many people as possible, anywhere it can find human hosts. You asked about anthrax before . . . we can deal with that because it's not transmitted by people. Smallpox is just the opposite. It's transmitted by respiratory secretions conveyed by coughing, sneezing, or wiping your hand across your nose and touching someone else."

Paul shifted his weight from side to side. Nervous. "Wouldn't these cases be caught by the person's doctor? And stopped right there?" he asked.

Dr. Samson removed his big glasses. "Maybe not because most medical doctors today have never seen the symptoms and since the disease has been eradicated, probably wouldn't even look for it to make a correct diagnosis. In the early stages, when the patient is contagious, the symptoms look like the flu."

"Look at the medical examiner in our case," Joan said from the corner. "She's good, but she missed the smallpox completely. Even with the rash on the hands. It's lucky she didn't get infected."

Valentini walked around the end of the table and looked back at everyone. "I may be the only one here who's not buying all this, but we're living in the U.S. of A. Not Jakarta or some shit-bag slum. Why can't we simply contain an outbreak? I just don't get that."

At a wave of his hand, Dr. Samson motioned a small man to step forward from the corner. "This is Dr. Kumar, our expert on that issue."

A young Indian man with straight black hair walked to the conference table. He wore a black jacket and black skirt and leather sandals. He looked nervous and uneasy at having to speak before everyone.

"It's true that we public health experts know how to respond. At the federal level we have vaccinated small teams of experts who can move quickly to an infected area to confirm the diagnosis and work to contain it. We call it 'quarantine-ring vaccination.' That's the simple part." He reached his arm around behind to scratch his back.

"Keep in mind however, that vaccine is useless if administered more than four to five days after exposure because the virus will already have grown in the body and overwhelmed the immune system, which won't be able to kick-in fast enough to stop it. Think about the technical difficulties of administering huge doses of vaccine to the population of Minneapolis or St. Paul. Other than getting people together for a Vikings game, I can't think of anything we can do to congregate people fast enough to be vaccinated. It could take up to two months—too slow and much too late."

No one spoke. Valentini looked down at the carpeting. *He must be worried,* Paul thought, *like the rest of us.* "Yeah, and half the public wouldn't believe us anyway. They wouldn't cooperate," Valentini mumbled.

Dr. Kumar put his hand inside his jacket and scratched his chest. He shuffled his feet. "Folks, there's more."

Paul saw all heads around the table come up to stare at him.

"If the sample stolen from Vector is here, we don't know how 'heated up' it is."

"What the hell does that mean?" Conway said.

"The Soviet scientists experimented with a number of enhancements to the virus. They exposed it to several antibiotics to force the smallpox to mutate into a drug resistant form. We call the process, 'heating up' a germ. The new, super-lethal strain enables the disease to crash through most vaccines."

The doctor rubbed his shoulder and shifted to stand on his left leg. "We don't know if that's the case with the stolen sample . . . we just don't know. So, if we can't contain it with vaccine fast enough or if the strain can crash through the vaccines we have, it's going out of control and we've lost."

Paul could hear his words echo in the silence of the room. No one moved. Finally Conway said, "We're here to help. What can we do, right now?"

Dr. Samson took a deep breath. "Frankly, Bill, the disease isn't our greatest problem. That's not the main reason a terrorist would introduce it."

Conway scowled. "What the hell? You've just scared the shit out of us and now you say, 'not a problem'?"

"Sit down, Bill," Samson ordered. "The fact is no pandemic has ever been controlled. We're hoping that the plan we've prepared will do that. In the meantime, we all have to deal with something far worse—the fear factor." He drained the last of his coffee, reached into his pocket, and pulled out another Snickers bar.

"Remember the panic that everyone felt after nine-eleven? Remember the anthrax scares, the flu scares, SARS?" He took his time looking around the table. "Multiply that by a thousand. If the population learns of a smallpox pandemic that's lethal, that no one is immune to, and travels faster than imaginable, what do you think people will do?"

Conway pressed his lips together. "See what you mean. So that's why they're really here. I can just see the problem if crowds of people try to stampede the vaccine facilities to get doses for their families. And then there's the transportation systems, schools, malls, and hospitals." He looked up with gray bags sagging under his eyes. "They'd all go down."

"And the medical facilities, if the personnel are immune themselves, will be quickly swamped. They'll lose all effective capacity to contain or treat the disease. If people flee, which they will, that's the worst thing to do because it amplifies the spread. Our local police and fire workers won't be immune and if they try to control an infected population, they'll succumb also."

"Katrina," Valentini moaned. "A complete breakdown of the civil society."

Conway took a deep breath and said, "What do we do? We can't sit here."

"We have one shot," Dr. Samson said. He licked chocolate off his finger. "You said you know where the delivery point is going to be. If we are able to quarantine a manageable area and vaccinate everyone immediately, we may stop it. We've already contacted the CDC's 'war room.' They're sending us a vaccinated team while we talk. They should be here tonight."

"It's important to let these experts handle the situation," Kumar said. "I doubt anyone of us in this room is immune to smallpox. We'll need all the law enforcement help we can get to keep the outer perimeter of the quarantine area sealed." He spread his fingers and brushed them through his shiny hair several times. "Still, it will be a great risk to all of us to even be near the scene. Remember, smallpox will most probably be introduced as an airborne pathogen."

"What should we tell the public?" Paul asked.

"Tough question. Lots of studies have shown that when we tell the public the full truth about the risk, the natural human response is to ignore it," Samson chuckled. "In the past, we've tried to reassure people not to panic, that we've got things under control—the response is panic. So, I suggest we mention very little of this to the press. If you do, believe me, it'll spread faster than the disease itself—and even if the disease isn't introduced, we'll have problems."

Conway waved his arm around the room. "Okay people. I want the Bureau and ICE agents to follow me. We'll contact the local police for assistance and put our plan together. Paul, I want you to take point on this." He nodded at Paul and hurried through the door.

A chair tipped over as people scrambled out of the room.

THIRTY-EIGHT

Z ehra didn't have to force herself to concentrate on the trial preparation—fear did that for her.

On Friday, in the conference room down the hall from Zehra's office, Jackie sat at the round table near the window. "I'm so like, blown away with all this work. Will we be ready for trial?"

"No matter how much you prepare, things always pop up you didn't expect. Trials are dynamic things. You've got to be able to think on your feet."

Stacks of papers, briefs, law books, half-empty coffee cups, CDs with witness' statements, file folders, and scattered chairs filled the room.

Jackie sifted through layers of notes. "Let's see . . . BJ got all the subpoenas served." When she looked up quickly, her black hair fluttered to the sides of her face. "What about Dr. Stein?"

"Payment? I've had a running battle with Mao about coughing-up the money for Stein. At first, Cleary wouldn't give me an extra dime. When I pointed out this guy could blow the lid off of DNA testing for every other case for public defenders, he got the point." Zehra crossed her eyes and shook her head. "Duh . . ."

"Okay. So, he's coming for sure." She twisted her hair in her fingertips. "How are you going to handle things if El-Amin insists on going pro-se?"

"I want to be prepared to try the case ourselves."

"But he's said he doesn't want the help of an 'infidel.'"

Zehra waved her hand. "Every time I've had a pro-se client, once they see twelve, mostly white faces staring at them or when the judge asks them about their motion to sequester, they all cave. Then, we have to take over. So, we keep working."

"I'm really tired. Josh has taken care of my apartment for me. He's brought over food for me. Sushi almost every night. Am I lucky? Hey, what about the suppression motion?"

"Yeah, that's our first line of defense. If we can get Goldberg to keep the clothes and the knife out of evidence, we're okay." She thought of the knife. "When the jury sees that knife . . ."

"But it's just a knife."

"The psychological effect of actually seeing the knife . . . well, El-Amin's gonna be sunk."

"This is like a wicked smart chess game."

"You're right. We've got to anticipate the different ways the trial can go and have a strategy for whichever direction it does. Like Plan A, B, and C."

Jackie sighed. "Okay, boss. That is, if our client even lets us help him." She stopped keying and looked over at Zehra. "How can you represent him, considering what a racist and sexist he is?" The overhead lights reflected off her large glasses.

Zehra shrugged. "It's tough. He stands for everything I have worked against in American Islam. That backwards, sexist, inflexible, hateful . . . ugh. I've got to ignore it." She shook her head to clear it. "If he would listen to us, I'd suggest he cut his beard and dress in clean western-style clothing. Try to get him to look middle-class. The jury may feel more comfortable with him."

"Plus, our guy's got like, a major bad attitude."

"Tell me about it," Zehra said. "It's the defendant's choice to testify or not, but he shouldn't. His attitude alone will convict him."

They both buried themselves in the work and remained silent. When Jackie wasn't looking, Zehra reached into her briefcase and pulled out a chocolate cupcake. She leaned down and took a big bite. Probably go right to my thighs, she thought but then justified it by all the work she labored through.

"Is this the worst case you've ever had?" Jackie interrupted her.

Zehra pushed back in her chair. "No, I think the toughest ones are when you think your guy may be innocent. Usually, the prosecution wins about ninety-some percent of the time. In some ways, the easiest are those where you know the defendant's guilty. If he's found guilty, it doesn't bother you as much."

"So, this case is tough 'cause maybe he's not the killer?"

"Yeah, but I hate the guy so much, it's going to be hard no matter what." Zehra's head jerked up. "Hey, where's BJ?" She looked at her watch and pulled out her cell.

He answered after four rings. "Z . . . I'm sorry. I'm on my way to Chicago. Momma's got some problems." His voice had a sharp edge to it. "I'll be back Sunday, for sure."

"Don't worry. You've done all the heavy lifting up to now. Take care of her, and I'll see you soon."

"Hey, babe, you see that friend of yours, you be sure to let somebody know where you are. He paused for a moment. "I know you didn't want me to poke my nose into it, but I did a little checking. And besides, you got the best of the federal government baby-sitting you. Heard anything about your car yet?"

"BJ! I told you to butt out."

"I'm worried about you, Z. Here's the problem: my sources can't find any record of this guy. If he's a legitimate scientist at that company, wouldn't he have some history?"

"I don't know. I can't think about it right now."

"I'll be okay." She hung up and told Jackie what happened.

"What about Dr. Stein's testimony?"

"Harmon will fight like hell to keep Stein's testing out of evidence. The issue for the judge is to decide if Stein qualifies as an expert or not. The jury will decide if the DNA testing exonerates El-Amin. Again, we don't have to prove that, just create doubt that the original testing was accurate. I think Goldberg will let it in, but if he doesn't, we'll go downhill fast."

Jackie stood up and lifted a four-inch notebook off the table. She carried the three-ring binder to Zehra's side of the table. "Here's the trial notebook. Everything. And I got it all backed-up on my laptop, just in case." She opened the front cover. "See . . . I've got all the legal motions right here, the pleadings, Complaint here." Jackie flipped through a few more sections.

"Good work. It's tedious, but we have to know every detail and every fact of the case before hand. During the trial, we won't have time to learn it. I remember a case I helped prosecute where we charged a guy with strangling his girlfriend to death—first-degree murder because of the premeditation. We figured the defendant had lots of time to think about what he was doing as he cranked down on her neck."

"Sounds like premeditation to me." Jackie walked back to the table to pick up her cup of Starbuck's tea.

"We thought so too until the medical examiner testified truthfully, that the victim's neck was broken within seconds from the pressure of the guy's hands. Any effort on his part after that, didn't add to her death. Since death was almost instantaneous, he didn't premeditate it. Jury found him guilty of second-degree murder instead."

"Were you mad?"

"Not so much mad as disappointed. The guy got about half the time in prison as a result."

"And you didn't see it coming in trial?"

Zehra shook her head. "We'd read the ME's autopsy report and had interviewed him beforehand. It was just something that came up. A fluke. And the defense jumped on it."

"How are you gonna handle the judge?"

"I'm happy to get assigned to him. He's honest and pleasant to work with. Trying a case is hard enough without having to work with a jerk for a judge. If we had a more sympathetic client, we could pull on Goldberg's social worker strings."

Jackie sipped her tea. "What's that?"

"Before going to law school, he was a social worker. He's always got a soft spot for people in trouble. Our problem is El-Amin won't generate any sympathy from anyone. My strategy, if he'll cooperate, is to keep him as quiet as possible. The less Goldberg hears from him, the better for us."

"This is like, overwhelming. How do you keep it all going?"

Zehra stood and laughed. "An old prosecutor who trained me often called it a circus act: you've got to keep three or four plates spinning in the air at all times. One falls and you lose." She stretched her arms above her head then ran her hands through her hair several times.

Zehra thought of Mustafa. She wanted to see him and hoped the relationship could work out. Because she wanted to date in her religion as much as she could, it was hard to meet men. And her mother's 'friends' were usually losers. In Mustafa she saw an intelligent, attractive and faithful Muslim man who was interested in her. The combination was hard to find. And she had to admit she felt some lust for him. If only he'd respond.

But doubts nagged at her. Beyond BJ's warning about Mustafa's truthfulness, there were other odd things he'd done and hazy feelings she couldn't identify that bothered her about him.

"Jackie, do you go out with men other than Vietnamese?" she asked.

"Sure. But then, I'm Christian so it works out easier. Lots of the white guys say they find me 'exotic.'" She laughed and cocked her hip to the side. "Can you imagine? Actually, I don't meet that many Vietnamese men. But then, I'm an American, so who cares?"

Zehra turned to the window and watched flashes of green off the trees, tangled in the blowing wind. The quality of green in the leaves deepened as summer came closer and the temperature rose. A storm was moving in from the west.

She was anxious to meet Mustafa tonight. A break in the trial prep would be wonderful. The event sounded interesting and fun with the students. How would Mustafa react around them? It would be fun to see that side of him.

Zehra thought of her promise to BJ. She keyed on her cell phone. The only other person connected to the case that she could think of was Paul Schmidt. She decided to text him a message. Zehra told Paul she was meeting Mustafa and gave Paul the location of the school. She closed the phone and had a guilty feeling. Should she have done that? The FBI agent would be with her. Was there really any problem?

THIRTY-NINE

The only quiet place Paul could find to think for a minute was a corner of the conference room with the large window. He practiced deep breathing and let his eyes float up into the sky. Thunderclouds trundled in from the west.

He'd been trained with both the Rangers and the FBI to remain calm in a crisis. He had to force his anger at Joan Cortez out of his mind until later. Paul thought of the humiliating raid on Ammar's house. This time, he couldn't screw-up—for the sake of his career or for the lives of thousands of others.

Paul turned around to see Dr. Samson back in the room talking on a cell phone. Techs set up several computer monitors on the conference table. More coffee had appeared on the small table on the side.

Conway bulled his way through the crowd at the door and ordered everyone to clear out except the crisis team, which included Paul. Conway lit up a cigarette in spite of the pained look on Samson's face. Conway drew in deeply, exhaled, and asked Samson, "Where do we start?"

Joan Cortez, followed by two older men, filed into the room and stood near the door.

"I said to clear the room." Conway barked.

"No." Joan looked at him directly. "What if the perp's bringing in more people across the borders or they try to escape over the borders? No, this is our jurisdiction too. We're staying."

Conway frowned and turned back to the doctor. "So, where do we start?"

Dr. Samson shook his head. "We need a containment strategy first."

Conway called for Valentini who came into the conference room quickly. Conway said, "I want you to notify the state Department of Health and . . ."

"No," Samson shouted. "This is much too sensitive to share with them right now. They're not normally privy to classified intelligence. Think about it—there aren't any security or clearance procedures set up. What if this is a nation-wide plot? We don't know the parameters of the problem yet. When I said 'containment strategy,' I meant not only containment of the virus but of information, also. We don't want information leaks to cause a panic."

"Oh, yeah," Conway said and drew from his cigarette again.

Dr. Kumar came into the room. "The team from the Center for Disease Control has landed at the military base by the airport. They've got three Epidemic Intelligence Services officers with them, the nurses, dosages of vaccine, and other personnel." He smoothed his hair. "They'll be at the site in less than a half hour."

"What if they don't have enough vaccine?" Valentini said. "Then what? Should we consider a mandatory quarantine?"

"How big should we draw the circle around the site?" Conway said.

Paul said, "I'm not sure a mandatory quarantine would be legal. I mean, how can you force people to stay in their houses for days?"

Heads dropped and the conversation lagged.

Paul spoke again, "We're going to need local law enforcement at the site."

Dr. Samson agreed. "But don't tell them why," he cautioned.

Conway nodded and told Valentini to make the contacts with the chief of police for the city. "What's the location again?" he asked Paul. The details were relayed to the chief.

Valentini held the cell phone away from his head. "What should I tell them to do?"

Dr. Samson said, "They are to maintain order and make sure no one leaves the area of the mosque. Paul, you should get out there immediately with Dr. B and meet the team from CDC. Post the police at all points where people may enter or leave the suspect area. When the CDC team arrives, they'll set up a mobile medical center to assess the problem and administer vaccinations to those people inside the containment circle as soon as they decide to release it. Hopefully, we won't miss anyone that could get out."

"Should we quarantine the entire suburb?" Conway asked.

"It may be necessary. But we don't know yet since the CDC team isn't on site to assess the extent of the release."

Conway added, "I've got to notify the mayor and the governor, too. The FBI director's already called me twice since we alerted their war room. Anyone else?"

Samson sighed and his face drooped. "We have to face the possibility that this is a national release. The Department of Homeland Security, Defense Department, and the National Security Council will have to come in at some point, along with the president."

Joan interrupted, "Hey folks, hate to burst your bubble, but we're here and that means Homeland Security already knows."

"It's too early for all that, Stan," Dr. Kumar said.

Samson's eyes lifted to meet his and then moved around the room. "How do you know?"

After a silence, Conway cleared his throat with a low gurgle. "How do I protect my own people?"

Samson said, "When the CDC team arrives, they can vaccinate everyone who'll have primary contact with the release. Law enforcement and health workers have priority. The closest hospitals and emergency rooms get second priority. We must maintain the viability of the medical personnel. If they're overwhelmed, we all lose."

"What about the kids who could be infected?" Valentini said.

"If the CDC has enough vaccine, of course anyone that's determined to have been infected will get the vaccine. They'll also be isolated at the closest hospital and monitored in quarantine."

People in the room attacked their cell phones and made the necessary calls.

Dr. Kumar sat down beside Samson and said, "Stan, it's damn lucky we participated in the national symposium back in '99. Did you ever think . . . ?"

Paul's cell phone buzzed. He opened it and read the message from Zehra. It confused him since she texted him that she would be going with Mustafa to Hiawatha High School for a science fair. Zehra also included the address. Why would she send him the text? Wasn't Mustafa some guy she had met or was dating? Paul didn't have time to think about it. He saved it and closed the phone.

Conway walked over to him. "You know where this mosque is, Paul?"

"Yeah. I was there earlier, and the witness Abraham, told me about it."

"Do you know when the meeting was supposed to occur?"

"Sometime tonight." Paul caught his breath. "Wait a minute! The services at the mosque began already, at noon. The meeting could be at anytime after, or even during the service."

"Like right now?" Conway crossed his beefy arms over his chest.

"I'm moving." Paul hurried toward the door.

They jumped into the elevator and fell to the basement. Paul jogged to his car.

He roared up the ramp, swiped his access card over the exit machine, and came out into the bright sun of the afternoon. Heat and humid air surrounded the car. Paul rolled the windows down and swerved through the traffic.

At his house, Paul took only enough time to grab the olive drab Glock 21, the one that shot the big .45-caliber bullets.

Removing his suit jacket, he twisted into his shoulder holster and settled the gun under his arm. He picked up his vest, just in case, and raced up the stairs.

Back in the car, he lurched out of the driveway. He glanced at his watch. He calculated about thirty minutes to the mosque. What about the CDC people? he wondered. He called Dr. Kumar on his cell phone.

"They'll set up things as fast as they can. I'll help you work with them," the doctor answered.

"When we get there, will they be able to start vaccinations?"

"Not immediately. Because the dosages of vaccine are limited, they'll insist on an accurate diagnosis first. Depending on what they discover, we'll react."

Paul sat back in his seat. "Wait a minute. You mean when we get there, I can't just seal-off the area and let them get to work?"

"You should set up the containment perimeter with the local police to help, but no, things won't work that fast."

"But don't they understand that the release could be going on right now? That we've got to arrest Ammar, that the stuff could be spreading as we're waiting for them?"

Paul could hear him sigh. "In this situation, they run the show and no one can tell them what to do."

He barked into the phone as he pushed the car faster. "Well, how long does this diagnosis take? I hope they can do it on the spot. We may already be too late."

"Uh . . . first, they'll have to fly it by a military plane to Atlanta to be analyzed in their maximum containment laboratory."

FORTY

Joan Cortez had armed herself earlier and brought along the two agents she trusted the most. George Eppert and Teddy Vang sat with her in the unmarked Immigration and Customs Enforcement SUV as they raced south toward the mosque.

She didn't have to ask if they were armed. Besides, the SUV had back-up weaponry if necessary. Extra pistols, two short-barreled shotguns, and a Taser rested in the back end.

They had all changed into lightweight Kevlar vests, covered by blue jackets with large yellow letters identifying their agency. Joan pulled her hair back and tucked it under a baseball cap. The vest hugged her chest and felt hot and tight.

"What's the plan, Boss?" Teddy asked.

"Simple." Joan glanced at him in the driver's seat. Teddy was small but one of the toughest agents she'd ever worked with. "We ignore all this epidemic shit and go for the gold. We're gonna be the ones to take down this guy, Ammar."

"You can ID him?" Teddy asked.

"Close enough. I've got a description. He's an Arab. Should be easy."

Teddy frowned. "You sure about this . . . ? What if we get the wrong dude. You know how these Somali religious guys are. We'll get sued and worse yet, get our faces on TV. The director won't be happy."

"I'm taking responsibility for the mission. If we get this guy, our future's made. The rest of these idiots will be running around with test tubes while we save the country." She rolled down her window to let warm afternoon air into the SUV. "Besides, the way the FBI treats us, I'd love to stick this up their ass."

Teddy shrugged and swerved between open slots among the cars heading south on the interstate. He pushed the vehicle up to eighty.

George leaned forward from the back seat. "What happens when we get there?" He wasn't the smartest agent she had, but Joan knew he was competent, loyal to her, and the best agent she could get for back-up.

"I've got the address for the mosque," Joan said. "We cover all exits and force our way in. I figure we'll trap the guy in there or at least, be ready when he shows. If necessary, we'll rescue the kids and still make the grab."

"Expect any problems from the local Somalis in the mosque?"

"Who knows?" Joan turned to face George. "Speed is our best weapon. Make the grab, secure him, get him in the vehicle, and get the hell out of there before they know what's happened."

George grunted and sat back. "So we need the shotguns."

"Right. Both of 'em."

In ten minutes, Teddy arrived at the area of the mosque in Burnsville. As they cruised the adjacent streets, it was obvious they'd beaten everyone else.

A long, low row of attached offices stretched along the road to their right. One story, flat roofed, with a single door in the front of each office unit. Teddy slowed to turn around the backside of the building. A large parking lot butted up to the loading docks on the backside. Each office had two rear entrances—the loading dock and a regular door. The loading dock door rested in a closed position.

"George, you'll take down the front," Joan ordered. "Take one of the shotguns."

Teddy circled around to the front of the building again.

"Teddy and I will take the back side. Keep your radio channel open. On my word, we'll storm the doors. The guy's name is Ammar. He's about six feet, dark skin, shiny black hair, no beard, good-looking dude. Maybe they'll give him up right away, but be prepared for anything. These people are crazy. Once we make the grab, we'll get him out the back to avoid attention."

After they dropped off George, Teddy parked near the back door with the front of the SUV facing the exit. They got out and left the doors cracked open. Teddy took the other shotgun, and Joan grabbed the Taser, which she hooked onto her waist belt. She removed the Smith and Wesson pistol from the holster that rode over her back right hip.

They walked quickly to the back doors.

Joan talked softly, "We'll both go in here. If we hear the loading door start to open, you cover it. I'll go straight ahead." Teddy nodded and stood to the left of her. Both of them flattened on either side of the regular door with their weapons up. The Kevlar vest dug into her armpits and hurt. After all the cop shows on TV, Joan felt a little stupid, but this was proper training.

She spoke into the radio clipped to her shoulder. "George . . . Go!"

She and Teddy folded into the door, which was unlocked. Inside, they spread immediately and raised their weapons, announced themselves, and demanded Ammar.

The room they entered was small but opened to a long hallway. Coming in from the summer warmth, it felt cool. Ahead of them, a lone man in brown robes bolted down the hall. They ordered him to stop, but he kept moving.

Joan and Teddy hurried after him. To the right and left of the hallway, sat several rooms. They cleared each one before moving on. In the front, they could hear George doing his work.

As they approached the end of the hallway, it opened to a large room covered in Persian rugs, which Joan assumed was the worship area. Several older, bearded men stood in a semi-circle in front of George with their hands in the air.

Joan approached and studied them carefully. They looked scared, and all of them stared at the ground. Excitement surged through her body like a wave of heat coming up from a hot sidewalk. She loved this part. To have people like this cower before her, to obey her. The power and anticipation of success intoxicated her.

"Everyone take it easy. All we want is Ammar. Where is he?" she shouted.

No one responded.

Joan holstered her pistol, pulled the Taser off her belt, and walked to the guy who seemed to be the leader. "You in charge?"

When he nodded, he flicked his eyes up to hers for a moment. Instead of fear, she saw hate and anger. That would make her job easier.

Joan held up the Taser. "I'm only asking once more, old man. Where the fuck is he?"

The man's mouth moved without opening. Finally, he said, "Are you looking for Dr. Kamal? He is not here."

"Kamal . . . ? Whatever. Where the fuck is he?"

"He was supposed to be here, but he is not here yet," the man said. Saliva dribbled from the corner of his mouth over his gray beard.

Joan turned to Teddy. "Search the place."

In five minutes, he returned with a group of young boys. They straggled in front of him until they reached the bigger group. Joan smiled and dropped her Taser to the side. "All right, relax," she said. "Now we're making progress." Both other agents lowered their weapons and the circle of clerics put their hands down also.

"When's he coming?" Joan demanded.

The old man opened his hands, palms out, toward her. "I do not know. We are waiting for him. What is this about?"

"You know damn well what we mean," shouted George. "The smallpox epidemic. Some new 'gee-had' of yours."

Frowns creased the faces of several of the men. They looked at each other. "Smallpox?" one asked.

"That's enough!" Joan ordered. "We'll just wait for your friend with you. No one will leave until Ammar gets here. Let's be cool here, guys. All we want is Ammar. No trouble. We'll take him out for questioning and leave you alone," she lied.

When she saw their eyes darting amongst themselves, she moved closer to Teddy and George. To be safe, Joan ordered a search of each one for weapons. Then, she'd isolate them in one of the small rooms.

After the search had been completed, they moved the group, including the boys, down the hall to the first room on the right. It took a long time for each one to file through the narrow entrance. As she was about to walk away to guard the outer doors while waiting for Ammar, Joan noticed one of the men in the back talking fast on his cell phone.

Alerting Teddy, she stormed through the crowd, pushed people aside, and grabbed the man by the arm with the phone. With her other hand, she slammed the end of her Taser into his face. He dropped the cell and screamed in pain. His lower lip cracked open. Blood spurted out.

"What the hell do you think you're doing?" she said.

With Teddy holding the shotgun on the man, Joan reached down to pick up the phone. He had managed to click it off but she keyed into it and went to the menu for recent calls.

Her breath stopped when she saw the man had called Channel Six TV news.

FORTY-ONE

rom her balcony, Zehra saw his Mercedes pull into the parking lot far below. Up where she was, the hot breeze blew in from the west. It carried the metallic smell of new rain. She hurried back through the condo.

She wore jeans, tight but not too much. Although he was conservative, Mustafa was still a man. Something had to awaken him. She studied her makeup in the mirror and pulled at her thick hair. The humidity didn't help. Curls threatened to burst out all over her head. Satisfied she couldn't get it any better, she draped the scarf he'd given her around her neck and switched off the light.

Mustafa was at the entry downstairs.

Zehra buzzed him in and arranged some tea cups. The water bubbled and popped softly.

Like the air pushed aside by a speeding semi truck, he entered the condo behind a burst of energy. "Hello. You look beautiful. Are you ready?" he chattered.

"Well . . . yeah, but don't you want some tea or pop? I've got a Diet Coke." She tried to tempt him.

He squinted. "Uh . . . no thanks. We do not have much time." He touched her briefly and from far away.

"What's wrong?"

"Oh, I'm sorry. I have worked with these students on their projects for so long. I want everything to go well."

"Relax. I'm looking forward to meeting them." She paused and pulled on his arm to slow him down. "Are you missing something?"

He stopped, turned, and looked her up and down. Finally, he said, "Oh, the scarf! Thank you for wearing it. It is very beautiful on you. It complements the color of your skin."

Zehra felt a hot blush flash quickly across her face. "Well, if you don't have time for anything, I guess we should go, huh?"

They hurried across the hall to the elevator. Waiting for it made her nervous. She'd never seen Mustafa so agitated. Usually, he was in complete control of everything. He prided himself on his scientific approach to things—too much, Zehra thought, when it came to relationships. Those kinds of things weren't meant to be controlled. How many times had she wished he would go "out of control" with her?

The FBI agent met them in the lobby. He would follow them in his car.

In the Benz, she sank back into the soft butter-colored leather seat and felt the cool wisp of air from the vents. Mustafa drove erratically and fast.

"Hey, slow down. I know this means a lot to you, but the traffic is still the tail-end of the rush hour." Zehra looked over at him. His eyes bored straight ahead and his nostrils flared a little. She became concerned. "Don't drive so fast. I want to enjoy the night."

He jerked toward her. "Sorry. You are right." He eased off on the speed and leaned back into the leather. "I have been so busy. It is nice to see you again. You make me feel calm and good."

She pushed her question toward him carefully, "Is it because I'm not wearing the scarf over my head? Is that upsetting you?"

"No . . . no, it's not that."

"Okay." She rearranged the scarf but left it around her neck. Pulling the visor down with the mirror, she turned her face left and right. Wearing the *hijab* was strictly up to each Muslim woman to decide. It wasn't that big a deal for her.

They rode in silence for ten minutes while Mustafa eased through the jammed lines of cars.

"What's the science fair about?" she asked.

"I have worked for months with the students. They will have all the projects displayed on the lab tables in various rooms." He looked at her and his features squeezed together.

"Do you expect lots of people?"

"We always get hundreds. It's very popular."

In fifteen minutes, they entered the southern suburb and drove through a neighborhood of small, single-family homes. Zehra lowered her window. Rows of stately trees spread over the streets reaching out from both sides, shading them as they drove.

Cars stood in front driveways and some adventurous kids had turned on sprinklers to jump through. She heard the squeals and laughter of children let free for the afternoon. Windows and doors stood open to invite the warm weather and summer inside after a long Minnesota winter. Zehra heard the rumble of thunder far off to the west. She looked back and saw salmon-colored clouds streaked with gray heaviness, underneath.

As they turned a corner, a half dozen kids spread apart before the car like fish in a tank. They had been kicking a soccer ball around in the school parking lot.

"Here we are," Mustafa said. He parked in the faculty lot next to the school. Already the rest of the lots were full of cars.

Zehra stepped out and walked across a small section of grass.

A sidewalk with broken concrete sections led to the door. The grass needed mowing. Two sets of tall bushes shrouded the parking lot on both sides. They were so thick Zehra couldn't see anything beyond them. A red maple arched over the bushes on the right side, like a protective umbrella. Around them, the air cooled as night came on.

Mustafa led her inside and immediately took her down a long hallway to a classroom in the middle of the hall.

Zehra followed him inside. The room was small, with several tables in the middle, all covered with displays of various science projects. It smelled musty, as if the room and had been shut-up for a while.

Students in the classroom shouted when Mustafa entered. They were happy to see him, but he scowled at them and spoke sharply.

Zehra took a deep breath. Maybe this wasn't such a good idea. He was so upset, she doubted they would have a good time. Hopefully around the kids, he'd chill out.

In fifteen minutes, more kids and people started to arrive. One by one, parents came through the room, stopping to admire all the projects and listen to the students explain them.

The FBI agent had followed them into the room. When he saw what the situation was, he told Zehra that he'd be in the hallway and left.

There were a variety of people. Many were Somali. Zehra didn't know much about them except that Minnesota had accepted thousands of the refugees to create the largest community of Somalis in the United States. Although few women came, she admired the men. Tall, with dark shiny skin, they all smiled a lot with beautiful, white teeth.

They greeted her warmly.

The men surrounded Mustafa and thanked him for all he did for their children. One father in a white shirt, gray slacks, and pointed black shoes said, "We are thankful, Dr. Ammar. Of course, we love our children, but we work very hard. We try to keep the family and religious traditions together . . ."

Mustafa nodded and assured them it was okay. "Remember to be faithful, no matter what happens to you in this country. It is most important to be obedient to Allah."

The men nodded but didn't seem as fervent about their faith as Mustafa. They gave their children hugs. It was obvious to Zehra, they were close families.

After each group of people moved on, the boys jumped and pushed and laughed with each other. It reminded Zehra of a club. Carefree and excited, they crowded around the newest member of their club. They pelted Zehra with questions. What job did she have? Where was she from? Was she Muslim? Did she like men? Did she like pizza?

"Are you and Dr. Ammar going to get married?" a skinny boy asked. The others giggled.

Zehra felt her face blush. "We're just friends . . . good friends."

Mustafa came over and told the boys to get ready for more visitors.

Zehra had to chuckle to herself. He looked so serious in contrast to the disheveled exuberance of the kids.

Another group marched into the classroom. Mustafa nudged Zehra into the corner. He said, "I have to run out to the car. I will return soon. Would it be a burden for you to stay to watch the boys? The parents trust me and you are the only one who could fill my place."

Zehra waved her hand before her. "Of course. These guys are sweethearts. Reminds me of when I was that age and I used to get together with my girlfriends for sleep-overs."

"Thank you. You will do something of great favor for Allah."

Zehra frowned. "Watching the kids?"

"I'll be right back." He looked at his big watch and gave her arm a squeeze. He hurried out the door and turned down the hall.

Zehra walked around the room and sat on a stool and watched the people come through. She thought of Mustafa. What was he doing? Her mind drifted back to him, and the old doubts and questions rose again. He was so smart, handsome, and dedicated to these young men. Why did BJ insist that Mustafa had lied?

Outside, Zehra heard thunder rumble closer. In ten minutes, she heard the spattering beats of rain on the windows of the classroom. Zehra glanced over her shoulder and noticed the long shadows creeping into the room through the windows.

Bored, she got off the stool and walked to the nearest exhibit. The boy next to it said his name was Sergio. He showed Zehra his project.

"It's a model of the human heart where I show how open-heart surgery is done." He pointed to the squishy looking model on the table. "See, here are the chambers. Here's the instruments the surgeons use." He held up a scalpel, sharp with a curved blade. "And I even got blood."

He reached behind him for a jar of red liquid. "This is the same stuff they use in Hollywood. See . . . ? It's so awesome. It's like real." He insisted Zehra put her finger inside the jar. When she finished, he set the open jar on the table.

Zehra wanted to wipe her hand. When she reached for a napkin, the strong breeze from the vent in the wall blew it off the table. She hadn't noticed it before. Why would they have the air conditioning on at night? She looked at her watch. It read 8:05.

FORTY-TWO

Paul rocked to a halt in the parking lot of Tarryville church, five blocks from the mosque. He both clamored out quickly. A circle of Burnsville police cars occupied the corner of the lot. Several cops stood around, waiting to find out what to do.

"Paul Schmidt, FBI." He stuck out his hand to the chief.

"Bob Rasmussen. We're ready for your orders."

He looked so young. Paul was surprised Rasmussen could be the chief of police. He wore a pressed uniform, burdened with a heavy belt that contained weapons, his night stick, radio, extra speed loaders, and cuffs. He had an athletic build and stood straight.

"You know where the mosque is?" Paul asked.

"Roger that."

"Right now, I don't want anyone to go in. The idea here is to contain the activity from the outside until we get support."

"What's the mission, sir?"

"Uh . . . for right now, containment. Get your men out on a quadrant, spaced at intervals to intercept anyone leaving or arriving. They are to be detained and brought to me immediately. In the meantime, I want you to maintain order."

"Are we looking for a suspect?"

"Not right now. We have good reason to think he's inside the mosque but containment is our objective."

"Okay. I've gotten permission from the church to utilize the lot for as long as we need it."

"That's great, Chief." Paul looked around at the expanse of asphalt. "This'll make a good staging area."

"Staging area?"

"For our support."

"Should we prepare for any . . ." His face clouded over.

"Chief, we just need you and your men to form a net around the mosque. Hurry!"

Rasmussen squinted at Paul. "Okay. We're all over it. What support are we waiting for?"

Paul started to move away. Too many questions. "I'll explain when they arrive."

The chief shook his head, squared his shoulders, and turned toward his men and women. He gave them orders and watched as the squad cars left the parking lot. The chief remained.

Paul flipped open his cell phone. In a few calls, he learned the CDC team would arrive in about five minutes. Conway and the team of ten more agents from downtown would get there right afterward. Paul noticed he had several messages but closed the phone.

When Dr. Kamur arrived, Paul asked him, "When CDC gets here, I'm out of my league. Tell me what to do."

"Sure. The most important thing they'll need is some space to set up the mobile lab. It's a tent, really. The cops should keep the area free and clear so the experts can do their work."

Paul looked toward the chief. He stood alone. Paul waved him over. "Can you get a squad back here to set up security for the support team?"

Rasmussen unhooked his phone from his belt and called in the orders.

Paul noticed a crowd gathering at the edges of the parking lot. Several people stood, their hips canted to one side, and watched silently. Some had kids in strollers with them. The police cars drew many out from their homes. Paul wanted to warn them to get the kids as far away as possible but of course, he couldn't say anything.

The sky darkened, and he heard thunder.

A large group filed out from the side door of the church. Led by an older man with a halo of white hair and a deeply tanned face, they approached Paul. He held up his hand to stop them. They kept on walking toward him.

"Pastor Heinz," the older man said as he reached Paul.

"Pastor, I need your help to keep this area clear of everyone. And I need it done now." Paul shouted at the man.

He jerked back in surprise but followed the orders. The group joined the other people at the edge of the lot.

Suddenly, a large white van curved into the lot and stopped abruptly. People exploded from every door, including the back end. A black woman in a white coat and short dread-locks came directly to Paul and Kumar. "I'm Dr. Johnson, CDC, who's in charge?"

"I'm Agent Schmidt, FBI. Dr. Kumar's from USAMRIID."

See looked at him, then at the doctor. "I don't mean to offend you, Jack, but is this all you got? From what I understand, we'll need an army."

Paul told her adequate back-up was on its way. Kumar spoke fast, telling her the latest information they knew. Chief Rasmussen came over and brought two cops with him. He stood beside Paul and propped his hand on his hip. "What's going on?" he asked Paul.

Paul glanced at him. "National security. Chief . . . this is very big. You can't let this information out, but these people are from the Center for Disease Control in Atlanta."

Rasmussen's eyes popped open. His mouth dropped. "Uh . . . what . . ."

"Not now, chief. We're too busy. Just keep the crowd away."

When Paul turned back, seven people scurried around the van. They had already erected a large tent and were wheeling equipment inside. Side flaps were lowered to conceal their work. They carried small suitcases and two laptop computers. One man lifted a heavy generator from the back of the van. He rolled it to the side of the tent, ran cables underneath the flap, and pushed his finger on the electric starter. The generator roared to life until it settled down to a steady hum.

Kumar spoke to Dr. Johnson. "What can I do?"

The doctor stopped working. When she lifted her head, dreadlocks danced over her face. "Let's get a map of the area. We're about to measure wind speed and direction. I need to know where the source is exactly. The first patient you have, we want to see, of course. We'll take a swab and put it on the helicopter to Atlanta. If it tests positive, we'll make a decision to release the vaccine. Anyone who's come within six feet of the infected parties will receive it. Plus, of course, all law enforcement on the scene."

Kumar scratched his back and nodded.

Two marked FBI vans and three cars shot into the parking lot. Conway was out and charging toward the tent before his car stopped. Agents poured out of the other vehicles. Another car, marked with USAMRIID on the side pulled up, and Dr. Samson stepped out. As Paul watched, he wondered why Joan Cortez and the ICE agents weren't with them.

Conway demanded, "Where's Agent Schmidt?"

Paul came from around the back side of the tent. He told Conway the cops were deployed around the mosque.

Valentini and Dr. Samson gathered beside them. "Should we storm the mosque right now?" Valentini asked.

"I'd advise against it," Samson said. "If any of the infected people scatter and we lose them . . ."

"Right," Conway agreed. "I've ordered a chopper to do surveillance. Should be here soon. Hopefully, they can tell us more."

"Besides, if Ammar is as dangerous as we think, there could be violence. We don't want to risk the lives of any of the boys or religious people in the mosque."

Conway wiped his damp forehead. "Can you imagine the media shit storm we'd get? I agree. We'll wait for now."

For now, Paul felt impotent. The disease could be spreading as they talked. What if it had already jumped the quarantine line guarded by the cops? He walked over to Dr. Kumar. "What can we do?" Occasional drops of rain plopped onto the asphalt lot.

He frowned. "Wait."

"Hey, guys!" Dr. Johnson shouted from the corner of the tent. "Get these people out of here."

Paul turned to see Pastor Heinz and a large group of people edging around the tent. They swarmed over the cables, and one person even lifted the flap of the tent. The two police struggled to move the mob back, but they couldn't budge them.

Paul and Valentini moved into the crowd. They flashed badges and shouted for people to back up. Paul found Heinz and yelled at him. "I told you to keep these people back!"

"This is our church. We have a right to know what's going on. This many cops and FBI means you're not out here looking for lost kittens."

"I'll explain later, but for now, get the fuck back. This is an emergency!"

People swore and shouted but started to fold back into the grass edges of the parking lot.

Paul noticed several more new people streaming in from the houses to the south of the lot. He hurried over to Chief Rasmussen. "Can you get more muscle out here?"

Sweat trickled down the side of Rasmussen's face. "I've got every man and woman out on the line right now. I can call for help from the next city over but that risks bringing more officers into this. I thought you wanted to keep things quiet?"

"I know, I know but we need the help. Call 'em."

Rasmussen pulled out his cell phone and made a call.

Paul's phone buzzed, but he ignored it.

Suddenly, a squad car crunched into the gravel of the parking lot. The side door flew open, and a cop pulled out a small man. He hustled the man over to the tent. "Found this man leaving the quadrant. Says he wasn't in the mosque but walked by it."

Dr. Johnson stepped up. "Good work, officer. Get him in the tent. We'll take a swab." She followed the man inside the tent and closed the flap. In a few minutes, they both came out. "Keep him in the back of your squad for now. We may need him quarantined at the closest hospital."

Paul's shirt felt steamy and damp. He wanted to take off his sport coat but was afraid to show his weapon and holster. As it was, the larger crowd bulged out from the south side of the lot to reach within twenty feet. He motioned Conway to use the other agents for crowd control.

As the agents moved toward the crowd, Paul could tell they were at the tipping point. The crowd could easily overwhelm the law enforcement and CDC, if they wanted to. He ran to find Rasmussen. "Where are the other police?"

"I got 'em coming, but it takes awhile to round 'em up."

"Can't you see it's about to blow-up here?"

Rasmussen stopped and looked into Paul's face. "Hey, we're doing all we can. This is your show, pal."

A surge of noise interrupted them. The crowd shouted and cheered. Paul looked over their heads to see a green van pull up with an antenna mounted on the roof. "Oh, shit!" he shouted as he ran toward it.

Large yellow letters on the side of the van said, "Channel 6 News." Three people spilled out of the sides. Two had cameras on their shoulders, and a blonde woman dressed in a starched blouse and blue blazer over blue jeans, waded through the crowd. Carolyn Bechter smiled and waved at people.

Paul's stomach tightened when he saw her. The short fling they'd had didn't work out. He knew Carolyn blamed him for everything. She'd be tough to deal with.

Paul heard Conway, who stomped around so much he looked like he was dancing. "Who the hell called those assholes? Get 'em out of here!" he ordered.

At the edge of the crowd, the cameramen pointed toward the news woman who started talking to Pastor Heinz. Someone opened an umbrella over the two. Angry shouts carried around the crowd. Paul moved to the interview.

Then Bechter started her interview, "We received an anonymous tip about the break-out of a small pox epidemic, a deadly contagious disease. Can you comment on that, pastor?"

Paul's breath stopped. How did they know about it already? When that news spread, could law enforcement control the crowd? For a while, he couldn't move.

Paul could see the heads of people bobbing back and forth in unison in a mindless push of panic. A scuffle broke out. People shouted and clawed at each other to get away. He looked around for more police. Bechter looked behind herself. Paul could see fear shadow her face. She sheltered herself next to the burly cameraman.

A second news van pulled in behind the first.

As Carolyn backed up quickly, someone ripped the microphone out of her hand and started yelling into it. She kept backing while the cameraman to her side tried to film. The person with the mike jerked it backward, causing the camera to tumble off the black guy's shoulder.

He and Carolyn looked at each other. Paul could see they were afraid.

Her head swiveled, searching around behind her, saw Paul, and worked her way through the crowd to reach him.

"Paul?"

"Carolyn," he said. He felt like they were two cats, circling each other.

"We need help."

He let his breath escape. "Here. Get inside that tent. I'll go with you." He looked her in the eyes. "Get into a corner and don't you dare ask any questions. Those people working in there may be the only ones who can save us now."

She nodded and sighed in resignation.

Paul's phone buzzed again, and he reluctantly reached for it, flipped it open. There was a voice mail from FBI headquarters in Washington. He listened.

"Agent, we've developed more intel about your suspect, Michael Ammar. He's got deep cover, so most data bases couldn't find him at first. He's Egyptian. Member of the Muslim Brotherhood, an extremist, violent group. And . . . his real name isn't Michael. It's Mustafa Ali Ammar."

Paul dropped the phone.

Mustafa . . . Mustafa, where did he hear that name . . . ?

Zehra!

He picked up phone, keyed in Zehra's earlier message, and caught his breath. He punched the address into GPS, checked to make sure he had both his weapons, shouted at Conway that he was leaving. He heard the faint screams of his boss' protests as he roared out of the lot, nearly hitting the civilians.

FORTY-THREE

Zehra felt dreamy. The crowds of people kept passing through forever, it seemed. Her mind wandered through the recent several days. Exhaustion tip-toed around her. She thought of the trial starting on Monday, her violent client that she would fight with, the threats and bombing, her mother's desire for her and Mustafa to get together, her loneliness, and Mustafa himself.

Her fatigue made it hard to think objectively. Maybe she shouldn't be objective about love. All her life, she'd been analytical, hard working, dedicated to her career, her mission in life. Look where it had gotten her. She longed to let go, to trust him.

"He's lying . . ." BJ's words echoed in her mind.

"But look at all the wonderful things he's done," she said back to the absent investigator. "His work in the mosques, his kindness, intelligence, worldly charm, and look at these kids." She glanced at the group, their faces lit up by pride—both the parents and the students.

She sighed and focused on the people again. They hugged their children, laughed, and moved on. Zehra's eyes fell on the curbed scalpel sitting on the table next to her.

The curved knife . . . Zehra's mind snapped to electric attention.

What was it about the scalpel? She tried to remember some thought from the past, but it rolled over and disappeared from her mind. Then it struck her hard. Her chest tightened painfully. One of the boys looked back at her in concern. She waved him off. Rain drummed on the big windows and ran down in slow, torturous streams.

When BJ and Mustafa had been at her condo watching the video of the murder, Zehra had been unable to see the actual knife in the film. She knew from the evidence room that the knife found in El-Amin's apartment, the murder weapon, was curved. She recalled holding it in her hands.

But no one, including Mustafa, could see the knife in the video. He'd said the "curved" knife slicing through the victim's throat really upset him. How could he know it was curved?

Zehra started to shake.

Her hands quivered. She couldn't breathe. She fought to gain control. Everything crashed down on her like a tsunami hitting a harbor. The thought of Mustafa killing the young man sickened her. He must be involved in the disappearing Somalis . . . but why? What was he up to? The bombing . . . ?

The betrayal, the lies, and the gifts he'd given her. The long talks about progressive Islam—all of it staged and false. Tears filled her eyes, and she sniffed repeatedly. How could she have missed it? An intense pain slammed into her chest. Two of the boys turned to her and asked if she was okay.

She calmed herself. Took several deep breaths. She stood and walked to the window and looked outside. Balanced herself against the wall. Cool air streamed over her ankles from the vent on the floor.

Purple clouds hung low over the roofs across the street. Underneath dark bushes, shadows filled in, hiding the lawns and sidewalks. Where the warmed vegetation met the cooling rain, a fog rose from the grass to further obscure things.

What should she do?

She worried about the boys. What did Mustafa have planned?

Zehra thought to run but remembered he had given her a ride. Besides, she didn't know what to do. Anger, furious anger, replaced her fear. Somehow, she had to escape as soon as possible. Was he still in the school? Would he insist on her coming with him? Could she fake him out? Pretend she didn't know anything?

She hurried into the crowded hall and looked around for the FBI agent. She couldn't find him.

Another large group surged out of the classroom. Zehra went back in. The boys stood up, stretched, and pushed at each other, young and carefree.

Amongst the noise, she thought she heard Mustafa's familiar footsteps in the hall. She forced herself to turn and look. Just another parent. Where was the agent?

Fewer people came through the classroom now. Zehra ran back into the hall. Didn't see Mustafa or the FBI agent. Around her, the parents unfurled umbrellas to protect them from the rain outside.

Zehra returned to the table where she'd waited. When she calmed down, it seemed simple. She'd leave with a big crowd of people and get to the parking lot. Once there, in spite of the rain, she'd hide or leave. She thought of her cell. Call for help now, but she'd still have to get away from him.

If only she could make it out before Mustafa came back. Zehra didn't think she could fool him. At the table, she felt dizzy and grabbed the edge of the counter to steady herself. This would be tough.

Her cell phone rang so loudly that her hand swept the table top, knocking off Sergio's jar. It smashed on the floor, splattering fake red blood across her shoes. She fumbled to open her phone. It was Mustafa.

"I am sorry to be late. I was delayed. How's everything?"

Zehra gulped a breath of air. "Uh . . . yeah. The parents are starting to leave. Where are you?"

"I'm just about there. Wait for me."

"Sure . . . sure. I'll watch for you." She hung up and grabbed for her purse. She hurried toward the hall and the side door of the school.

With a dwindling group of people, she emerged from the school onto the grass outside. Zehra searched the night for Mustafa. With the rain, it was difficult to see much of anything.

In a few minutes, she saw the lights from his car turn on and slice through the rain in the parking lot. She moved in the opposite direction. Started to walk quickly. She could beat him.

He was out of his car faster than she planned. Mustafa came toward her in long, graceful strides. "I am so sorry. Is this all right for you?" He had a rain jacket on with the hood pulled up, hiding his face. The lights from his car glistened on the bushes beside the school.

She avoided his face. "Sure. Let's go. I've got a lot of work left to do tonight."

He stopped her with both his hands on her arms. Black shadows hovered along the sides of the building. The rain drummed without interest and the fog rose around them. He looked down at her. "Thank you for your help tonight."

Mixed emotions flooded through Zehra. His hands felt strong and confident and that scared her. Should she try to run? She glanced at him. "Hey, no problem." When she tried to move past him, he held her firmly. She felt the rain seeping through her thick hair. Her face was wet.

"What is wrong?" His voice dropped to a lower register than Zehra'd ever heard before.

"Uh . . . nothing. I've got a lot of work . . . Hey, it's raining."

"Something is wrong." He pushed her toward the bushes. "We will find out."

"Let me go . . . please," she pleaded.

His hair fell forward on either side of his face. Even in the dim light, she could see his eyes bulge and his nostrils flare. His arms started to shake in anger. "What did you do?" he demanded.

"Do? Nothing, I didn't do anything." Zehra twisted her body to the left and slipped from his grip. For a moment, they both were surprised. Then, she started to run down the sidewalk.

"Stop!" he bellowed and chased her. A few people stopped to look.

She screamed at them, "Help me."

She picked up speed until her foot caught on one of the broken concrete slabs. She fell hard onto her side. With her face on the ground, she smelled pungent earth. Her arm hurt, and it was hard to breathe. Her face lay in wet grass.

Mustafa towered above her. He reached down and yanked her up. When she went limp, he dragged her toward his car. Zehra kicked at him with her left foot but missed. She tried to jam her foot into the greasy ground. She slipped. Mustafa pulled harder.

"No . . . please . . ." she begged.

"You cannot be allowed to reveal anything. I have worked too long," he screamed.

"Why?" she screamed at him. "Why?"

"For the glory of Allah. Why else, you fool." He tugged on her wet legs.

"Killing an innocent boy is for the glory of Allah?"

"You would not understand. You are an infidel."

Suddenly, Zehra's fear coalesced into hatred and anger. She twisted her body around until he lost his grip. She put her foot underneath her to shove off for a run. She pushed. In the wet grass, her foot slipped, and she slammed into the ground.

Mustafa fell on top of her. His weight suffocated her. His arm went around her neck. She felt her head jerked up until it hurt and realized her throat was exposed. No . . . no, her brain screamed. She saw the glint of a knife off to the side of her head. Rain fell effortlessly and without concern on her face.

Zehra flailed with her arms to hit him but only struck slippery shoulders.

He mumbled something that sounded like a few words of prayer. He shifted to the left side, and he pulled her head in the same direction. He stiffened along the length of his body.

Zehra tried to scream but his arm around her throat made it impossible. An image of her parents flashed through her mind. She started to cry. She saw a beautiful kaleidoscope of colors in the reflections on the sidewalk. Blue and yellow and green from the refracted headlights of the car, like flowers in a garden.

She tried to fight to the last but realized it was hopeless. Zehra collapsed onto the ground. She braced for the pain. Suddenly, Mustafa's weight disappeared. His body lifted off her. Zehra gagged and rolled to her side, gasping for air. Her lungs sucked hard at staying alive.

She heard shouting and thumping from behind her. People yelling. Someone shouting at her.

When Zehra rolled over and propped herself on an elbow, she saw Paul wrestling with Mustafa in the grass. They struck at each other, twisting to get an advantage. Slipping in the mud. Mustafa no longer had a knife but he was strong and seemed to be winning.

Paul separated from him, inching back on his butt along the sidewalk. He reached behind himself. Drew out a pistol. As he brought his arm forward, it tangled in his wet sport coat.

Mustafa pounced like a tiger. He kicked the gun from Paul and shoved him over on his side. The gun skittered across the sidewalk. Before Paul could get back up, Mustafa grabbed it and stood.

Zehra screamed at Mustafa to stop.

A loud bang echoed off the wall. Zehra looked at Paul. Saw a bloody mist explode from his thigh. He yelled and jerked to his side. Zehra crawled to him.

He writhed in pain. Zehra turned to beg Mustafa to stop.

Mustafa leaned forward and raised the pistol again, pointing at Zehra. "This must happen," he mumbled. Long wet hair stuck to his face. His clenched teeth shown brightly in his dark face.

Zehra squirmed to the side. "No . . . no!" As she lifted her hands in protest, Paul moaned something to her. Pointed at his ankle. She reached along his leg, pulled up the bloody pants cuff, and found a small gun. Paul collapsed onto his back.

Mustafa's gun barked but he missed.

Zehra held the small pistol in both shaking hands. It was wet, and she fought to keep from losing her grip. She pointed it up at Mustafa's chest. He started to turn away. Her mind drifted into the fog around her. Zehra closed her eyes and jerked the trigger.

FORTY-FOUR

Zehra shook so badly, the gun fell from her hand and clattered onto the sidewalk. Great sobs tore through her chest. When she looked across the lawn, Mustafa was lying in a still lump, facing away from her. Rain bounced off his upraised hip.

She heard Paul moan and turned to him.

"Tourniquet . . ." he gasped and pointed at his belt.

Zehra pulled on the buckle while he rolled to his side. When she had it out, Zehra wrapped it around his thigh, just under his crotch, and stretched as tightly as she could, tying the loose end underneath the strap.

Paul fell back and rested for a while.

"What . . . what happened?" Zehra said.

"Call nine-one-one."

"Oh, yeah, of course." Zehra pulled out his phone, sheltered it under her jacket, and called. Curious people edged toward them.

"Your friend is a terrorist, Zehra. I'm sorry to tell you."

"I guessed that earlier tonight." Her stomach turned over and she felt sick. "I . . . I killed . . ."

"You didn't have any choice. You probably saved my life."

"I don't know what . . ."

Paul interrupted her. "Why were you here?"

"He invited me to the science fair."

"What?" Paul shouted. He propped himself up on one elbow. "Here, tonight? Were all these people inside?"

"Yeah, why?"

Paul's face contorted in pain while he thought. He grabbed the phone from Zehra. Keyed in a number. "Bill," he grunted, "get everyone over here right now! We got the wrong place. Ammar was here for the release. Get the CDC here." Paul slumped back and repeated the address.

In five minutes, an ambulance and a police car pulled into the lot. Two emergency techs jumped out. One ran to Paul, the other to Mustafa. The second one came back to the group quickly. "Gone," he said.

Within a short time, they had cut Paul's pant leg, dressed the wound, given him several shots, and helped him sit up. They threw a blanket and tarp over him.

"Hit a lot of muscle, but I don't think it touched any bone," the tech said.

When Zehra looked back at Paul, the color had returned to his face. "You just sit there and take it easy." She felt her hair hanging in sodden clumps around her face. Suddenly, Zehra felt cold. She started to shake. Another tech wrapped a blanket around her shoulders.

"Someone's got to get inside the school," Paul said. "Check the heating system. If he was releasing the stuff here, there should be an aerosolization device." He was handed a pair of crutches as he stood, dropped the tarp, wobbled, and righted himself.

The cop stepped up and asked, "What's going on?"

Paul identified himself as FBI, told the officer more people were on their way, and he couldn't say anything until later. Pulling Zehra aside, Paul gave her the ten-second version of the smallpox threat and what was being done to contain the spread.

"But there isn't any smallpox in the world. How could . . . ?"

"Later. When the CDC gets here, they can give us both the vaccine." He grunted in pain and glanced around.

Looking up, Zehra saw dozens of cars and vans in the backyard, parked all over the lawn. The rain had tapered to a light drizzle. A burly man charged toward them. Paul's boss, he told her.

"Paul, you okay?" He tossed a cigarette away.

Zehra saw people in white coats erecting a small tent in the corner of the yard. Two of them came over to Paul. The black woman seemed to be in charge.

"Did you find any evidence?"

Paul grimaced and, tight-lipped, said, "There's probably something inside."

The black woman motioned to her partners to go inside. Masked, they left immediately.

Someone had found chairs for both Zehra and Paul inside the small tent. They slumped into them. Paul told Zehra more of the background of the plot and the fears law enforcement had about it.

As she relaxed, Zehra started to cry. She couldn't stop. The unbelievable horror of it all, the deception, lies, and the smashed hopes, flooded out through her tears.

Conway and two other FBI agents surrounded them. The black woman, Dr. Johnson, was there also.

She spoke to Zehra. "Take it slow, honey. What can you remember here?"

Zehra sniffed and told her about the program.

"How long was the fair?"

"A couple hours."

Johnson frowned and looked at Conway. "Shit." She turned back to Zehra. "Was Ammar with you?"

"No, he left shortly after the fair started. Why are you . . . ?"

"Honey, two hours is more than enough time to zap all of you with, maybe triple the dose necessary for infection and transmission." She shook her head. "Who's left in the school?"

Zehra felt sick at the thought of the disease. "Paul says you have a vaccine?"

"We do, but I have to tell you, we're not one hundred percent sure it'll work. Depends on the strain of this virus." Johnson's eyes grew round and soft. "Now who's in there? Talk to me, dear. Talk to me."

"Lots of people left, but they're still some inside."

"God damn it! My black ass is too old for this," the doctor slapped her hands together and sighed. In a moment, she collected herself and said, "Okay . . . at least we've got the sample in the basement. I'll authorize that to be choppered over to the airbase and flown to Atlanta. The testing takes about an hour."

"Meantime, we've gotta quarantine the neighborhood right now," Paul said.

"Right. Where are the closest hospitals?" Johnson asked. "If these kids get sick, or their families, they'll show up there and we've got to warn the staff to be prepared."

Conway spoke, "But how wide do we throw the quarantine net? We don't know where the hell these kids went." Conway's stomach jiggled as he started to move around quickly. He pulled out his cell phone.

Dr. Johnson held up her hand. "Hold your butts, boys."

"Huh?"

"Don't you see? All of these people are hot. Everyone they've been in contact with it will carry the transferred virus. Families, friends, neighbors, gas stations they stop at on the way home, potentially dozens of other victims." She paused and looked at the group. "Quarantine? Shee-it! It has to be big."

Kamur's face clouded over. "She's right. We've already lost the first line of defense. Even with a low multiplier, this will spread like mad. It may already be too big for the limited supply of vaccine we have available."

Conway stomped the ground. "I hate to say it, but where the hell is Homeland Security? We better call the mayor to help coordinate the containment."

Dr. Johnson said, "We gotta go public with this soon. We need major help. The message has to be worded carefully to avoid a panic. For instance, if we describe the initial flu-like symptoms to the media, hundreds of noninfected people with colds who are afraid, will flood the hospitals and emergency rooms. They'll crash the medical staff so they won't be able to help the truly infected patients."

Dr. Kamur said, "I'll try to determine the perimeter of quarantine. Hopefully, we can still catch it."

"I'll work on the statement," Conway said.

Kamur interrupted him, "Sir, you need to call the governor and the FBI director and get all the troops. This is too big now."

Wᴀᴇɴ Cᴀʀᴏʟʏɴ Bᴇᴄʜᴛᴇʀ ɢᴏᴛ ᴡᴏʀᴅ of the shooting at Hiawatha High School, she and her crew raced over there. It took them twenty minutes to fight their way through the growing ring of law enforcement.

Thoughts of Paul swirled in her mind. There was no doubt, he'd saved them from the crowd. When this was all over, maybe she'd call him for a drink . . .

She was wet from the rain and used a small hair blower to dry herself in the van. She reapplied her make-up as best she could in spite of the jolting van.

When they jerked to a halt at the edge of the school parking lot, she burst out of the side door. "Come on, Ray," she called behind herself. "We're the first ones here."

She saw several small white tents across the lot, pitched near the entrance to the school. Dozens of people scurried from one tent to the other. The rain let up to a slow drizzle.

Carolyn started to work her way around the line of law enforcement people, flashing her press credentials as she went. Within ten feet, both she and Ray were stopped.

A young cop pushed them backward. "Can't go any closer. Don't you know what's over there?" His eyes opened wide. "There's a plague."

Carolyn started to shove her way forward. She'd been in these situations many times and remembered that sheer guts usually worked. Before she could break through the line, she heard rumbling behind her. She turned to look.

Four large dark-green trucks lumbered along the street next to the lot.

Brakes squealed as they all stopped. From the back end of each truck, dozens of soldiers erupted into the street and circled around the edges of the parking lot.

They all carried weapons and wore gas masks. In the drizzle and darkness, they looked like actors in a cheap thriller film.

Carolyn found herself pulled back toward the street. She tried to fight forward, but several soldiers grabbed her and shoved her out of the way. "Who are you?" she called out to the knot of soldiers closest to her.

"National Guard. We're taking over the city."

FORTY-FIVE

Too exhausted to continue, Zehra went to the hospital with Paul. Physically, she was okay except for a bruised throat and scrapes to her arms and legs. Warm blankets piled around her body, up to her chin. She was quarantined.

Mentally, she was a wreck.

Although she didn't know the full story about Mustafa and his plot yet, Zehra still felt guilty. In her mind she replayed the details of the shooting. Would he have shot again? Wasn't he turning away? Was there something else she could have done? It became too much, and her brain shut down.

She awoke when her mother and father looked through a glass window into the bay.

"What have you heard on the news?" Zehra asked.

"It doesn't sound good," her father looked grim. "The governor's called out the National Guard for the Twin City area. The rain has stopped so everyone's worried people will start coming out again. The best place for you is right here where you can be taken care of. We're old enough that we received vaccinations as kids. Hopefully, it's still effective."

She worried there wouldn't be enough vaccine for her and that it wouldn't work. "How's Paul?" she asked.

"Your friend from the FBI? He's right next to you. Here . . ." Her mother pointed to the curtain beside Zehra.

Paul lay propped up in his bed, talking on his phone.

"How can you keep going after all you've been through?" Zehra asked.

Lowering the phone, he said, "This is why I became an FBI agent. We're fighting for the state now. If we lose, the battle's for the country." He resumed talking.

Zehra took a deep breath. No one spoke. Her parents found chairs and sat beside the window.

Suddenly, Paul whooped. He laughed and cheered. "Dr. Samson, are you certain?" he said into the phone. "I can't believe it—there's one honest person left in the world." He shut his phone and looked to Zehra and her family. A smile split his face open.

"What's so funny?"

"You won't believe it. The CDC flew the sample of the virus they found in the basement to Atlanta to be tested. The tests were run three times. It turns out the virus was already dead. Ammar and his terrorists bought worthless stuff. The Russians found the guy who stole it, and he confessed. He knew the virus was dead. He cheated the terrorists."

"So, what does that mean?" Zehra turned sideways and put her feet on the floor. Didn't feel like she could stand yet.

"It means, we're okay. There's no epidemic! False alarm."

Zerha's family flooded into the room and hugged her.

Two DAYS LATER, PAUL INVITED Zehra to the FBI office in Minneapolis. When she arrived, she found him propped in a lounge chair in the conference room. His leg stuck out, wrapped in a colorful, plastic brace. Conway was there and several people she hadn't met.

Paul called to her. "Hey, Zehra. Come on in. How's your trial going?"

"Under the circumstances, we got a continuance. It's pretty clear Mustafa was the killer. Until things are sorted out, the prosecutor isn't dismissing the case yet."

"Why didn't the defendant tell you all this in the first place?" Paul asked.

Zehra shrugged. "He thinks I'm an infidel, so he'd never reveal anything to me. And, he's a zealot. Maybe he felt it was his duty to take the fall and be a martyr in his own way. Who knows? What about the DNA?"

"Looks like Mustafa doctored the samples at the crime scene to frame El-Amin. Then, he planted the murder weapon in El-Amin's apartment. It almost worked." said Conway. He looked at Paul. "What do you know?"

"Well, I can't tell you everything, but Ammar had been planning this for years. Embedded himself at Health Technologies as a cover and infiltrated three different mosques in order to recruit the young Somali men."

"Why did they disappear?" Zehra asked.

"Testing. He and others recruited and sent them to Somalia. Most stayed to fight. But a few of the boys were isolated in the desert and infected with smallpox to see how it worked."

"How horrible. Have you found the young men?"

Paul shook his head. "Unfortunately, we probably never will."

Conway lumbered next to Paul's bed. "We're lucky here, that Paul's alive— thanks to you."

Zehra shrugged and wondered if that were true. "What about the threats to me? My car?"

"We assume Ammar did all of it. But there're probably others still out there. Local police haven't found any suspects for the deli shooting yet. We think it's tied to Ammar's scheme, so we're involved in that now."

Conway interrupted, "For your safety, I've authorized an agent—a new one—to stay with you for a few weeks. I fired the other one."

Zehra felt somewhat relieved but not completely.

Paul looked away from the group.

"Once they had the transmission process worked out and knew the incubation period, the plan was to introduce it in the U.S.," Conway continued. "Although they wanted people to get sick and die of course, the main goal was panic."

Paul interrupted, "Hysterical, mass panic would tear the country apart faster than any army or bomb could ever do. They could've easily destroyed us." He tried to stand but fell back into the chair.

"Where'd they get the smallpox virus? I thought you said it was dead?"

"Looks like they bought two batches from the Russian. The first one was hot but the guy felt so guilty about selling it to terrorists, that when he sold the second batch, it was the dead virus. The world owes a debt to a crook with a conscience."

Conway cleared his throat in a loud gurgle. He looked nervous and shifted his shoulders. "I need a cigarette," he announced. He lowered his head and leaned down to Paul. "I've been so damn busy I haven't had a chance but . . . congratulations." He shook Paul's hand. "You got a good shot to take over for me when I bail from here next year."

"Thanks, but does that mean I'm not fired?" Paul's face lit-up. "Zehra Hassan saved me and hey, what happened to the agents from ICE, Joan Cortez? Where'd they go?"

Conway stepped back and laughed deeply. "You didn't hear?" He wiped his eye. "They busted the mosque in Burnsville before the rest of us got there. They were waiting for Ammar to show so they could grab him and all the glory."

"What happened?"

"Nothing. Sat there for three hours until someone finally got through to them. The mosque's suing the ass off of their agency, and I think Cortez got busted back to working for security at the airport."

"Righteous, Joan," Paul said.

"What about the victim in my trial?" Zehra asked.

Conway shook his head, "Poor son of a bitch. They infected him and were ready to roll out the transmission when the kid refused to cooperate. We figure Ammar had to kill him to keep things quiet. The fact the kid was hot explains why the killer wore all the protection."

The conversation rolled on but Zehra lost interest. Most of it revolved around the federal bureaucracy and its internal struggles. Conway talked quietly with Paul. Zehra stopped when she heard Conway whispering.

"Luckily, the governor's statement did it."

"What do you mean?" Paul asked.

"We worked with him and all the brass you can imagine from Washington to get it right. We decided to call the whole thing a 'training exercise.' The possibility of the real deal was never mentioned. If the public ever knew the truth . . . Well, all I can say is, thank God it worked."

Paul looked up at him. "I wouldn't say it 'worked'. I'd say we were damn lucky." He turned back to Zehra. "How're you holding up?"

"Oh . . . I've got my family and garden but . . ."

"Don't worry. We're not done chasing these guys down. I promise."

Zehra didn't want to hear anymore. Guilt and fatigue haunted her, but she found herself angry, instead. Angry at all the violence and fear the terrorists caused. "Thanks Paul, but we all have to do something. If moderate Muslims like me don't stand up and fight these extremists, they'll win."

She stood to leave. Looked out the window at sun lighting up the piles of white clouds to the east. Turning back to the group, she said, "It's about time some of us progressive Muslims declared our own 'jihad' against the terrorists."

ACKNOWLEDGEMENTS

The creation of any story is always the result of an author who is helped and supported by a number of others. In my case, I'm particularly thankful to my wife, Pam for her ideas, editing, and encouragement. To Christopher Valen for his friendship and editing, Mary Logue, and Imani Jaafar-Mohammad for their reviews and wonderful comments. To Mary Stanton and Carol Epstein for the time they took to read and critique the manuscript. To NorthStar Press and Corrine Dwyer and Cecelia Dwyer for their belief in the story and for bringing it successfully to book form. Finally, to my parents Vern and Sherry Nelson, long gone but never forgotten, for their support of me and for always telling me to "just try it."